Wild DARLING

First published in Great Britain in 2026
by Electric Monkey, part of Farshore

An imprint of HarperCollins*Publishers*
1 London Bridge Street, London SE1 9GF

farshore.co.uk

HarperCollins*Publishers*
Macken House, 39/40 Mayor Street Upper,
Dublin 1, D01 C9W8

Text copyright © Alexandra Moody 2026
Cover illustration © Andra Murarasu 2026

The moral rights of the author have been asserted

ISBN 978 0 00 879414 9

A CIP catalogue record of this title is available from the British Library

Printed and bound in the UK using 100% renewable electricity
at CPI Group (UK) Ltd

3

All rights reserved. No part of this publication may be reproduced, stored in a retrieval system, or transmitted, in any form or by any means, electronic, mechanical, photocopying, recording or otherwise, without the prior permission of the publisher and copyright owner.

Without limiting the exclusive rights of any author, contributor or the publisher of this publication, any unauthorised use of this publication to train generative artificial intelligence (AI) technologies is expressly prohibited. HarperCollins also exercise their rights under Article 4(3) of the Digital Single Market Directive 2019/790 and expressly reserve this publication from the text and data mining exception.

Stay safe online. Any website addresses listed in this book are correct at the time of going to print. However, Farshore is not responsible for content hosted by third parties. Please be aware that online content can be subject to change and websites can contain content that is unsuitable for children. We advise that all children are supervised when using the internet.

Wild
DARLING

ALEXANDRA MOODY

*For my parents. My greatest
support and inspiration.*

Chapter 1

MACKENZIE

Summer of freshman year

"Hockey is just a guy's sport, you know?" It was the last thing I felt like hearing at the end of a hard first day at hockey camp. All I wanted was to eat my dinner in peace. But the boy sitting across from me in the dining hall wouldn't shut up. And between his casual misogyny and the way he talked with his mouth full of food, peace was hard to come by.

"See, girls are naturally weaker," he explained as he gnawed on a chicken wing. "They're not as fast, and nowhere near as strong."

I was far too horrified by the massacre taking place inside his mouth to respond. The way his chewed food sloshed around was putting me off my own dinner, and yet I couldn't seem to look away.

"Like you." He pointed his chicken wing in my direction. "Way too short, especially for a goalie."

I wasn't sure the guy even realized he was being insulting. Given his cheery tone, we could easily have been talking about something as simple as the weather. Not his belief that girls didn't belong on an elite ice hockey summer camp—or playing the game at all.

"Shows how much you know," my brother said calmly from beside me. "Shorter goalies are usually much more agile. Mackenzie's reflexes are insane."

"Whatever," the guy snorted. "I think we all know the only reason your dad opened the camp up to girls this year was to check the diversity box."

"Actually—" My brother tried to object but Chicken Wings kept on talking.

"I guess having a few girls around camp isn't the *worst* thing in the world." He was grinning now, a large piece of his dinner hanging from his teeth. "It *is* nice to have something pretty to look at."

"Watch it, dude," Max warned.

But I didn't need my brother to defend me. I was already leaning forward on the table, smiling as sweetly as I could at the guy. "Yes, I guess you're right, there's obviously no way I could ever be as skilled as you."

He winked. "You haven't seen half my skills. Yet . . ."

"Seriously," I continued. "It's really impressive—you can talk, think *and* chew all at the same time. I'm sure that's just what they're looking for in the NHL."

It took a moment for him to process, but then his grin quickly transformed into a scowl as a few girls at the other end of our table started to snigger.

His gaze flashed to my brother. "Can you get your sister in line?"

Max simply shrugged. "She's got a point."

Our friend shot me a glare as he gathered his things and stood up.

"Just because your dad played in the NHL, doesn't mean he passed any of his talent onto you two." He stormed away, and I swore I could still hear him chewing as he went.

I should have known the guy was a jerk the moment he sat down; the peroxide-blond tips were a dead giveaway. But while I was relieved to see him go, a small part of me—the insecure part I mostly tried to ignore—wondered if he might be right.

My dad had refused to let me play hockey competitively my whole life. He didn't usually take much of an interest in my hobbies, but something about me and hockey turned him into a stubborn, irrational tyrant. It didn't matter to him that I'd spent years practicing with my brother. That I'd been stopping pucks since the moment I first learned to skate, when Max realized he could prop me up in front of a net. No, as far as he was concerned, Chicken Wings was right. I didn't belong here.

Still, I *was* here. From the moment I'd heard my dad was adding a girls' team to his famous summer camp, I hadn't stopped bugging him. And he'd finally caved. Now, I had one chance to show him I deserved to play. The only problem? He hadn't once looked my way since the start of camp. The girls practiced with a separate coach, and Dad was too focused on his role coaching the boys. How could I impress him with my skills when he wasn't even aware I had any?

"Remind me to never piss you off," my brother said, smiling.

I sighed and rubbed a hand over my face. "I know, I should have just ignored him, but it's been a long day and he really got on my nerves."

"Hey, he deserved it. I'm surprised you didn't knee him in the balls for that 'something pretty to look at' comment."

"I'm surprised *you* didn't knee him in the balls for hitting on your little sister."

"Why would I do that? You've got knees of your own, and

I've seen you use them plenty of times before." His expression turned thoughtful. "Seriously though, I don't care what that dude says, you belong here just as much as anyone. You were brilliant out there today, Kenz. Didn't let a single goal in."

I raised an eyebrow. "You didn't even see me play today. You were busy trying to impress Dad, just like everyone else."

"Okay, fine," he admitted. "I *heard* you didn't let a single goal in. And I don't need to impress Dad."

"Uh huh."

Everyone wanted to impress Wade Foster, even Max. And not just because Dad was the founder of this camp and the head coach of the boys' team. He'd played in the NHL for years, but he took a break when my mom got sick. After she died, he tried to go back to playing but barely lasted a season. He retired and turned to high school coaching.

Over the years his reputation for nurturing young talent had become legendary. More of his protégés went on to become professional hockey players than any other high school coach in the country. And this camp was where the magic happened. At least, it was for those who our dad deemed worthy. He only selected the best players to train with him personally.

I glanced down at my dinner. My appetite still hadn't returned after I got put off chicken wings for life, so I pushed my plate toward my brother and stood.

"Where are you going?" he asked, barely hesitating as he happily took my food. The boy usually ate more in one meal than I did in a whole day. At least he knew how to do it with his mouth closed.

"Back to the rink."

"But we practiced all day."

"Yeah, I know. I just want to skate for a bit and clear my head."

He shrugged, then turned to the full plate in front of him.

It was getting cooler out as I made my way to the ice arena. The locker room was empty as I changed back into my gear, and I was pleased to find the rink just as vacant. I smiled as I slid onto the ice, which must have been freshly resurfaced because it was smooth and clean under my skates.

The coaches had told us the rink was off limits outside official practice sessions, but I figured if my dad was running the camp, I might be able to get away with it. And to be honest, it felt worth the risk. I'd been waiting for this opportunity for years, and I didn't want to waste a second of it.

As I warmed up, the sound of skates hitting the ice drew my attention. I turned to find my rink had been invaded by a boy. He was wearing one of the camp practice jerseys with the number twelve stitched to the back of it. He didn't look my way, and his focus was on the puck in front of him as he skated over to the net on the opposite side of the ice. I knew I should probably leave him be. But the ice *was* off limits, and I didn't really want an audience right now.

"You're not supposed to be out here," I called to him.

He spun around, and I swallowed as I took him in. Dark hair. Bright blue eyes. Lips that hinted at trouble. He was tall, about my age, and there was a cheeky grin on his face that told me he was unbothered by my warning.

"The rink is closed after practice," I continued, skating closer. "They told everyone at orientation. You don't want the coaches to catch you."

I came to a stop by him and pulled off my helmet, shaking out my blonde hair. His eyes widened with surprise, but it was only for a moment before pure mischief filled his gaze. "*You're* here."

"Yes, well . . ." I paused, not wanting to pull the Wade Foster card.

"You . . ." he prompted.

"I'm special," I finally replied.

"I can't argue with that."

The way his lips curved and his eyes glittered made it hard to remember what we'd been talking about. Boys my age were supposed to be awkward and annoying. Their eyes weren't supposed to *glitter*.

"Okay, good," I replied. "Bye then."

I went to turn away, but he called out. "Sorry, *special*, but I didn't say I was leaving. If you want the rink to yourself, you'll have to play me for it."

"What?"

"If I score on you, I get to stay. You stop me, I'll get out of your hair."

My eyes narrowed. "You think you can score on me?"

"I want to stay on the ice, and I'll do just about anything to make that happen."

I paused as I considered him. "Why do you want to stay on the ice so bad? Is it really worth getting in trouble for?"

"I think I'm already in trouble." The way he smiled was totally disarming. I got the distinct impression he was used to getting away with anything he wanted.

I shook my head. "You really expect that to work?"

"Kind of. I thought girls were into guys who fall in love at first sight."

"You haven't fallen in love with me."

"I'm already picking out our wedding playlist."

I groaned. "Be serious."

He released a breathy laugh. "Okay, you want serious?"

"Please."

"Apparently I made a bad impression on a certain superstar coach." He shrugged like it was no big deal, but the light in his eyes dimmed a little. "I need to prove him wrong."

He had to be talking about my dad, and the frustration in his voice was clear. It wasn't surprising. I knew first-hand how frustrating my dad could be. Perhaps we had more in common than I thought.

"But more importantly, I think I'm in love with you . . ."

I couldn't stop a laugh escaping me, though I did my best to make it sound like I was laughing *at* him.

"Fine, you're on," I said. "But only to shut you up. And I should warn you, I'm on a hot streak today."

I skated for the net, pulling my helmet on as I went. Although I'd preferred having the place to myself, I felt a rush of adrenaline at the prospect of competing against someone. One day into camp and I was already addicted to the thrill of testing myself against players who weren't my brother.

I was almost in position when I heard him take a shot, and I turned just in time to see the puck sail right past me into the net.

"Hey! I wasn't ready."

My mystery opponent laughed to himself before calling

back. "Damn, I guess that hot streak is done."

"Uh, because you cheated."

Still laughing, he skated over to me. "Don't worry. The streak might be over, but you're still hot."

My mouth dropped open. This guy might just be worse than the one at dinner. Though for some reason I wasn't completely revolted by his attempts to flirt with me. I tried to convince myself it was because he wasn't talking with his mouth full. It had nothing to do with his striking blue eyes.

"That doesn't count," I argued. "I want a rematch."

"Nope."

"Are you scared you can't beat a girl without cheating?"

"Yes, I'm terrified."

I scoffed. "So much for love at first sight."

"Okay, fine," he said. "We'll make it best of three. But why don't we up the stakes?"

His eyes started to do that whole glittering thing again, and I immediately grew suspicious. "What are you thinking?" I paused. "Actually, don't answer that," I said before he could reply. "I know guys like you. You're probably going to say something like 'loser has to take off a piece of clothing' or 'if you score, I have to kiss you.'"

He slowly started to smile. "Well, those are both excellent suggestions, but the kiss seems like a worthy prize. You're on."

"Wait, that's not—"

But he was already skating away. *Shit*. I hurried back to the net. He hadn't allowed me a moment to consider the terms of his bet, but I wasn't going to let him score another cheap goal. Thankfully, this time, he waited until I was in position.

I clanged my stick hard against each post and nodded that I was ready.

Instantly, he started pushing the puck down the ice toward me, switching it from side to side with impressive speed. I swallowed as I kept my eyes laser-focused on the puck. This guy was really good. But so was Max, and I'd been playing against my brother for years.

As he got closer, he suddenly deked left, then right, and flicked a shot toward the top-left corner of the net. My glove flashed out on pure instinct, and I smiled when I felt the impact of the puck hitting my glove.

He slid to a stop next to me and I smirked as I tossed the puck down at his feet.

There was a slightly stunned look on his face, but he quickly shook it off. "Good save," he said. "Maybe there really *is* something special about you."

His words surprised me, and I felt a fluttering in my stomach. Getting a compliment from your brother was one thing, but having my game praised by a stranger, especially a talented one, was something else. And he didn't try to come up with some list of excuses to explain why he'd failed to score on a girl. Instead, he flashed me an appreciative smile, scooped up the puck, and headed back to center ice.

"You better not be going easy on me," I called.

"Wouldn't dream of it," he replied with a cocky grin. "We're tied now, so there's a lot riding on this final shot, isn't there?"

"You're not getting that kiss." I realized I was enjoying this almost as much as him.

"We'll see about that."

He paused for a moment, as though planning something, but then, in a flash, he was speeding toward me again. I had to remind myself I was here to defend the net, not admire how well the guy moved the puck. It was practically impossible to keep my eye on it, but this time, when he took his shot, I almost lost sight of the puck completely. It streaked toward the net even faster than before, and I was too slow to react. This time, there was no thud of contact against my glove. But apparently, luck was on my side, and I heard a resounding clang as the puck struck the post and bounced away.

I pulled my helmet from my head, a relieved smile on my face. "You missed."

He stopped right by me and again I was surprised by his reaction. He was smiling too. "I did."

"You don't seem upset."

"I'm not."

"And why is that?"

"Don't get me wrong," he said with a shrug. "Your kissing idea was a good one. But I don't want you to kiss me because of some bet. When you kiss me, it's going to be because you really want to."

"When?" I lifted an eyebrow at him. "You're even cockier than I thought."

"You have no idea."

The mischief that danced in his eyes had my heart beating faster, and now he was standing so close I couldn't stop myself from wondering what might have happened if he'd scored.

"This was fun," he continued. "But a bet's a bet. I'll leave you to your rink."

The words had barely passed his lips when we were plunged into darkness. My heart leaped in shock. The lights had shut off, and it took a moment for my eyes to adjust. Apart from the dim glow of some safety lights around the rink, we were in total darkness. Were they closing the place up for the night?

He chuckled gently. "Guess we both lost."

"No, I'm pretty sure I still won," I replied. My heart was beating even faster now, but, as much as I wanted to, I couldn't blame it on the sudden blackout.

"Funny," he said, looking down at me, his eyes bright despite the darkness. "I kind of feel like I've won too."

He hadn't skated away. Neither had I. We were both staring at each other, like the rest of the world had disappeared. I wasn't sure who reached for who first. But suddenly, we were kissing, and the feel of his lips against mine sent electricity zapping all the way down to my toes.

I'd never kissed a boy before. Though it made sense that my first time would take me by surprise. I'd always been a little reckless, and as we kissed, I couldn't find it in me to care. My pulse fluttered, my breath stalled, and his lips were all I could think about.

When we pulled apart, he was smiling.

"You kissed me," I whispered.

"Uh, I think *you* kissed *me*."

I shook my head. "I don't even know your name."

"It's Parker," he said, a little of his cockiness returning. "Parker Darling. And you are . . ."

"What's going on here?" I jumped as my dad's voice thundered across the ice.

"Twelve?" he barked. "You know the rink is out of bounds after hours. Why am I not surprised it's you?"

I guessed Parker really had made a bad impression. My dad already sounded livid, and he was yet to notice me. There was no escaping this situation for either of us, though, so I drew in a breath before I slowly edged to Parker's side to face my father. As his eyes landed on me, I could clearly see his shock.

"Ma-Mackenzie?" he stuttered.

His features quickly hardened. I was used to seeing my dad angry—especially coaching—but I'd never seen him like this. His jaw tight, his eyes dark, and his expression totally leeched of warmth. It wasn't just anger; it was disappointment.

He walked onto the ice, and I backed up a step.

"Dad, I—"

"*Dad?*" Parker hissed.

I grimaced at the sound of betrayal in his voice, but there was no time to explain as my dad started yelling again.

"You said you were desperate to be here, Mackenzie. That you wanted a chance to prove yourself; to show me how passionate you were about playing hockey. How much *respect* you have for the game. Instead, on the first day, I find you at the rink after hours kissing some boy."

"I *do* respect the game, Dad. But how can I prove myself to you when you won't even watch me play?"

"So, what, this is all just a way to get my attention?"

"That's not fair. I didn't kiss some boy just to—"

"I knew this was a bad idea," he seethed. "I gave you a chance, but I don't see a hockey player before me. Just an immature little girl who can't be trusted. I'm not going to allow you to risk your neck on the ice if you refuse to take it seriously."

"I *am* serious!"

Dad ignored me as he turned to Parker. "I've had enough of you already, Twelve. The ice is prohibited after hours. Call your parents to come pick you up. You're done here."

"You're kidding, right?" Parker protested. "I just wanted to get some extra practice in, to prove I'm good enough to train with you."

"I don't care," my dad snapped back. "We have rules here, and you broke them. I don't want to see your face anywhere near my rink, my camp, or my daughter ever again."

"But Coach—"

"Dad, please—"

"Enough!" My dad waved his arm across his body, like he was physically cutting us off. "Mackenzie, let's go."

He turned and marched away without looking back. I stared after him, unable to move. Had I just destroyed my one chance to win over my dad because of a boy? Because of a stupid kiss?

"My parents are going to kill me," Parker groaned, before turning my way. "You could have warned me who your dad is!"

"I'm in as much trouble as you are." I scowled at him in return. "And just so we're clear, *you* kissed *me*."

"No chance. You leaned in."

"I was leaning *away*."

"And yet your lips somehow ended up on mine?"

"Accidents happen."

"Accidents? So how do you explain your arms around my neck?"

"Self-defense."

"Kissing someone in defense? Sounds about right. Is that how you plan to win hockey games, too?"

I gripped my stick tightly and tried to remember not to use it as a weapon. "I don't need to kiss people to win hockey games. You couldn't score on me. Not without cheating, anyway."

"You really think that? Well, the truth is, I *was* taking it easy on you."

"Oh, of course, you were."

"Want me to prove it?" He gave me an irritating smirk and skated back a few feet to where he'd taken his last shot. He slammed his stick against the puck, sending it flying toward the net. There was a familiar metallic twang as it hit the post in the exact same spot he'd struck before. My heart sank.

"I lied," he said. "You didn't win our bet. I can put the puck anywhere I want to. I missed on purpose."

"You . . ." I gaped as I stared at him. I could feel a sense of inferiority rising up inside me, but I quickly tamped it down. "You're an ass."

"At least I'm a hockey player."

Using my dad's condescending words against me was a low blow, and it made my blood boil.

"Ugh! I'm just glad I'll never have to see your face again." I started across the ice, my skates pushing hard so I could put as much distance between us as possible.

"I wish I'd never seen yours in the first place," he called after me, like he couldn't resist stealing the final word. Fine—it was all his.

I was planning to forget tonight ever happened. And I was most definitely going to forget that my first kiss had been with a jerk like Parker Darling.

Chapter 2

PARKER

Three years later

I'd always dreamed of being a famous hockey player. Of scoring goals, packed stadiums cheering my name, and girls falling at my feet. It all sounded pretty damn great. And while I might only be a senior in high school, I'd already experienced my fair share of all three.

"Are you going to make captain tonight, Parker?"

I was trying my best to get to practice, but I was penned in by a group of sophomore girls who'd just come off the ice after a figure-skating lesson. I usually didn't mind this kind of attention, but not when I was running late to such an important session.

It was the last week of preseason, and tonight was the night Coach Ray would announce the final varsity team roster and name the team captain. Ray had pretty much told me the position was mine at the end of last season. But nothing was guaranteed until I had a bold letter C stitched onto the heart of my jersey. Plus, Coach had been out sick last week, and I wasn't even sure if he'd show today, so I didn't want to get my hopes up.

"Uh, can't make captain if I don't make practice," I said with an awkward laugh. I tried to maneuver past the group, but the girls shifted in sync with my movements, refusing to release me. They were like a pack of wolves, and apparently I was their prey.

"Your brother was captain last year," one of them said. "Surely Coach Ray will make you captain too..."

"Yeah, that's the plan." I tried again to move beyond them but failed once more. I'd developed a bit of an infamous reputation with girls over the years, and I was usually quite good at charming my way both into and out of their clutches. But right now, I was outnumbered and struggling.

"He'd be crazy not to. You're by far the best player."

"Yeah, you scored so many goals last season."

"And practically won the state championship game singlehandedly..."

Okay, maybe this wasn't *so* bad. I could be a few minutes late.

"You guys are going to win it again, right?"

I paused as some lingering doubts crept to the surface. A lot of good players had graduated over the summer, including my brothers, Reed and Grayson. The Ransom Devils would be a very different team this season.

I started moving again, more urgently now.

"Like I said, if I don't get to practice, we won't be winning anything. Have a good night, girls."

"Bye, Parker," they all chimed.

I breathed a sigh of relief once I was free, but the nagging uncertainty stuck with me as I changed into my gear, a hovering dark cloud that followed me onto the rink. It wasn't just the team I was worried about. Would I be the same player without my older brothers alongside me? Despite all the praise my female fans had just showered me with, I'd always felt like I was playing in Reed's and Grayson's shadows.

But with them gone away to college, it was my time to shine; my time to cement myself as the best Darling ever to be a Devil. I'd already secured a place at Ryker University to play college hockey with my brothers next year. Now all I needed was to win another state championship and be named captain. *No pressure.*

By the time I got onto the ice, it was already full of players warming up with the assistant coaches. I headed straight for Seth. With his blond hair and blue eyes, girls often speculated whether my best friend was a long-lost Hemsworth brother. I thought he looked like a distant cousin, at best.

Unsurprisingly, Seth was lagging at the back of the group. Nothing fazed him. His laid-back personality was part of the reason he'd ended up on the JV team last year, even though he was easily the best skater at Ransom High. His mom had been a champion figure skater, and he'd clearly inherited her talent on the ice. But while Seth liked hockey enough to show up for games, he rarely bothered to show up for practice. He'd always been happy coasting. And not even his dad breathing down his neck made a difference.

But he'd showed up to every single practice so far this preseason. He'd even joined me for a few extra sessions as well. I got the feeling Seth might actually be ready to give hockey his all.

"Is Coach Ray back tonight?" I asked, falling in beside Seth. I couldn't remember Coach ever being sick. He'd certainly never let a cold stop him from missing practice before.

"Haven't seen him yet," Seth replied with a shrug. He was probably the wrong person to ask. Coach Ray could have been standing right in front of him and he probably wouldn't have noticed.

"Sorry I'm late." Owen was puffing as he joined us, as though he'd gotten changed too quickly. He was only a year younger, but Owen Cleaver was still far too wide-eyed and innocent to be hanging out with the likes of Seth and me. He'd made varsity for the first time last season, but he and I had become closer since our brothers had graduated. It felt like I'd gained an enthusiastic sidekick. I supposed every superhero needed one.

"You're fine, Cleaver, we haven't started yet." It was an attempt to reassure him, but as I looked more closely, I realized maybe he wasn't quite so fine after all. "You okay, Owen?"

"Uh, yeah," he replied. "Just a little nervous." He instantly corrected himself. "Okay, a lot nervous. It was a miracle I made varsity last year. What if I don't make it this time? What if my game suffers now that Matt's gone?"

"Calm down, dude. You don't need your brother here to play well." I tried to sound confident, but his words had struck a nerve. "We're both better off without them."

"Don't you miss Reed and Grayson?"

I didn't get the luxury of missing Reed and Grayson. They were only an hour's drive away and came home almost every other Sunday for dinner.

"I saw them this weekend," I replied. "Look, just do what I do when I'm nervous. Picture everyone naked."

"You picture everyone naked?"

"Well, no," I admitted, "I don't get nervous. But if it ever happens, that's totally my plan."

"And you think picturing our teammates naked will help me?"

I didn't seem to be helping. In fact, I think Owen's freak-out was only getting worse. "Maybe forget the naked stuff." I patted him on the shoulder. "Just do your best. I've got your back, Owen."

He gave me a nod, seeming just a little more relaxed.

"Have you seen Coach Ray?" I asked him. Owen tended to pay a little more attention than Seth.

"Oh." Owen's eyes darted nervously between Seth and me, and he lowered his voice. "Haven't you heard?"

My stomach twisted uncomfortably. Those words couldn't mean anything good when said in such an ominous tone. "Haven't I heard *what*?"

Even Seth leaned in to listen.

"Coach Ray, he . . ." Owen hesitated, as he searched for the right words. "Well, he's not coming back . . ."

A sharp whistle blew, and everyone turned to face the sound. Everyone except me.

"What do you mean, he's not coming back?"

Owen didn't answer. Instead, his mouth fell open as he looked past me. I turned to see what the big deal was and froze.

Owen's tone definitely hadn't been ominous enough. Because standing at the edge of the rink was my very own personal apocalypse: Coach Wade Foster. And he was wearing a Ransom Devils cap.

"Well, that's not good," Seth muttered, shooting me an uneasy glance.

"Is that who I think it is?" Owen asked.

"If you're thinking that's Wade Foster, ex-Minnesota Wild defenseman and high school coaching royalty, then yeah it's who you think it is," Seth replied.

"But what's he . . ." Owen drew in a sharp breath. "He must be our new coach."

Our new coach? That couldn't be true. If it was, then things were worse than I thought. My entire senior year season was about to go up in flames.

"Gather round," Foster called before I could get any more answers. He looked just as I remembered him. Tall, with broad shoulders and arms like tree trunks; still a physical force to be reckoned with. The only difference I could spot was how the firm line etched into his forehead had grown more pronounced, probably from a few more years of scowling. He might've been trying to smile at us, but it came across more like a grimace, as though he'd already decided we were a disappointment.

I'd done my best to erase the memory of my disastrously short time at Coach Foster's hockey camp. How I'd failed to impress him with my play on the ice and then been unceremoniously booted off it all together. But it was no use. There was no forgetting the way he'd had made me feel that day. Every time I laced my skates the following season, I got the same irritating sense that I wasn't good enough. I could have let it get me down, but instead, I used Foster's criticism and my own self-doubt as fuel. It motivated me to become such a good player I could never be overlooked.

The thought made me stand a little taller. I was the best player here. I deserved my place on this team. And a new coach didn't change that. I refused to let Wade Foster's menacing eyes make me doubt myself again.

"Good evening, everyone," Foster said once we'd formed a circle around him. His words instantly silenced all the mumbling whispers of excitement coming from the players. "I'm Wade Foster, and I'll be your head coach this season."

That got people whispering again. Not me. I was too busy wondering if I was stuck in a nightmare. There was no way this could actually be happening.

"I understand my arrival may come as a surprise, especially as you have your first game on Friday. But I've spoken with the assistant coaches, and we still plan on confirming this season's varsity and junior varsity squads tonight. I'll be watching and assessing you all closely, and remember, your spot on the team is still on the line."

He nodded for one of the assistant coaches to take over, and I immediately turned to Owen. "What happened to Ray?" And, more importantly, how the hell were we going to get him back?

"He's out for the season." Elliot Ford was standing in front of me, and he turned to reveal an unsympathetic smirk. "Back injury. Didn't you know?"

I had a natural talent for pissing people off, but Elliot was one of the few people who managed to irritate me in equal measure. What I wouldn't give to see him dropped to JV this year. It would never happen, though. He was a senior, and Ransom High was already seriously lacking in goaltending talent. Our backup goalie had moved to Florida over the summer and none of the guys vying to fill the vacant spot had impressed during preseason.

"That's what I was trying to tell you," Owen said in a hushed voice as Ford turned away. "Apparently, Coach Ray has always had a bad back, and it started playing up a few weeks ago. Turns out he needs surgery, so he's taking the year off. Although, I heard he might be retiring altogether. Leaving on a high after last year's championship win."

"Well, shit." This was a disaster. Coach Ray had been my coach throughout high school, and I really liked him. He was a brilliant mentor, and I knew the team wouldn't be the same without him. I couldn't even be pissed at him for ditching us. It's not like he could help it if he needed surgery.

"But can you believe it? Wade *Foster*." Despite Owen's excitement, he kept his voice quiet as the assistant coach was still explaining the plan for tonight's session. "I wonder what he's like."

"Yeah, Parker, what's he like?" Seth answered, sending me a grin. He knew all about my rocky history with Coach Foster. But as my best friend, wasn't he supposed to help ease my suffering, not revel in it?

"Didn't he tell you he never wanted to see your face again?" Seth added.

"Well, we don't always get what we want, Seth. I have to see your face every day, don't I?" Everyone started moving into position to begin our first drill, and I bumped Seth's shoulder as I skated past him. "I hope you end up in JV."

He laughed and called after me, "Don't lie, you missed me too much last year."

I pushed the shock of Coach Foster's sudden appearance aside to focus on the task at hand: impressing him. Something

I'd completely failed to do the last time we met.

When it came to the end of practice, it seemed I'd done enough, because I made the varsity squad. I was stoked to hear both Owen and Seth's names called, too. Elliot was also selected, so it looked like I was stuck with him for another season. Freddy Anderson, a sophomore I'd never even noticed until preseason started, was named as his backup. But I prayed we never had to use him. Whenever a puck went near him tonight, he'd just stood in front of the net and squinted his eyes shut like he was hoping his body might somehow make the save.

And by some stroke of luck, Coach Foster didn't appear to recognize me. I guess it made sense—he must have coached thousands of kids in his time, so while he'd left a lasting impact on me, it was hardly shocking that the feeling wasn't mutual.

Once Foster finished reading out the two rosters, he dismissed us and everyone started to make their way back to the locker room. I should have been happy; I'd made varsity, and that was what mattered most. But all I could think about was that Coach Foster hadn't announced team captain.

I knew I should leave it alone. That I shouldn't draw attention to myself so soon. But I'd been waiting for this moment for weeks—no, months. Hell, I'd wanted this ever since I first pulled on a Ransom Devils uniform. I didn't want to wait any longer. I was obviously the best player, and there was no way Foster could deny it this time.

I started skating over to him before I could reconsider. Perhaps he'd just forgotten, like he appeared to have forgotten me.

"Uh, Coach Foster?" I said as I approached.

Up close he cut an imposing figure, and I was taken right back to our first encounter three years ago. I'd grown taller since then, so he didn't tower over me quite as much, but he was no less intimidating. I remembered the way he'd bluntly told me I wasn't good enough. The look of disapproval on his face when I'd questioned the decision. And how that disapproval had turned to blind rage when he caught me on the ice after hours with—

I refused to let myself finish that thought.

Foster lifted his eyes to mine. "Can I help you . . ."

"Parker," I cleared my throat. "Parker Darling. I play center."

His ever-present frown deepened as he studied me, and I resisted the desire to swallow. I was already regretting my decision to come talk to him. I hadn't exactly made a good impression the last time I did. But he didn't remember me, right?

He nodded for me to continue.

"I, uh, you . . ." Why was I stuttering? Damn, maybe, I did get nervous. I would *not* be picturing Foster naked though. "You didn't announce your pick for captain," I finally said. "Coach Ray always announced his captain at the same time as the final team rosters."

Foster's eyes sparked with dark amusement. "And I suppose you think *you* should be captain."

"Well, kind of, yeah," I replied with a little more confidence. "I know what it takes to win. I've been playing varsity longer than anyone here, and I'm even on track to beat the school's all-time scoring record this season. I'm your best pick."

"That remains to be seen," Foster said. "I'm planning to assess how the team plays together over the coming weeks. I'm in no rush to announce a captain."

"Right." It was probably fair that he wanted to take some time. He had only just arrived, after all. At least he hadn't ruled me out completely.

"But, Parker?"

"Yeah?"

"Don't think I've forgotten exactly what kind of *player* you are. I'm watching you, *Twelve*."

"Actually, uh, I wear number sixteen now . . ."

I could almost hear him clenching his teeth, and I mentally kicked myself. I had a nasty habit of saying whatever came to mind.

He started to turn but paused. "Do you remember what I told you before I sent you packing that summer, Twelve?"

"Uh, have a safe trip home?"

Foster stepped closer and I swallowed. It suddenly felt like I hadn't had that sophomore year growth spurt.

"Stay away from my daughter."

I had to smother a laugh at the prospect. Three years might have passed, but I'd still rather lose a tooth to a high stick than even think about going near that girl again. Coach Foster wasn't the only one who could hold a grudge. Thankfully, I managed to keep that as an inside thought, and he finally stalked away.

Still, I was screwed. Completely and totally screwed. Forget being named captain, I'd be lucky to play a single game with this guy in charge.

*

It was raining when I got outside, and I pulled my hood up as I continued cursing my luck. Could my day get any worse? A low rumble of thunder answered from somewhere in the distance.

I started toward my truck but hesitated when I noticed a set of keys glinting on the wet concrete. I glanced around the dark parking lot, searching for their owner, and noticed a hooded, hunched figure moving between the rows of cars.

"Hey!" I called, but they didn't seem to hear me over the rain and wind. "Hey!" I yelled louder. This time, the person glanced over their shoulder, then immediately hurried in the opposite direction.

"Hey! You with the hood!" This time my shouting caused a couple walking out of the arena to pause and a few of my teammates who were getting in their cars shot me confused looks. The one person I actually needed to look my way still didn't seem to hear me though.

With a sigh I picked up the keys and started to jog through the rain after the retreating figure. I wasn't even sure the keys were theirs, but I needed all the good karma I could get right now. Returning lost keys seemed like a decent place to start.

As I closed in on the person, they suddenly quickened their pace and cut between two cars. I hiked my hockey bag higher on my shoulder and followed, matching their speed before finally catching up when they stopped next to another car.

I reached out to touch their shoulder. "Hey, I think you—"

They spun. I registered a flash of blonde hair and bright

green eyes. My heart stilled.

I recognized the girl instantly, but a second later her fist was flying toward my face. I didn't have a chance to duck.

Next thing I knew, pain exploded across my face. My head snapped to the side and I stumbled back, slipping on a patch of ice. The weight of my hockey bag pulled me down flat to the ground, where I lay staring up at the darkened sky. So much for my night not getting worse.

And so much for staying away from Mackenzie Foster.

Chapter 3

MACKENZIE

Shit. I just punched someone. And it seriously hurt. I shook my hand as white-hot pain cascaded across my knuckles. I liked to believe I was pretty tough. But punching someone was a first, and I had no idea it would hurt so much.

"What the hell was that for?" the guy I'd knocked to the ground complained. His voice was deep, but I realized he sounded younger than I'd first thought.

"Stay back." I lifted my fists again and edged away until I brushed the side of my car. "You picked the wrong girl to mug. I know ju-jitsu."

Well, I knew *of* ju-jitsu. My martial arts experience was limited to movies only, but I was cornered, so it seemed an appropriate time to lie. The ice arena was on the opposite side of the parking lot, and while I was standing right next to my car, I could hardly dive for the handle and escape inside the vehicle as I still hadn't found my keys.

I couldn't believe I was getting mugged on only my second day in Ransom. Although, I guess I had been warned. One quick Google search before we arrived in town had given me a bad feeling about our new home. And then, yesterday, when my stepmom and I were walking through the cute town on the other side of the river, Sunshine Hills, some old lady in one of the stores asked if we were new to the area. When we explained we'd just moved to Ransom, she recoiled in horror and warned us to be careful. Apparently, she hadn't been joking. I'd just discovered first-hand the town's bad reputation was well deserved.

You'd think my parents would care a little more about where their seventeen-year-old daughter spent her senior year of high school. But no. All consideration of what was best for me went out the window the moment my dad got offered the head coaching job with the reigning state champions, the Ransom Devils.

"I think you broke my nose," my assailant groaned as he slowly climbed to his feet. "And I'm not trying to mug you."

Now he was standing tall, he towered over me, and I inched even closer to my car door. He must have been at least six feet, and his broad shoulders seemed to take up all available space between my car and the next.

"That's exactly what a mugger *would* say."

"I'm *not* a mugger." He huffed and shook his head, like he couldn't be bothered to explain himself. Instead, he ran a hand through his hair, pushing his hood back.

Despite the dark, I could still make out his features, and I found his face almost more intimidating than his size. His tousled brown hair was wet from the rain and thick lashes framed big blue eyes. I couldn't see his whole face as he was gingerly caressing his nose with one hand.

Something about his appearance nagged me though, like I'd seen him somewhere before. I tried to recall if I'd come across any wanted posters around Ransom. No, just ominous warnings from little old ladies I should have listened to. I shouldn't even be in this town, let alone this parking lot.

"Look," the guy exhaled as he started again, "you can save your rear-naked chokehold for the next guy. I'm here for preseason training." He gestured at the bag on the ground which had a hockey stick strapped to it. "You know, at the ice rink we're standing outside. I'm on the school hockey team. The Ransom Devils. Any of this ring a bell?"

I stared at him blankly, still not sure I could trust him.

"I found these keys on the ground . . ." He opened his hand to show me the evidence. "You looked like you were searching for something, so I thought they might belong to you."

Slowly, the realization of what I'd done started to dawn, and I stared at the keys in horror. "You—you really weren't mugging me?"

"Do I have to say it again? No, I wasn't mugging you. The keys; are they yours?"

I couldn't bring myself to answer. This was so embarrassing. I was always getting myself in trouble for being too impulsive, and now I'd gone and punched an innocent boy who'd only been trying to help.

"Uh, yes," I stuttered. "They're mine. I'm sorry for punching you. It's just it's dark out and I'm new to town. I heard some rumors about this place, and I got nervous, and then you practically chased me through the parking lot . . ."

"Because I had your keys . . ."

"Well, I know that *now*." I swallowed again as I watched him. His nose looked like it was starting to bleed, which only made me feel worse. "Hang on . . ."

I took the keys from his hand and opened the passenger side door of my car. I grabbed a handful of tissues from the box in the glove compartment and passed them to him.

"Here, this should help." The internal light of the car wasn't particularly bright, but it was enough to bring his features more clearly into view. I noticed his sharp jawline, the soft freckles on his nose, how his eyes weren't just any old shade of blue but shone like a clear summer sky.

My would-be mugger wasn't just good-looking; he was beautiful. And he didn't just feel a *little* familiar. He looked scarily like an older version of the first boy I kissed. A taller, stronger, manlier version of the jerk who had helped ruin my one chance of ever playing hockey again.

Surely it couldn't be him. That had all happened at a summer camp four hundred miles away. What were the chances? But this guy was a hockey player . . .

"Parker?" I asked cautiously.

His blue eyes looked to the sky, then dipped back down to meet mine. "Took you long enough."

"Parker . . . Darling."

"The one and only."

Unbelievable. Face to face with my biggest mistake, I felt a surge of anger rush through me.

It seemed he was still just as cocky as I recalled. And he didn't look nearly as surprised as me by our little reunion. Though he had just come from practice with my dad, so I guessed he'd had more notice.

"And you play for the Devils?" I continued. "So, that means you go to Ransom High?"

"Sure do."

I was already pissed at my dad for taking this job. But now

it felt like his decision was truly unforgivable. I knew it was a great opportunity for him. That it meant we'd be close enough to Ryker University so my brother could visit easily and we could get to some of his games. But surely nothing was worth this.

"Me too," I muttered.

"Well, this day just keeps getting better and better." Parker's voice was thick with sarcasm as he adjusted the tissue on his nose. "Let me get this straight. First you kiss me. Then you punch me. I'm honestly not sure if I should be excited or terrified to find out what you've got in store for me next."

"*You* kissed *me*!"

He raised an eyebrow. "Look, Melanie, I might get kissed by a lot of blondes, but when one kisses you *and* gets you kicked out of the most prestigious hockey camp in the country, it kind of sticks in your memory."

"It's Mackenzie," I replied through clenched teeth. "And that's *not* how it happened."

"It's okay," Parker replied, leaning in a little closer. "I understand why you did it. Most girls can't resist me."

Irritation rippled down my spine. "I can resist you just fine."

"Can you?"

"I'm doing it right now, aren't I?"

"Thankfully."

I scoffed at the arrogance in his tone. "Do you want me to punch you again?"

The air between us was so tense, I swear the very molecules surrounding us wished they could be somewhere else.

"If my options are between that and another kiss, then

please, swing away."

My memories hadn't done Parker justice. He was far more annoying than I recalled. Unfortunately, he was also far better looking too, even with his potentially broken nose, and that only made me hate him more.

I grimaced as I inspected the damage I'd done more closely. Despite my hostility toward this guy, I didn't actually want him hurt. "Do you need that looked at?"

"I'm not letting you anywhere near it," he said, stepping away as if he was preparing himself for another attack.

I gritted my teeth. "I meant at the hospital. By a trained professional."

"I'll be fine."

"Just let me have a look first."

"No way."

"Don't you at least want me to check it's still straight?"

His eyes flashed with concern, and he lowered his tissue. "Okay, fine, be quick."

I stepped forward and this time he held his ground. We were still mostly shrouded in darkness, so I reached up on my toes to get a better look. A shiver went down my spine as I neared, like a silent alarm.

While I didn't really know what his nose had looked like before, it seemed straight to me. My gaze drifted upward slightly, until I found his blue eyes looking down at me.

"How do I look?" The way his words rumbled through me made me realize how close we were.

"Good—uh, I mean, *it* looks good. Your nose. It's fine." I dropped back onto my heels and stepped away from him, relieved to be able to breathe again.

"Glad to hear it." A knowing smirk was pulling at his lips.

"Yeah, well, I'm not an expert, so maybe the hospital is still a good idea. You are getting blood on the pavement after all. It's like a public health hazard."

"You're the only public health hazard around here," he replied. "You should come with bright flashing lights, warning tape, and a barricade."

I folded my arms. "This can't be happening." I said it more to myself than to him.

"Apparently, it is." He sounded just as frustrated.

The rain started to come down a little harder, and he glanced up at the sky. "Well, as fun as this has been, I better go before you decide to punch me again. I guess I'll see you at school tomorrow, Macy."

"It's Macke—" I didn't even get a chance to correct him before he turned and strutted away, leaving me fuming in his wake.

Chapter 4

PARKER

I was torn between feeling smug and furious as I stalked across the parking lot to my truck. Mackenzie *freaking* Foster. The hits just kept on coming tonight. She'd been back in my life for two minutes, and I already had a messed-up nose to show for it.

She was the kind of person you only had to see once to remember. With bright blonde hair and green eyes like shards of broken glass, she was probably seared into the memory of every guy who'd ever looked her way. I wasn't going to let her know that, though, and it was strangely satisfying to make her think I'd forgotten her name.

If only that were truly the case.

I'd thought about her far more often than I cared to over the years. The surprise I'd felt when she took off her helmet and I saw her for the first time. Her piercing glares and subtle smiles. Our shootout. The bet. The kiss ... and the fallout.

I liked making out with hot girls as much as the next guy, but no kiss was worth risking my hockey career. The thought pissed me off more than the pain in my aching nose.

I picked up my phone from where I'd left it on the dash during practice and saw a stream of notifications, all from my brothers.

Reed: How was practice?

> Grayson: Did Coach Ray make you captain?

> Reed: Is it finally time to teach you the secret captain's handshake?

> Grayson: Oh God, maybe you don't want to be captain after all, Parker.

> Reed: No need to get jealous, Gray.

They'd clearly grown impatient when I didn't respond, because they'd started speculating.

> Reed: Damn, maybe he didn't even make varsity.

> Grayson: I have always thought he'd be more suited to the junior Devils.

> Reed: Don't worry, little brother, at least you'll score a lot of goals in JV.

> Grayson: I'll get Paige to bake you some muffins, that'll cheer you up.

I drew in a breath as I considered how to respond. I didn't have it in me to explain how things had spiraled from one disaster to another. Easier to keep it vague.

> Me: It's all good, I killed it.

The truth was, tonight had nearly killed me. Still, I hoped it would shut them up.

No such luck.

> Reed: Proud of you, man! We'll talk about the handshake soon.

> Grayson: Never doubted you for a second, bro.

> Grayson: About this, I mean. Everything else? I still have doubts.

There was a knock on the window, and I jolted. I didn't need any more surprises tonight, and I wasn't ready for round two with Mackenzie. Thankfully it was just Seth peering through the glass.

"Forgetting someone?" he asked.

I reached over to unlock the passenger side door. He'd asked for a ride home earlier, but in my rush to escape Coach Foster, I'd left him behind.

"Nope," I replied. "Just waiting for the varsity team's new star defenseman to finish primping in the locker room."

He snorted and got in the truck. "So, you forgot."

"Maybe. But if it makes you feel any better, a girl punched me in the parking lot, and she might have broken my nose."

"Huh, that does make me feel better," he said. "Well, it was bound to happen eventually. Who was the girl?"

"Foster's daughter," I grumbled.

"She's here too? I guess that makes sense." He paused for a

moment. "Wait, she's not joining our class, is she?" The look on my face was all the answer he needed, and his grin only grew. "Damn, that's seriously bad news."

"If it's such bad news, why are you smiling?"

"Because it's bad news for you, not me." He was really enjoying this. "Oh no, you didn't try to kiss her again, did you?"

"I told you, *she* kissed *me*. I was just an innocent victim. And no, there wasn't any kissing this time. She punched me because she thought I was mugging her."

"*Were* you mugging her?"

I started the engine. "I'm seriously considering leaving you here."

"Okay, okay." Seth held up his hands in surrender. "Sorry, I just wish I'd been there to see it."

"Well, I'm sorry to disappoint you."

"It's all good. I'm sure you'll give her another reason to punch you soon. Especially if she's going to be at school with us."

That was almost the worst part of all this. Coach Foster had made it clear that if I made one wrong move I'd be off the team. It was going to be hard to obey his order to stay away from his daughter when I'd be seeing her every day at school.

"Nope, I'm avoiding her at all costs," I said. "If I do anything to piss off Coach Foster, I'm screwed."

"Guess that means he remembers you."

"Unfortunately."

"Guess that also means you're the last person he wants to name captain."

I swallowed and nodded.

"Sorry, man. I know how much you wanted it."

I shrugged. "I'll just have to show him he's wrong about me."

People often misjudged me. They thought I breezed through life, like everything was easy. That I was nothing more than a playboy who only cared about girls and hockey—okay, maybe they were right about some things. But I *did* deserve to be captain.

"I can worry about that tomorrow," I continued. "We should be celebrating the fact you made the team."

"Sure, we can," Seth said. "But is your nose okay?"

"It's fine. Just a little bloody."

"It's a *lot* bloody," he corrected. "Are you sure Foster's daughter did that? It wasn't some professional boxer out for an evening jog?"

"Yes, I'm sure."

"Maybe my dad should take a look..."

Dr. Walker had tended to plenty of my hockey injuries over the years, but I didn't want to bother him. Then again, if even Seth was concerned, this was probably more serious than I thought.

"You're getting blood on the seat..." he added.

I grimaced as I realized he was right. Perhaps I did need to get my nose checked out after all.

Thankfully, Seth's dad didn't mind taking a look. He told me my nose wasn't broken, but it might be a little swollen and bruised for the next few days. Luckily, there was no serious damage. Not physically, at least. Mackenzie had given my ego a big hit.

"If anyone asks, I took an elbow to the nose during practice," I told Seth as I left his house.

He scoffed. "That's boring. I'm telling everyone you've started bull riding."

"Bull riding on a school night after hockey practice?"

"Okay, what about that underground fight club you supposedly set up?"

"That rumor's like two years old. I started it to give Gray an alibi when he sprained his wrist."

"Why, what was he really doing?"

"He tripped while picking daisies with Paige . . ."

"Seriously?"

"Yep. Before they were even dating."

Seth's eyes lit up before he shook his head. "Fight club it is. We can't have people thinking you've gone soft without your older brothers around. You're supposed to be the wild one, not the mild one. And if word gets out you were punched by a girl . . ."

"Okay, fine, the fight club is open for business."

"Good. Just don't forget you've got a reputation to live down to." He grinned before closing the Walkers' front door on me.

As I drove home, I wondered if Seth might have a point. While our team had certainly been weakened by talented players graduating last year, that wasn't all we'd lost. The fearsome reputation my brothers and I had developed over the years had given us a distinct advantage on the ice.

Opposition players always seemed to think twice when it came to confronting us, and it often felt like we'd beaten them before the game even started. So, I'd been more than happy to encourage some of the ridiculous rumors that swirled around town about us, and I'd even added a few of my own when necessary. With my brothers gone, there was less reason to fear the Ransom Devils. Maybe it was time to let the rumor mill crank up again.

I was hoping my nose wasn't too bad to look at, but the moment I walked through the front door of my house, Cammie started to smile.

"You look terrible." My sister could be brutal sometimes, and I swore she had gotten even worse since starting her junior year. "Did you drop your phone on your face again?"

"That was one time."

"Stick to the nose at practice?"

"Fight club, if you must know. You should see the other guy."

"Does he look like he tried to stop a puck with his face too?" Like I said, brutal.

"He wishes."

"No one in their right mind would wish they looked like you."

I couldn't help but laugh, and Cammie smirked to herself before heading up the stairs.

"Parker?" my mom called from the kitchen.

I'd been hoping to sneak off to my room without her seeing me, but I hadn't had much luck so far today, why should it change now? With a sigh, I went to find her.

"Why are you home so—" She jumped from her seat when she saw me. "Your nose! What happened?"

She took hold of my jaw and lightly tilted my head to get a

better look. I hated it when my mom fussed, but I didn't shake her off. I hated worrying her more.

"I'm okay, Mom. Just a little knock at practice. Nothing broken."

"Why didn't you call?" She tutted before turning her head toward the living room. "Danny, your son's injured again."

"*Again?*" he replied.

"It's fine," I insisted. "I've already had Seth's dad check it out, and he gave me the all clear."

"You went to see Seth's dad?" My dad walked into the room. "Don't tell me I owe him another case of beer."

"You owe him another case of beer," I replied. "Sorry."

My dad winced when he got close enough to see my nose properly. "Catch the wrong end of a stick?"

"Something like that," I muttered. I didn't want my dad inspecting it too closely. He might quickly realize this was not a hockey-related injury, but a fist-related one.

"Aren't you going to ask me about practice?" I said, trying to divert my parents' attention.

"I'm more concerned about your nose," Mom said. "You sure it's okay?"

"Yes, I'm sure," I said, wriggling free of her grasp. "I promise. You can call Dr. Walker if you don't believe me."

That seemed to calm her somewhat, but I had no doubt she'd call Seth's dad as soon as we were done here.

"So, how was it?" Dad asked. "Did Ray name his captain?"

"Nope," I muttered. "Coach Ray's gone."

"He's gone?" My dad frowned. "What do you mean?"

"Apparently he needs back surgery," I explained. "He's out

for the season. People are saying he might have to retire."

Mom drew back with surprise, but my dad looked thoughtful. "I'd heard his back was causing him some issues, but I had no idea it was that bad."

"How awful," Mom said. "I hope he's okay. We should send him something. Maybe I'll bake cookies."

"He's already got a bad back, Mom. I don't think we should give him a bad stomach to go with it." I loved my mom, but we all knew she was a terrible cook.

She slapped me on the arm, then instantly apologized with another look at my injured nose.

"This is all very sudden," my dad said, his brow still creased in thought. "The season starts this week. Are they getting a replacement coach?"

"They've got one. And you'll never guess who it is." I didn't wait for suggestions. "Wade Foster."

My parents instantly shared a concerned look, and I wasn't surprised. They weren't big fans of Coach Foster either. They'd listened to me rave about the guy for months in the lead-up to his camp three years ago, and then they still had to foot the massive bill after I got kicked out. I'd spent the rest of that summer working at Dad's garage to help cover the cost. Unlike my brother Reed, I was more of a liability than anything else when it came to cars, and the whole ordeal wasn't a happy memory for any of us.

"The coach who kicked you out of his camp?" My mom asked the question like she knew the answer but hoped she was wrong. Like perhaps there was another high school hockey coach named Wade Foster, and this was all just an unfortunate coincidence.

"The very same. And apparently he not only remembers me, but he also holds a grudge. I'll be lucky to ride the bench this year, let alone make captain."

My dad rubbed a hand over his head, and I swore I spotted another three gray hairs magically appear. You could probably chart every time I'd stressed my dad out by tracking the grays dotting his hairline.

"I'll talk to him," Dad said. "Make sure he gives you a fair shot. I think his son plays at Ryker with Reed and Grayson. I'm sure he'll take a call from me."

It was tempting, but I sighed and shook my head. "It's fine, Dad."

I knew he just wanted to help, but I didn't need him fighting my battles for me. Plus, I'd bet a call from Dad would only make Foster hate me more. "Just give me a few weeks. I'll win him over."

I wasn't exactly sure how I was going to do that. But I'd have to start by proving myself on the ice. And avoiding his daughter, of course.

"That's the spirit." Dad patted me on the shoulder. "I'm sure he'll come around. He'd be crazy to leave his best player on the bench."

My mom wasn't so easily reassured, though. She was staring at me, clearly desperate to spill her thoughts.

I sighed. "What is it?"

"Well, it's just, you know you're going to have to stay out of trouble, Parker."

"Yeah, I know."

"Do you?" She tilted her head. "That means no detentions. No saying whatever comes to mind. No mystery injuries. No rumors. No *police*."

"Mom, the police was a one-time thing. A total misunderstanding. I swear."

"You and Seth were caught on the Sunshine Hills Prep grounds in the middle of the night with sixty-four toy devils and a wheelbarrow full of feathers."

"I still maintain I was sleepwalking."

"And I suppose you were also sleepwalking the time you painted a Devils logo on Jeremy Hoffman's car?" Dad asked.

"I can't help that I'm artistic when I sleep."

"What about skinny-dipping in the town pool at midnight this summer?" Mum pitched in.

"Sleep-swimming."

Dad grunted. "We're just saying—don't give Foster an excuse to kick you out again."

My parents were right. We all knew it. But I could see they needed my word.

"Okay, okay. I'll be good. I'll stay out of trouble."

Mom's lips twisted to the side. She didn't believe me. "I hope so. You've worked too hard to let it all go to waste in your senior year."

"I won't do anything to jeopardize my spot, Mom, I swear."

"Okay." Neither of my parents seemed convinced though, and I didn't really blame them. I wasn't great at staying out of trouble. And it was going to be even harder to avoid it now that Mackenzie Foster was in town.

Chapter 5

MACKENZIE

"So, this is where I'm spending my senior year?"

I stared up at the red-brick building my stepmom had just pulled up outside, trying to comprehend how my life had changed so drastically in the past week. I was supposed to be back home preparing for the fall art exhibition. Instead, I was staring up at a new school where I didn't know a soul—well, I knew one person, but it was debatable whether Parker Darling had a soul.

"I know it's not as flashy as Lakeview High, but it's a good school."

No, this school wasn't nearly as flashy, but apparently it had flash-*ers*. I pointed to the second floor. "Is that some guy's butt hanging out the window?"

Tessa grabbed my hand and lowered it, doing her best to hide her shock. "So, your new classmates are a little spirited..."

"Oh, that's the term we're using?"

"And I know it was hard leaving your friends behind, but I'm sure you'll make new ones in no time."

"Hopefully ones wearing pants," I muttered.

"Mommy, can I have a snack?" Skye called from the back seat. My three-year-old sister sounded sweet and innocent, but she was always one wrong answer away from unleashing her inner demon. With dark curly hair and big brown eyes, she and Daisy, who was sat in the car seat next to her, looked just like Tessa.

Their features couldn't have been more different to my brother and me, who took after our mom with blond hair and green eyes. At least, according to the pictures I'd seen of her. I was only a baby when she died, so those photos were all the memories I had. My dad rarely talked about her. Even now, I think it hurt him too much. But he'd once told me I had her smile, and her determination.

"When we get home, Skye," Tessa replied.

"But I want one now."

"You better get her a snack, Mom . . ." Daisy warned. My other sister was only four years old, but she'd always been a bit of an old soul, and the concern in her voice right now made her sound far wiser than her years. She knew just as well as me what would happen if Skye didn't get what she wanted.

"When we get home," Tessa repeated.

That was my cue to leave. Nothing inside Ransom High could be worse than the tantrums of a three-year-old who wanted a snack.

"I better get going." I jumped from the car before I missed my opportunity to escape. "Bye, you guys."

"Don't forget your father's driving you home tonight," Tessa said.

"Okay."

"Good luck. Love y—" The sound of her response was swallowed by Skye's pterodactyl screams.

Perhaps Tessa needed the luck more than I did. I gave her a sympathetic smile before I shut the door and waved as she pulled away from the curb.

When she was gone, I turned to face my new school. Between the warnings I'd heard about Ransom, the flasher whose butt was still poking out a second-floor window and the fact this place had produced Parker Darling, I had serious concerns.

My hand was still sore after my encounter with Parker last night, and I bristled as I thought of him. While a twinge of guilt for punching him remained, I had a plan to get over it: avoid him like the plague.

I drew in a deep breath, but just as I went to step forward a truck came screaming down the road behind me. I heard the splash of tires slashing through a puddle, and a split second later freezing gutter water hit me like a tidal wave. It sprayed across my back, soaking my top, jeans and sneakers. I didn't have a chance to even try to jump out of the way. One moment I was dry. The next, I stood there dripping, cold and fuming.

I spun to search for the driver. They were already pulling into a parking space. Of course they drove an oversized truck. Probably compensating for something. The driver's door opened and as they jumped from the vehicle my blood started to boil. Parker.

He smoothed a hand through his hair as he placed a Devils cap backward on his head, like he was gearing up for another day of making bad choices. My hands clenched into fists at my sides. Was this his revenge? Drenching a girl on her first day at a new school was low, even for someone like Parker. I wondered if it was too soon to punch him again.

He started walking toward me, and my anger slightly diminished when I caught sight of the damage I'd inflicted last night. A bright bruise had formed under his eye and there seemed to be a small cut on his nose. I was surprised by how bad it was—and also by how attractive he still looked.

A cool wind made me shudder and I looked down at my soaked clothes. I didn't want to give Parker the satisfaction of knowing he'd upset me. I started peeling off my wet sweater only to find my top underneath was drenched too. I was going to need a whole new outfit.

When I looked back up, I saw Parker had stopped near me. A frown creased his brow as he glanced between the puddle and me. For a moment, the dash of uncertainty in his expression made me wonder if he had only just realized what he'd done. But then his eyes started to dance with joy and his lips lifted in that annoying smirk of his.

"I'm not sure what your old school was like, but you should know, wet T-shirt contests are frowned upon here."

Screw being the bigger person. I wanted to kill him.

"You did this on purpose," I seethed.

"Hardly. I didn't see you there."

"I was standing right by the road."

"And I was focused on driving."

"You really expect me to believe this was an accident?"

He gave a one-shouldered shrug in reply. "I mean, I know I seem godlike, but even I can't control puddle trajectory."

Was this guy for real?

"If you need a dry top to wear," he continued, "I've got a spare jersey with my name and number on it in my locker..."

Irritation clawed through me. "I'd rather roll in that puddle than wear something with your name on it."

"Guess you better try the front office then." He smiled and set off up the steps to the front entrance. "Welcome to Ransom, Mallory."

"It's Mackenzie!" I shouted after him, making a few nearby students jump and look my way.

I took several deep breaths and tried to remind myself that murdering Parker would be a bad idea. Jumpsuits didn't flatter me, and I looked terrible in orange. If I was ever going to end up in prison, I refused to let it be because of Parker Darling.

Another breeze sent a shiver up my spine. My wet top clung to my skin, while my jeans and shoes felt like leaden weights. There was no salvaging this outfit. I was just going to have to hope Parker was right, and the front office had a spare set of clothes.

With my shoes squelching and my arms wrapped around my body, I hurried up the steps and through the front doors. There were students laughing and shouting, and a constant clanging of lockers opening and shutting. It was weird to feel such a strong sense of familiarity and total foreignness at the same time.

I felt a fleeting desire to turn and flee back out the front doors . . . but I never backed down from a challenge. So I stuffed my nerves deep inside and focused on finding the front office.

Luckily, it wasn't far from the entrance, and when I arrived, I was greeted by a girl with a cautious smile and kind hazel eyes behind heavy-set glasses. She was wearing a thick, knitted cardigan and jeans, and her light brown hair was messily piled on her head. I was immediately jealous of how dry she looked.

"Mackenzie Foster?" Her voice was soft but friendly.

"Uh, yeah, but Kenzie's fine."

"Well, welcome to Ransom, Kenzie. I'm Jaz. I'll be showing you around the school today. I . . ." Her voice drifted off as she looked me up and down. "What happened to your clothes?"

"I lost a fight with a puddle."

"On your first day?" Her eyes filled with dismay.

"Wrong place, wrong time, I guess."

"Well, don't worry. We can fix this. Come on, let's get your schedule and then we'll check the lost and found for something you can wear."

I nodded and gave her a grateful smile as I followed her into the office. My gratitude was extremely short-lived, though. While there was a box of spare clothes for me to look through, the options were severely limited. It was mostly boys' clothes, and nothing looked like it would be the right size.

After I'd found the best possible combination I could, Jaz took me to the closest bathroom to change. I cringed as I left the stall and caught sight of myself in the mirror. The faded red Devils hockey sweatshirt I'd selected was so big it hung to my knees. And while there were shorts underneath it somewhere, the sweatshirt swallowed them whole. I supposed things could be worse. At least I wasn't wearing a jersey with the name Darling printed across my back.

"I look like I raided the Ransom High uniform shop," I said, quickly tying my hair back. I hadn't realized it was wet too. The list of things Parker Darling had to answer for was growing by the second.

"It's not that bad," Jaz said, trying her best to sound positive.

"You look cute."

"Cute?"

"With lots of school spirit," she added.

"Right." I lifted a half-hearted fist in the air. "Go Devils."

Jaz giggled. "Okay, well, if you're ready, we should probably get to homeroom. I can give you a quick tour on the way."

I risked one last look in the mirror. I didn't want anyone seeing me like this, but we were already running late, so there wasn't much choice. At least I was no longer wet. "Okay, after you."

The corridor was much quieter now. The bell had rung while I'd been getting changed so most students had gone to class.

"So, what do I need to know?" I asked Jaz.

"Well, I'm a Pisces. Pescatarian. I have two super annoying brothers, a BookTok account with ten followers, and I'm almost ninety-nine percent certain aliens walk among us. You should see the lunch lady, she . . ." Jaz trailed off as she caught my confused expression. "You're talking about the school, aren't you?"

"I was." I laughed. "But your views on extraterrestrial life sound far more interesting. What exactly makes you think the lunch lady is an alien?"

Jaz scanned the hall before lowering her voice and saying, "She never blinks, and I mean *never*."

"Highly suspect," I agreed with a smile. "And I know all about annoying siblings. I have an older brother who's so perfect it hurts, and my two younger sisters are cute, but one of them can scream so loud I sometimes think she's part dinosaur."

"Oh, my older brother is the golden child too. He's at college now. My younger brother's a junior here. But Owen rarely screams."

"Lucky," I said. "Okay, what about the school? Just tell me the important stuff."

"The important stuff?"

"Yeah." I nodded. "Like, which of the cafeteria food is edible? Are there any places I should avoid? What are the other students like?" I had to hope this wasn't a school filled with Parker Darlings.

Jaz laughed lightly. "Hmm, well, most of the cafeteria food is fine. Don't go down the alley that runs along the east side of this building, unless you're into weed. No judgement if you are, by the way."

"I'm not," I said with a laugh.

"And most of the students are good eggs."

"And the others?"

"Some are a little scrambled," she said, smiling. "But I've always liked my eggs slightly messy."

Jaz showed me to my locker before taking me to our homeroom. Along the way she pointed out things of interest like the library, the cafeteria, and classrooms I'd need to find later in the day. It was impossible not to notice all the Ransom Devils posters papering the walls, too. Most of the images were promoting the first game of the season this Friday night. But there were also plenty of pictures showing Parker and his teammates in action. Like I needed to see any more of his face.

As we entered homeroom, every student's eyes darted my way. I did my best to ignore the attention and resisted the urge to pull my sweatshirt lower. I'd been conscious it was too long at first, but now I was wishing it would make me disappear entirely. I kept my gaze on the teacher, trying to ignore the whispers and giggles my arrival had sparked.

"Mackenzie Foster?" he asked.

I nodded and silently prayed he wasn't about to make me introduce myself in front of the class. Thankfully, he gestured toward some free seats near the back of the room.

"Welcome. I'm Mr. Green. It's great to have you here; take a seat."

I released a breath and rushed to the free chair he was gesturing to. A couple of girls were still giggling to each other as I went to sit in front of them. I preferred that to the guys whose eyes were lingering on my legs.

Jaz slumped into the seat at my side.

"I thought he was going to make me stand up front and tell everyone my life story," I whispered.

"Oh, no, Mr. Green's pretty cool," Jaz replied. "He teaches art."

He was still calling roll, and now that I looked a little closer, I noticed his fingers were covered in paint stains. Art was my favorite subject, and my hands were also sporting a few marks from spending that morning working on a mural for my bedroom wall. I hadn't gotten too far with it yet, but I was eager to keep going.

"This is my friend, Isaac," Jaz continued, leaning back so I could see the guy sitting on her other side. "Isaac, this is Kenzie."

Isaac was hunched over a book on his desk, and as he lifted

his head, he pushed his glasses up his nose. He wore a faded sci-fi tee under a zip-up hoodie, and as he met my gaze he gave me a welcoming smile. "Joining a new school midway through the semester," he said. "Military family?"

"My dad's the new hockey coach."

"Ah." He nodded.

Jaz gasped. "I should have known. We can't believe Coach Ray's gone, but your dad sounds like he's a big deal. It's all been kind of a shock though."

"For me too," I agreed.

"Jasmine Cleaver?" the teacher called.

"Here!" Jaz waved her hand in the air for emphasis.

Isaac laughed and shook his head before returning to his book. The thing was massive. I didn't realize they made books that thick, and the writing looked tiny.

Jaz smirked when she caught my curious look. "It's the *Lord of the Rings* trilogy," she said. "I've lost count of how many times he's read it."

"You can't count very high," Isaac muttered without lifting his eyes from the book. "This is the fifth time."

Movement at the door caught my attention and I glanced up to see someone leaning into the room. "Here, Mr. Green."

My spine stiffened at the sight of Parker. I'd already crossed paths with him more than enough times since I got to Ransom; did we have to share the same homeroom too?

He seemed primed and ready to dart right back out the door, but his eyes flashed in my direction as if he sensed my loathing glare. His gaze dipped to my old Devils sweater and then my bare legs, and the corner of his lips twitched with amusement. *Ass*.

Thankfully, he quickly decided homeroom wasn't for him and disappeared once more.

"Did you see Parker's bruise?" I heard someone whisper behind me. "I wonder what happened." It was one of the girls who had giggled at my outfit.

"Maybe he got in a fight," her friend replied.

"Probably on the ice," the first added.

The guy beside me brushed a hand through his blond hair before he leaned back to join their conversation. "Actually," he said, "there was a fight last night, but it didn't have anything to do with hockey."

I couldn't resist glancing behind me.

"What happened?" both the girls asked in unison, leaning forward in their chairs.

The blond guy lowered his voice. "Parker's started a new fight club. You know, the sketchy underground basement kind. No gloves. No ref. No rules. Just a crowd yelling for blood."

The girls gasped and I had to stop myself from spluttering out a laugh.

"The dude Parker was up against fought dirty, but our boy came out victorious. He might look a little rough today, but the other guy ended up much worse."

What the hell was he talking about? I knew exactly how Parker got his bruise. Even if I didn't, I never would have believed the story. The whole thing was ridiculous.

But one of the girls crooned, "Oh, poor Parker," and the other one added, "He's so brave."

They both sounded well and truly under Parker's spell.

Noticing my confused expression, Jaz leaned in close and nodded to each girl as she whispered, "That's Vanessa and Britt. They're talking about Parker Darling." As if that alone was enough explanation.

When my expression didn't change, she continued. "He's one of the Darling Devils."

"The who?"

She looked startled for a second, as though she'd never heard the question before. But then she seemed to remember it was only my first day at this school.

"The Darling Devils," she repeated. "The best hockey players Ransom High has ever had. Reed, Grayson, and Parker Darling." She pursed her lips as she considered something. "The older two graduated last year though, so I guess Parker's just *the* Darling Devil now. Anyway, that fight club story is one of the tamer rumors you'll hear about him and his brothers."

The Darling Devil. Of course, Parker had a little nickname for himself, and an infamous reputation to go with it. No wonder he walked around like he owned this place. Even my punch hadn't dented his image.

"Actually, you're all wrong," I said, unable to stop myself from turning to the girls and entering the gossip circle. "Parker has a black eye because he snuck up behind me in a parking lot last night and I punched him."

The girls stared at me with equal amounts of confusion and horror.

"And you are?" one of them asked. I think it was Britt. There was a skeptical look in her eyes, like she'd already judged me and decided I wasn't worthy.

"Mackenzie Foster," I replied. "I'm new here."

"Obviously," the girl answered with a laugh. The way her eyes dipped to my loaner outfit made me feel like I'd shown up at school in a clown costume.

"Well, Mackenzie, I don't know if you're trying to be funny or what, but you don't have to lie about Parker like that." It was Vanessa who spoke this time, and I knew immediately she was the one to watch out for. There was a crafty intelligence in her eyes. Combined with her dark silky hair and sultry beauty, I could easily picture her ruling over this school at Parker's side.

I could also see she wouldn't make a good enemy. So I simply shrugged and said, "Maybe, instead of gossiping, you should ask *him* what happened?"

Vanessa scoffed and turned back to her conversation with Britt. It seemed I'd been dismissed.

Jaz leaned over again. "Did you really punch Parker?"

"Yeah."

"*Why?*"

"Like I said, he snuck up on me in the parking lot. It was dark. I thought he was about to mug me."

"Oh, my God," she laughed. "That's hilarious. Although, I have to admit, I'm a little surprised a girl hasn't punched him sooner."

"Because he's a total jerk?"

"He's not a *total* jerk..."

"Because he's a player?"

"I mean, he is, but that's common knowledge. No one's going to punch him when they know exactly what they're getting into."

"It has to be that annoying smirk of his then, right?"

She smiled and shook her head. "I don't know how to explain it. He's just Parker, I guess. You either want to kiss him or punch him. And most girls want to kiss him."

"What about you?"

She laughed and shrugged. "Kiss, I suppose. But only so I could see what all the fuss is about. He's definitely not my type."

"What's your type?"

I could have sworn her eyes darted toward Isaac. And I was certain his head lifted a fraction from his book.

But Jaz answered, "Fictional."

"Fair enough," I said with a laugh.

The bell rang and everyone jumped from their seats to file out of the room.

"Come on, I'll show you to your first class," Jaz said. "See you at lunch, Isaac."

He gave us a wave, though he was still reading his book as he walked. I glanced at my schedule to find I had math next. The rocky start to my first day wasn't getting any smoother.

As I left the room, the guy who had been spreading rumors about Parker fell in beside me.

"So, you're the girl who punched Parker," he said, smiling broadly. "I'm Seth."

I was beginning to understand why Ransom had such a bad reputation. The guys here were all too good-looking and intent on causing trouble.

"You knew I punched him?"

"Oh yeah. I've heard a lot about you, Mackenzie."

Seeing as the only person I knew in this town was Parker, I could only assume Seth already had a terrible opinion of me.

"You play hockey, right?" he went on. "Goaltender?"

His comment took me off guard. Parker had told him that? It was the last thing I'd expect him to know. My goalie days were over, and I never really spoke about it with anyone except Max.

"Uh, not anymore," I muttered. "And don't change the subject. If you knew the truth about what happened last night, why'd you tell those girls that story about the fight club?"

"Just trying to help out a friend," Seth said. "Parker's got a reputation to uphold. Although, it's kind of difficult when you immediately debunk my carefully crafted rumors."

"Parker's reputation is not my problem."

"It is if you don't want the whole school to think you're crazy."

"I'm not crazy. He really did sneak up on me."

"That's not how they'll see it," he replied. "Parker has a very dedicated fandom."

Perfect. I'd picked a fight with the popular playboy hockey star and was destined to be a pariah at my new school after only one morning.

"Leave her alone, Seth," Jaz said, coming to my rescue. She tucked her arm through mine. "We've got to get to class."

"Well, it was nice to officially meet you, Mackenzie. You're welcome at the fight club anytime." With a wink, he turned and strode away.

I sighed. "I really need to learn to keep my mouth shut."

"Are you kidding?" Jaz laughed. "Please don't. I haven't had this much fun at school before the first class all year."

"I only just got here, and I've already got a growing list of new enemies."

"I always say you're not doing life right if you don't step on a few toes."

"What about punching hockey players on the nose?"

She laughed. "Yeah, that might not be the smartest thing to do at Ransom High. But personally I'm fully in favor of it. Come on, let's get you to math."

Chapter 6

PARKER

"What the hell is that?" I stared in horror as Elliot Ford slowly and carefully moved into the art classroom, a pair of crutches clicking with each step he took. His foot was elevated off the ground in a large protective boot.

"Ford, what did you do?" I cursed. Only he could be selfish enough to get injured before the season had even started.

His eyes narrowed in response. "*I* didn't do anything."

"Well, it sure looks like you did! Or is this some kind of joke?"

"I wish," he grumbled, gradually making his way to the front of the room. Still, I had no answers.

"Do you know what happened?" I spun to face Seth who was leaning against the table beside me. Although he didn't take art, he had a free period now and had come to gleefully update me on how Mackenzie Foster was letting everyone in school know the truth about my injured face. She'd already tried her best to ruin my hockey career three years ago; now she was back to ruin my reputation. It wasn't even lunch on her first day.

"Apparently, he slipped and fell while *stretching* in the shower last night," Seth said with a smirk.

"Stretching?"

"Yeah, probably had a bit of tension to release..."

"Well *that's* a graphic I never want to picture again."

Seth laughed, but I couldn't find the humor. This was a serious problem.

"How long are you going to be wearing that thing?" I called across the room to Elliot, who had taken a seat.

"Not sure." He shrugged. "I need to go back for more tests, but the doctor said it could be at least six weeks."

I couldn't believe what I was hearing. Don't get me wrong; I had often dreamed of some terrible mishap befalling Elliot so another player could take over as starting goaltender. But our first game of the season was on Friday, and we didn't have a backup goalie. Not a good one, anyway. Elliot was quite literally the devil we needed.

"What are we going to do?" I groaned.

"To help Elliot?" Seth asked, clearly confused.

"No, idiot. The *team*. He's the only goaltender in Ransom who can stop a puck. Since Micah moved to Florida, the only other option we have is that kid Anderson."

"There's really no one else?"

"No, everyone else who tried out at the start of preseason was even worse. Don't you remember?" I almost shuddered at the thought. Most of them could barely stay upright on their skates.

"I didn't really notice." Seth shrugged.

"Trust me, they played like they'd never held a hockey stick in their lives."

Seth nodded, as though he was finally starting to understand my urgency. "Sounds like a problem for the new coach."

"It'll be a problem for all of us if Anderson plays in our first game this Friday. We're up against some strong teams to start this season, and in just over a month, we've got the homecoming game against Sunshine Hills."

"You worry too much."

"You don't worry enough. It's homecoming. My whole family will be there. And the Saints are our biggest rivals. I refuse to lose to them."

"I'm sure it'll be fine." Seth lowered his voice. "Besides, I think you've got a bigger problem."

He nodded toward the door as Mackenzie came barreling into the room. She was still wearing her borrowed outfit from the school office. The sweatshirt was way too big on her, and she must have been cold with such bare legs. An uncomfortable feeling swirled in my chest. Surely it couldn't be guilt, could it?

Was I an asshole for getting her wet today? Probably. But I'd been telling the truth when she confronted me earlier: splashing her was genuinely an accident. But that didn't mean I was sorry she got soaked. It was just a little water—not, for example, a black eye.

I'd mostly managed to avoid Mackenzie so far today. So why, of all the classes, did this have to be the one we shared? Art was the only subject I didn't totally hate or suck at. There were no right or wrong answers when I entered this room, and it was the one place that could take my mind away from the pressures of hockey; where I could switch off for a little while and relax. She was the last person I wanted here.

"I still can't believe you soaked her with your car," Seth said.

"I didn't mean to," I replied. "It was a happy accident."

He rolled his eyes at me and glanced Mackenzie's way again. "Yeah, well, I think she won this round. Even in those lost-and-found clothes, she still looks pretty hot. And I'm not the only one who's noticed."

I glanced around the room to see several other guys looking at her with interest. Another uncomfortable swirling started in my chest. As much as I hated to admit it, Mackenzie *was* hot. And something about seeing her in a Devils jersey only increased the appeal. I shook the thought from my head. Her looks didn't change anything.

"Let's see how interested they are once they've actually met her."

Mackenzie had found a seat near Elliot at the front of the room and was yet to even glance in my direction.

"She doesn't seem too bad," Seth said.

"Easy for you to say." I gestured toward my face. "She hasn't tried to break your nose."

"I'm sure it was just a happy accident."

I glared at him. "You're also forgetting the time she kissed me, knowing full well her father was psychotic and would kick me off the camp."

"Yeah, you really need to get over that."

"Get over it?" I growled. "I feel like I'm reliving it. Only this time, if her dad decides he wants me gone it'll ruin the most important season of my life. That girl is like a walking tornado. I need to stay well away from her or I'll get torn to shreds."

Seth started to laugh.

"It's not funny."

"It is kind of funny. Only you would mess up your entire future in hockey because of a kiss with some girl."

"I was fourteen."

"And you haven't changed one bit."

I sighed and dropped my head into my hands. Seth was the worst person to talk to if I was looking for sympathy.

"Seth Walker, don't you have your own class to get to?" Mr. Green had finally decided to make an appearance. He was only five minutes late, which had to be a record for him.

"Actually, I have a free period."

"And you should be using that time to study. Now stop distracting my students. Out of my classroom, please."

"Okay." Seth grinned at the teacher. "But don't miss me too much."

Mr. Green sighed and continued to the front of the room.

"All right, everyone, let's get started." He raised his voice as he made his way past the easels and desks peppering the room. "I want you working on your personal portfolios today, please." He stopped next to Mackenzie's desk.

"Mackenzie, why don't we have a chat in my office?"

I snorted under my breath as I pulled out my tablet. Mr. Green's "office" was just behind me at the back of the room, and it was no more than a paint closet. It was tiny, but he'd somehow squeezed a desk and two chairs in there. He used it for most of his student meetings so we could talk about our work more privately. Mr. Green was always trying to encourage us to search for deeper meanings in our art, and conversations in his office often felt a little like being on a psychiatrist's couch. I liked art, but that definitely wasn't my style.

As Mackenzie followed the teacher to the back of the room, her green eyes landed on me. They glinted like gems, sharp and cold. She seemed just as annoyed as I was about sharing this class.

"Nice outfit," I said as she walked past.

"Nice nose," she snapped in reply, barely breaking stride.

A smile crept onto my lips, but I quickly quashed it. I was supposed to be avoiding this girl at all costs, but I couldn't seem to let an opportunity to mess with her pass me by. There was something about the way her eyes narrowed whenever she saw me and her fists clenched whenever I spoke that I enjoyed a little bit too much.

I leaned back in my chair as I watched her continue to Mr. Green's office.

As she reached the room, she glanced back and caught me staring. The glare she sent me was so piercing, I wondered if it was possible to punch someone with a look alone. She truly hated me, yet the thought only made me smile.

But then my chair started to wobble beneath me. I'd leaned back too far, and my arms shot out as I tried to rebalance. I must have looked like a flailing octopus as I desperately attempted to stop myself from falling. I threw my weight forward and just barely managed to save myself from crashing to the floor.

I glanced at the students sitting nearby. A few shot me confused looks but most hadn't noticed. However, when I looked back at Mackenzie she was biting her lip, trying to withhold her laughter before she disappeared into Mr. Green's office.

I attempted to focus on my project, an illustrated comic strip inspired by a box of old superhero comics my dad found in the attic over the summer. Flicking through them, I'd started to wonder why superheroes were always stuck saving the world. I knew with great power came great responsibility, but what if Clark Kent didn't want to fight for truth, justice, and a better tomorrow? What if instead he used his secret powers to become an unstoppable hockey player?

I was quite proud of how the comic was coming along, but I was struggling today. I found myself constantly glancing toward the back of the room. I shouldn't have cared what Mackenzie was talking about with the teacher. But a part of me was curious. And when there was a lull in the noise of classroom conversations, I realized I was close enough to the slightly ajar door of Mr. Green's office that I could hear him talking.

"Your love of hockey really shines through in some of your previous pieces, Mackenzie," he said. "Is that the focus of your current project?"

"Yeah, I'm planning to explore the changing face of the sport over the years," she replied. "I'm looking into how it's developed visually, socially, and culturally. I was thinking it could be a mixed-media piece..."

I glanced down at my tablet, suddenly questioning whether my work was as good as I thought. Mr. Green was always telling me my artwork needed more voice and meaning, while it sounded like Mackenzie's had plenty. I didn't want someone else using the same subject matter as me because I didn't want to be compared—especially not with her.

"Well, I'm really looking forward to seeing how it turns out," Mr. Green was saying. "Do you play hockey?"

"No, not anymore."

The chatter in the classroom increased so I couldn't hear the rest of their conversation. Why didn't Mackenzie play hockey anymore? Her dad was a coach, and her brother played at the same college as Reed and Gray. Hockey must have been as much a part of her family as it was my own.

And while I might have despised every fiber of this girl's being, even I couldn't deny she'd been a decent player when we'd squared off against one another. I'd scored countless goals that day, not that Coach Foster had noticed, but Mackenzie had saved my best effort with impressive ease. Whatever her reason, she would have been out of luck at this school anyway; Ransom High had never had a girls' team.

When they emerged from the office, Mr. Green was beaming. It was hardly surprising; it sounded like he'd just found a new star student. "If there's anything I can do to help, Mackenzie, I'm always here. This classroom is all about experimenting and expressing your ideas in unique ways, and I'm excited to see more from you."

"Thanks, Mr. Green."

The teacher nodded for Mackenzie to return to her desk, but when he caught me watching, he lifted an eyebrow. "Parker, you're next."

I sighed and gathered my tablet before heading to his office. As I passed Mackenzie in the aisle my arm brushed against hers. I felt a jolt of excitement dance across my skin, but I stayed strong. No teasing comment. No cocky grin. I completely blanked her, and she did the same to me. Maybe I could pull this off after all.

"How's your comic strip going?" Mr. Green asked, once I was sitting in the cramped closet.

"Great."

"Parker..."

"Okay, I haven't made much progress since last week. But preseason has been full on, and we've got our first game coming up. You understand, right?"

A frustrated breath left my teacher's lips as he placed his arms on the desk between us. "I know how important hockey is to you, but the season is only just starting. You're only going to get busier. You need to manage your time better. I don't want you falling behind."

"I know. I won't."

"Good, because I'm running an exhibit at the Ransom Community Center for homecoming weekend next month. I've been asked if a few of my students would like to display their work. I think you should be one of them."

"You do?"

"Yes, Parker. You're very talented, when you're focused. I think it would be good for you to have a deadline and something to strive for this semester."

I swallowed. What happened to art class being my sanctuary from pressure and expectation? I didn't think I was ready to share my work with other people. It was hard enough sharing with the teacher.

Mr. Green held out his hand. "Anyway, let's see how your comic is shaping up..."

I passed him my tablet, and he adjusted his glasses before studying the screen, occasionally scrolling, swiping and pinching his fingers together as he zoomed in to get a closer look. I watched him just as closely, waiting for any hint of the feedback I might be about to get, slightly surprised by how eager I was to receive it.

"You know," he said, without looking up from the screen. "Mackenzie, the new girl; she's selected hockey as a subject area too."

"Uh-huh." Where was he going with this?

"I'm looking forward to seeing the different approaches you both take to the same topic."

That was teacher talk for *I'm going to compare and judge you both against one another*, I was sure of it.

"Well, Parker," Mr. Green said, when he finally lifted his eyes from my work and handed the tablet back to me. "I have to say, I'm very impressed."

"You are?"

"Absolutely. Your illustrations are excellent, and you've done a fine job of capturing the art style used during the Golden Age of comics."

"I have?"

"Yes, but . . ." Of course. There was always a 'but' with Mr. Green. "I want to hear more about your vision for the project as a whole and the themes you intend to explore."

I hated this part. As much as I loved art class, it always eventually reached the point where Mr. Green wanted to get deep about things.

"Uh . . . it's about a superhero hockey player. The theme is hockey."

I knew instantly it wasn't the answer my teacher was looking for. Did my art really have to hold a hidden meaning? I just wanted to draw something that looked awesome. What was so bad about that?

"Think about it," he continued. "What message can you send through the story and your portrayal of the player?"

"That having superhuman speed is a really useful skill for a center?" Mr. Green sighed, and I didn't blame him. I sounded like an idiot, but it was my own fault. I knew this talk was coming, but I'd put it off, and now I was winging it.

"I think you can do better than that," he said. "The traditional comics your work is based on often explored interesting themes like identity, ethics and politics. They're more than just good vs. evil. And you're more than just a super hockey player, Parker."

"Am I though?" The corner of my mouth lifted.

Mr. Green's remained a firm line. "Just think about how you could add depth to your hockey-playing superhero."

I gave him a small nod. "Okay, I'll think about it."

But as I escaped his office I thought, *More than just a hockey player?* Maybe Mr. Green had been hanging out with the stoner kids in the east side alley. My whole being started and ended with hockey—I didn't have any added depth, so why did my work need it?

And even if Mr. Green was planning to display my work publicly, I had much more important things to focus on right now. Like finding a way to win our first game of the season now our goalie was on crutches.

Chapter 7

MACKENZIE

Finally, it was Friday. I'd barely survived my first week at Ransom High and wanted nothing more than to hole up in my room and pretend the rest of the world didn't exist. But unfortunately, my prize for enduring one week living in a new town, attending a new school, and existing on the same planet as Parker Darling, wasn't blissful solitude. Instead, I found myself sitting in the stands that evening watching the Ransom Devils' first game of the season.

My stepmom had pretty much guilt-tripped me into coming to support my dad. Watching hockey was like a cruel form of torture for me. Knowing I could never take to the ice myself, I both loved and loathed watching others play. I'd still gone to plenty of games over the years, but mostly to support Max. I never missed a chance to cheer on my brother. But there was always a quiet voice in my mind reminding me I'd never get to follow in his footsteps.

My dad probably would have understood if I hadn't shown up tonight, but Tessa kept pointing out what an important game this was and how much it would mean to him to have all of us watching. It was a little ironic, then, that after only one period, my stepmom had to take my sisters home because Skye was having a meltdown. I wondered if Tessa might have let me leave if I'd started screaming and kicking my feet too.

It was just as well they weren't here to watch the game

unfold. The Devils were currently being ripped apart by the Westfield High Tigers. It would be bad to laugh, right?

"Do you think if I just close my eyes, you can tell me when it's over?" Jaz was sitting beside me in the stands and had been chewing her nails the whole game. Her brother Owen was playing and, unlike me, she actually cared whether the Devils were successful or not.

"You should have brought something to read," Isaac said from beside her. He hadn't lifted his eyes from his book since the game began, and I had a strong feeling he was only here because Jaz was.

She shook her head at me. "He always comes but never watches."

"I have ears," Isaac replied. "I can hear if there's a goal."

"Not really the point, Isaac."

A smile hinted at his lips, but he continued reading. Bringing a book wasn't the worst idea—I could also use a distraction. Unfortunately, despite the inner turmoil hockey caused me, I didn't have it in me to look away. Whenever the Tigers got near the Devils' net, my palms began to sweat, and every time Ransom forced a turnover my heart raced as the crowd urged them on. Hockey was as much a part of me as the blood rushing through my veins, and I couldn't ignore it even if I tried.

"This team really won the championship last year?" I said to Jaz.

"It was a different team back then," she replied. "Lots of guys graduated, and I guess they aren't the same without the full might of the Darling Devils."

That stupid nickname again. I resisted the urge to roll my eyes.

"Grayson and Reed left big shoes to fill," she continued.

"They were the best players in the league," Isaac added. "And they're already starting for Ryker University as freshmen."

This wasn't the first time I'd heard about the older Darling brothers. Their names were mentioned around school almost as much as Parker's. Many of the comments I'd overheard had been about how the Devils would fare without them this season and how the boys were performing at college. And I'd heard more than a few rumors about them that were just as ridiculous as Seth's fight club story.

I'd been surprised to find out Parker's brothers were at Ryker with Max. My brother and I had messaged regularly and spoken on the phone a few times since he'd started at college, but he always seemed to keep his hockey-related updates short and sweet, like he was worried it might upset me to hear about them. However, I did know that Max was also getting plenty of game time for the Raiders as a freshman, so he must have been giving the infamous Darling Devils a run for their money.

"It doesn't help that Anderson couldn't stop a beach ball tonight," Jaz added. "We might not be losing quite so badly if he actually made some saves."

I nodded involuntarily in agreement. She was right; the Devils' backup goalie was completely out of his depth. When I looked back to the ice, the Tigers were on another breakaway and Anderson was completely out of position. It was like he'd forgotten where the net was. My dad must have been having a meltdown on the bench. If this was the best goaltender

Ransom had, there was no hope for the Devils this season.

It wasn't all Anderson's fault though. The rest of the team were also struggling. Their passing felt clunky and uncertain, and with every mistake they seemed to get increasingly frustrated with each other. Of course the team was new, and my dad had only just started as coach, but he definitely had his work cut out for him.

Just as a Tigers forward went to shoot the puck past the stranded Anderson, a Devils player appeared almost out of nowhere. It was number sixteen; Parker. He swiped the puck from his opponent, preventing a certain goal, and shot off down the ice.

"God, he's fast," I murmured. I'd been trying not to appreciate just how talented Parker Darling was, but it was impossible. Certain players just had something special about them. They moved like they were born to play and seemed capable of doing things no other player on the ice could. I couldn't take my eyes off Parker when he was out there—though I'd rather chew my hand off than ever admit that out loud.

Even though he was moving at breakneck speed, he somehow managed to weave his way past multiple Tigers players before firing the puck past the goalie into the net. The crowd erupted in hopeful cheers, but I knew it was too little too late. Parker had now scored two goals for the Devils, but the Tigers were still winning by three, and there were only a few minutes left. Parker couldn't win the game on his own.

"You think that was good." Jaz nudged my arm, making me realize I was still staring at Parker. "You should have seen him and his brothers. When all three of them were playing together it was crazy."

"Honestly, I think Parker might be the best of them," Issac argued.

Jaz folded her arms and turned to him. "How can you tell if you don't watch the game?"

"Because Parker got recruited to college earlier. Plus, his stats are off the charts. Did you know he's on track to surpass Reed as the all-time leading goal scorer at Ransom High?"

"How do *you* know that?" she asked.

"Because I listen." He glanced up at her and grinned.

"Yeah, well, he won't be beating any records if the Devils play like this for the rest of the season," Jaz replied.

"True," Isaac agreed before returning to his book.

It was almost a mercy when the game came to an end. Anderson let in another two goals before the final siren meaning the Devils had lost 7–2. A massacre. Every player's head was hung low as they made their way back to the locker room.

"They lost," Jaz said, shaking her head in disbelief. "I can't believe they lost. The Devils never lose."

"I think that's actually their biggest loss since we started high school," Isaac added. "Might be one of the worst ever."

Jaz huffed out a frustrated breath. "Seriously, are you hiding stat sheets in that book of yours?"

Isaac closed the massive novel and tucked it under his arm. "Sorry, I just mean that this is obviously a freak occurrence. I'm sure they'll get back on track next game." I could tell he was only trying to reassure Jaz.

"I hope so," she replied. "Owen's going to be devastated."

"My dad too," I agreed, although in truth he didn't really do devastated. When it came to hockey, he only seemed capable of showing different shades of fury. He'd taken all the aggression he had as a player and used it to fuel his passion as a coach. Most of the guys who played for him were half terrified. He got results though. At least, he usually did.

We rose from our seats, and I went in search of my dad. Thanks to my stepmom leaving early, he was my ride home. It didn't take me long to find the locker room, but with the game only just finished I knew he would be a while, so I leaned against the opposite wall to wait.

Eventually, Devils players began to filter out of the locker room. Most of them wore forlorn looks, like the game had broken something fundamental in their souls. Anderson looked especially devastated, and his eyes were red and puffy like he'd been crying. Poor kid.

Another five minutes passed. Then another. There was still no sign of my dad. I sent him a text but wasn't at all surprised when he didn't respond. He was probably already busy analyzing everything that went wrong.

When Seth emerged, I stepped away from the wall. "Hey, Seth."

"Oh hey, Mackenzie."

"Tough game. I saw you took a hard hit in the third. Are you okay?"

"Bit of a headache, but I'll survive." He gave me a tired smile. "I always thought brain cells were overrated anyway."

I laughed, but I could see Seth had forced out the joke. He

looked as bummed as every other player who had shuffled past me.

"Have you seen my dad?"

"I think he's still in the locker room," Seth replied with a nod toward the door.

I sighed as I followed his gaze. Guessed that meant I'd have to keep waiting.

"I'm the last one out though," he added. "It should be fine if you want to go inside."

"Oh, really? Thanks."

"No problem." He smiled. "Have a good night, Mackenzie."

"Yeah, you too. And don't worry, I'm sure you guys will win the next one." After what I'd just seen, I was far from sure, but it seemed like the best thing to say. It must have helped, somehow, because Seth was smiling more brightly as he set off down the corridor.

I took a deep breath and pushed through the door to the locker room. It was silent inside, but as I turned the corner and stepped into the wide-open room I froze. While there was no sign of my dad, the place certainly wasn't empty.

Parker was sitting on one of the benches in nothing but a towel. He was facing away from me, with his hands gripping the bench on either side of him and his head bowed, like the weight of the world was pressing down on his shoulders. After that game, it probably was.

The way he was sitting made the muscles on his back tense, and I found myself wondering how a high school boy could be this ripped. Suddenly, as if he had sensed my presence, he turned, and his eyes snapped up to look at me.

Surprise flittered through his gaze, but it quickly transformed into an arrogant smirk. My fingers clenched at my sides. Seth had totally set me up. No wonder he'd had a spring in his step as he walked away.

"So, you like to spend your evenings punching unsuspecting victims *and* peeping in locker rooms," Parker said in a thoughtful tone. "I'm impressed the police haven't caught up to you yet." There was something devious about Parker Darling's smile. Like it had been fed a strict diet of mischief and mayhem.

"I'm not here to peep at anything," I growled. "Certainly not you."

As he stood, it took all my willpower not to immediately contradict myself by looking down at the hard planes of his chest. I knew he was an athlete, but I still hadn't quite been prepared to see the evidence of it chiseled into his bare skin.

"And yet you couldn't keep your eyes off me today," he replied. "I saw you watching me from the stands."

I folded my arms as irritation rippled across my skin. "It kind of sounds like you were the one watching me. Maybe you should have kept your eyes on the puck."

The way his eyes sparkled with dark delight, you'd think he got off on this kind of thing. The thought immediately had me biting back any more snarky responses.

"Look, I'm just trying to find my dad."

"In the boys' locker room?"

"I was told he was in here."

"And you just go charging into male changing areas whenever the need strikes?"

"I thought it was empty!"

His smirk only grew. "Don't worry, I'm not ashamed of my body, and I don't like to let my fans down . . ."

"I'm not your fan."

"I think you might be. You do seem kind of obsessed with me. I'm afraid the fan club is already full, but I can add your name to the waiting list if you want. It's Mary, right?"

My teeth were gritted so tightly right now, I thought they might crack under the pressure. "Did you see how you guys played today? I'm surprised you've got any fans left."

His expression dimmed slightly, and I knew I'd hit a nerve. I almost felt guilty, but then he said, "Yeah, well, it's easy to judge when you're sitting on the sidelines."

My eyes narrowed. Now *he'd* hit a nerve. "I don't want to sit on the sidelines, *trust me*." I would have given anything to swap places with Parker. "You walked away from that summer camp with a slap on the wrist. Consider yourself lucky."

He frowned, waiting for me to say more. But his concern quickly disappeared. "Whatever. I need to hit the shower."

"Fine, I was just leaving."

"Glad to hear it. I'd hate to have to take out a restraining order, especially against my biggest fan." He was smirking again as he started to walk away.

"I'm not here for you!" I yelled after him, but he'd already disappeared behind the wall that separated the shower area from the locker room, and I soon heard running water.

I started for the door but hesitated when I caught sight of Parker's clothes on the bench. I'd been itching to get him back for splashing me earlier in the week.

Clothes for clothes seemed like a fair revenge...

I knew I shouldn't do it, though. Not after he'd suffered such a brutal loss. I could find another way to punish him—perhaps on a day when life wasn't already doing it for me.

I turned to leave, but then stopped in surprise as Parker started singing. His voice actually sounded quite good. Then I heard the lyrics and recognized the song. "Obsessed" by Mariah Carey.

Without thinking, I started moving back toward him. He was standing in a cubicle, only a thin frosted white door blocking my view. I knew this was a bad idea. *A terrible idea.* I almost reconsidered, but then he started belting out the lyrics even louder.

I snatched his towel off the hook outside his cubicle and bolted back into the locker room, where I gathered his clothes, hockey gear, and everything else on the bench and shoved it all into his sports bag. Then I slung it over my shoulder and left the room without a shred of guilt holding me back.

After this, we'd be even. Well, closer to even.

As I hurried from the locker room, I almost collided with my dad.

"There you are." He glanced at the door behind me, his frown deepening. "What were you doing in the locker room?"

"Looking for you," I quickly replied.

"In the boys' locker room?"

"Someone said you were in there." I shrugged. "Don't worry, it was empty. But someone left their bag behind." I pulled Parker's bag off my shoulder and passed it to my dad.

He grunted as he glanced down at the name printed on it.

"Darling," he muttered. "Figures. I'll go put this in my office. I just have a couple of things to wrap up before we go. Why don't you grab a drink from concessions? I'll meet you out front."

"Sure, Dad."

He headed for the door on the other side of the locker room. I didn't linger. I had no idea how long Parker took in the shower and I needed to be well out of range when he figured out what I'd done. He was going to be so pissed. Perhaps he'd be taking out that restraining order after all.

Chapter 8
PARKER

I stood in the shower, allowing the warm water to run down my face, hoping it might wash away memories of the game. Mackenzie must have by left now—if my attitude hadn't driven her away, my terrible singing should have done the trick. I didn't want to see anyone after such an embarrassing loss, let alone Mackenzie. Though, I had to admit, teasing her was a lot of fun, and it took my mind off the game, if only for a little while.

Soon, of course, I was replaying every missed shot, every failed pass, every defensive error over and over again. I might have scored two goals, but it wasn't enough to make up for our wide-eyed rookie goalie. Could I have done more? Maybe. Or maybe I just wasn't good enough to inspire this team to victory without my brothers. That was what troubled me most. We never would have lost a game that way if Reed and Grayson were still on the team.

I shut off the water. There was no point hiding in here forever. Taking a deep breath, I reached for my towel. But the hook I'd placed it on was empty. Frowning, I opened the door and glanced around. The towel was nowhere to be seen. What the hell had I done with it? Could I have left it in the locker room?

A wave of cool air rippled over my skin as I stepped out of the shower. But when I got to the locker room I stopped in my tracks. The bench was totally bare.

I gaped for half a breath and then started swearing. Loudly.

This was Mackenzie Foster's doing. Apparently, I *could* despise that girl more than I already did. If it weren't me this was happening to, I might have laughed. I might even have appreciated her revenge tactics. But it *was* me standing naked in the locker room, and I was livid. I'd get her back for this.

First, I had to figure a way out of this situation. I scanned the locker room for something to wear. But for once, my teammates had actually taken all their stuff home. All I could find was some stick tape, a plastic bottle, and a stray glove that had fallen on the floor.

What the hell was I going to do? My phone was in my bag, along with my truck keys. Walking home wasn't an option. I'd either get frostbite or thrown in jail. I just needed to find someone with spare clothes or a phone I could borrow to call for help. Hopefully, I'd find the clothes first; the only phone number I knew by heart was my mom's.

My gaze landed back on the lone glove that lay on the floor . . . better than nothing.

Grumbling and muttering curses, I picked up the glove and did my best to cover up. With a deep breath, I prayed the arena was mostly empty and pushed open the door.

The corridor was deserted, which was both a relief and a disappointment. I didn't *want* to see anyone, but I would need to find another person eventually.

I glanced at the office door. I had no idea whether Coach Foster was in there, but I couldn't risk him catching me wandering around naked. I was going to have to search a little further afield.

My heart was racing as I stepped from the safety of the

locker room. It was much colder out here, especially with water droplets still clinging to my skin. I repressed a shiver and tried to ignore the icy air. Perhaps if I just acted like I didn't mind being naked, no one else would care either.

I started toward the arena entrance. All I needed was to find someone from my team. Or maybe someone who worked here. Hell, even a Tigers player would do. I'd happily pull on one of their jerseys right now.

The girls' locker room was up ahead, and I considered sneaking inside. Maybe I'd find some discarded clothing in there.

As I approached the door, it burst open, almost hitting me in the face, and a group of girls skipped out. They were all looking down at their phones or in close conversation with each other as they walked, totally oblivious to the naked boy they'd almost collided with. Still, I edged away from the door and hid behind a tall pot plant against the wall. Although it had plenty of height, the plant did little to shield me. Its stupid fronds were far too thin. Thankfully, the girls continued in the opposite direction without looking back.

Just as I was about to try the locker room door again, it opened once more. This time, a familiar face stepped out. My sister Cammie. The prospect of asking her for help was almost as bad as facing Coach Foster. She would never let me hear the end of this. But I was running out of options.

I leaned out from behind the plant. "Psst, Cammie."

She paused and glanced around her.

"Cammie," I repeated. "Over here."

She turned, and when her gaze landed on me, her eyes widened with horror.

"Parker, what the hell?" she gasped, approaching me warily. "Are you naked? Oh. My. God. Are you trying to embarrass me?"

I rolled my eyes. "Yep. You got me. I decided to walk around the arena naked *just* to embarrass you."

She folded her arms. "I wouldn't put it past you."

"Funnily enough, Cam, my nakedness is not about you."

"Well, what is it about?" she demanded. "Wait, are you doing some kind of post-game punishment? Like how Reed used to run home after a loss? I know I'm superstitious, but I think walking home naked might be taking it too far. Even though you guys were terrible today."

"My clothes were stolen!"

"Really?"

"Yes, really."

She tilted her head. "Why would someone steal your clothes?"

"Because I pissed them off."

Her expression cracked and she let out a laugh. "Brilliant."

It was probably a good thing Cammie and Mackenzie didn't know each other. I could only imagine the kind of torture those two would inflict on me if they ever teamed up.

"Do you have something I can wear?" I asked.

"No," she replied, still laughing. "Oh, wait, actually . . ." I felt a wave of relief as Cammie opened her bag, but it quickly disappeared when she pulled out a bright pink scarf. I didn't even know my sister owned anything pink. Her entire wardrobe was black, grey, and more black.

"Gabby left it at our house," she said. "She's always telling me how hot you are, so I'm sure she won't mind if you borrow it."

"What the hell am I supposed to do with that?"

"I mean, if I were you, I'd tie it around my waist as soon as possible."

"I thought you had some actual clothes for me."

"Sorry." She shrugged. "This is the best I can do."

I cursed under my breath but gestured for the scarf. "Okay, fine, just give it here."

She passed it to me, and I retreated behind the plant. The scarf was just wide enough to reach around my waist like a flimsy miniskirt.

"I think I preferred my glove," I grumbled. "At least Reed and Grayson aren't here to see this."

"Hmm, lucky," she agreed with a smirk.

"I can't get to the car looking like this. There are too many people around."

"I already said that's all I've got."

"What about in the locker room?"

"There're still girls in there."

"Well, maybe they have something?"

Cammie huffed as if me being stranded naked in public was more of an inconvenience to her than me. "I have a meeting with my coach now."

"*Please*?"

"Okay, fine. Just go back to the boys' locker room before someone sees you. I'll find you something."

"Thank you! Have I told you you're my favorite sister?"

"I'm your only sister."

"Still." I grinned. "Also, maybe call Mom and see if she can drop off my spare keys? They're gone too."

Cammie lifted her eyes to the ceiling. "Don't worry, I'll find you a ride."

Sorting out a ride wasn't the same as getting me my keys. My eyes narrowed. "What do you mean?"

She just waved me off and headed back into the girls' locker room. I couldn't help but feel suspicious. Cammie rarely went out of her way to help me. But this wasn't exactly a common scenario.

Slowly and strategically, I started back to the boys' locker room. Hopefully, now I had Cammie's help, I could keep this whole thing between just me and her. No one else would ever have to know.

But just as I was nearing safety, the door to the coach's office opened, and out stepped Coach Foster.

I didn't hesitate. I didn't think. I turned and started running in the opposite direction as fast as I could without causing my little pink skirt to fly off.

As I turned a corner, I risked a glance over my shoulder, almost expecting to see Foster stalking after me like the Terminator, silently and relentlessly pursuing with one objective in mind: elimination.

Much to my relief, he hadn't followed, but in my panic, I hadn't considered where I was going. And when I finally faced forward again, I skidded to a halt.

I'd found my way to the foyer. And it was full of people. Lining up at the concession stands. Milling around the front desk. Making their way out of the building, while more hovered near the entrance. And every single one of them turned to look at me.

As I stood rooted to the spot, scanning the horrified faces gazing back at me, my eyes found Cammie. And she wasn't alone.

Reed frowned at me and shook his head. Grayson was standing next to him, his mouth hanging open as he held a chip frozen in place in front of it. He looked like he was questioning what he'd done to deserve a brother like me. Probably not for the first time. Or the last.

I stood tall, lifted my head high, and started toward them, acting every bit like I didn't care about the countless sets of eyes, and more than a few phones, tracking my every move.

"You couldn't wait in the locker room for five minutes?" Cammie hissed.

"Me? I thought you were supposed to be finding something for me to wear. How's that going?"

"We've been gone for one week." Reed had finally shaken off his shock. "*One* week. Did you lose a bet?"

"He must have," Grayson agreed.

"Nope, no bet, I just like to keep life interesting." I grinned, trying to convince myself a cold breeze from the entrance wasn't getting playful with the back of my scarf.

"He pissed someone off," Cammie corrected me without missing a beat. "They stole his clothes. I can't believe *this* is why I'm going to be late to my meeting. He's your problem now, Reed. If anyone asks, I'm not related to him."

"I've been telling people that for years," I replied as she stalked away.

"Something like this was going to happen eventually," Reed murmured as he rubbed a hand across his creased forehead.

"To be honest, I'm shocked it hasn't happened before," Grayson added.

"What are you two even doing here?" I could still feel the eyes of everyone in the foyer on me. The urge to run and hide was pretty strong right now. But, unfortunately, for both me and my onlookers, I had a reputation to uphold. Running and hiding in embarrassment wasn't something I would do.

"We thought we'd surprise you by coming to your first game," Reed said.

"Yep," Grayson continued. "Although, kind of feels like we're the ones getting the surprise."

It seemed like they were starting to see the funny side of all this. I was still looking for it myself.

"Tough loss," Reed said. "What happened out there?"

"Can we talk about this on the way home, please?" I asked.

"No time like the present," Grayson replied, the corner of his lip twitching.

"I always say the best time to analyze a game is immediately after it's finished." Reed was smirking now too. "Why don't we get a drink and debrief."

"I'm already debriefed," I grumbled, glancing down at my improvised skirt. "Let's *go*."

My brothers laughed but then nodded. "Fine, let's get you home."

As they started to move away, something caught my eye behind them. Mackenzie was leaning against a pillar, just a few feet away, watching us. She held a large soda, the straw pressed against her grinning lips.

Her green eyes trailed down my body, studied my bright

pink scarf, sparkled with joy, and then flicked back up to my face.

"Nice outfit," she said.

Maybe I'd met my match with this girl. She'd pulled off the perfect revenge for splashing her at school. But as I stared at her, I got an idea that was too good to pass up.

Without giving myself a chance to second-guess it, I plastered on my most mischievous smile and stepped toward her. With one swift movement, I pulled the scarf from around my waist and handed it to her. Gasps filled the foyer and Mackenzie's eyes grew wide, her mouth dropped open, and her cheeks went as pink as the scarf she was now holding.

"If you wanted to see me naked," I whispered, "all you had to do was ask." Then I turned and strolled toward the arena entrance, walking as if I had all the time in the world.

When I got outside, I was instantly struck by a freezing wind. Still, it had been totally worth it to see Mackenzie blush.

My brothers hurried out the doors behind me.

"What the hell was that?" they both asked at the same time.

"Just tell me where the car is," I said. "I'm ready to get out of here."

"Same." Reed laughed. "Come on, it's this way."

"We should have known this had something to do with a girl," Grayson muttered, finally handing me his sweatshirt.

"Yep, there's always a girl," Reed agreed.

I couldn't really argue with them. But as I followed them through the parking lot, my bare feet crunching on the snow, it occurred to me: Mackenzie Foster wasn't just any girl.

Chapter 9

MACKENZIE

"Huh, maybe the rumors about Ransom were right."

I jumped at the sound of my brother's voice, turning to find him standing behind me. He was frowning as he watched Parker's naked figure strutting out the door.

"Max?" I gasped before quickly recovering and giving him a tight hug. "What are you doing here?"

He laughed as he hugged me back. "Came to watch Dad's first game. Thought I'd surprise you both."

"Well, I'm definitely surprised. You shouldn't sneak up on people."

For a moment, I almost forgot about my run-in with Parker. Almost, but not quite. It was a little hard when I was still holding the pink scarf he'd given me. I thought stealing his clothes would even the score. But with one bold move, Parker had stolen my victory.

"I was hardly sneaking." Max smiled. "You were a little distracted."

Who wouldn't be? Parker was distracting with his clothes on, let alone without them. But I wasn't going to get into that with my brother.

Max scrunched his nose as he carefully plucked the scarf from my hand and tossed it in the closest bin. "Just how many guys in this town are stripping for you, Kenz? Do I need to have a word with anyone?"

"Don't worry," I assured him. "He was only naked because I stole his clothes."

Max raised an eyebrow as though he needed a little more information. "Did he deserve it?"

"Definitely," I replied. "Not that it seemed to bother Parker all that much."

"Parker?" Max asked. "As in, Parker Darling?" He nodded toward the front doors. "Your naked friend is Reed and Grayson's brother?"

"Uh, yeah." I shrugged. "Though I wouldn't call him my friend."

"You know I play with his brothers at Ryker, right?"

"Yeah, I'm aware. It's all anyone talks about around here. It's almost like being a college hockey star is a big deal or something." I nudged him playfully, and he lifted his eyes to the ceiling.

"Well, they were my ride here," he explained. "This should make for an interesting journey back to Ryker. Remind me again why you stole Parker's clothes?"

"If you knew him, you wouldn't need to ask."

He gave me an expectant look, waiting for me to elaborate, but I folded my arms and stayed silent.

"Fine, keep your secrets," he eventually said, laughing again. "It's good to see you, Kenz."

"You too." I smiled back at him. "Does Dad know you're here?"

"Not yet. It was a kind of a last-minute thing. Reed and Grayson decided to drive back and asked if I wanted a ride. We were late, though. Missed the first period."

"I think Dad would have preferred you to miss the entire game."

"Yeah, it wasn't great. He won't be happy."

"When *is* Dad happy?"

"True." Max stole the soda from my hand and took a sip before passing it back to me. "So, what's Ransom like? How was your first week at school?"

He was the only person in our family to ask like he actually wanted to hear my answer. It wasn't that my parents didn't care, but Tessa was busy with my little sisters, and my dad had his new job to focus on. I just wasn't their top priority. "School was fine."

"Wow, interesting. You've really painted a picture for me."

I probably should have resented my brother. He was the superstar hockey-playing child my dad had always dreamed of having. I would have done just about anything to trade places with Max, but no matter how jealous I was of him, it was impossible to dislike him. He was the best person I knew. Being closer to him was the one positive thing about our move to Ransom.

"Come on, Kenzie," he continued. "You've been here less than a week and you're already stealing a boy's clothes. You must have a little more to share than *fine*."

Max had always been persistent, so I knew I was going to have to give him something. "I guess school's been a bit of an adjustment, but I've made a couple of friends and I'm not too far behind with classes. I'm just finding my feet still."

His expression softened. "If it makes you feel any better, I'm still finding my feet at Ryker too."

"I find that hard to believe." My brother could fit in anywhere. He got voted prom king at his girlfriend's school last year—he didn't even go there.

"Seriously," he replied. "The expectations are so high, and it feels like they're trying to kill us with practice and games. It's going to be tough keeping up with schoolwork on top of that, and I'm still getting to know everyone."

"So, things are fine for you too then?" I replied.

"Pretty much," he agreed with a grin.

My brother stiffened as he caught sight of something over my shoulder. I turned to see my dad walking toward us. Dad's face was stoic and unreadable. When he wasn't pleased with the way his team had played, you could always count on him either being visibly angry or repressing his emotions altogether. I guessed tonight it was the latter.

Tessa and my sisters were all delighted to see Max when we arrived back at the house. My stepmom pulled him in for a warm hug while Daisy and Skye eagerly introduced him to their dolls and stuffed toys.

"It's lucky I made extra pasta," Tessa said as she led Max into the living room. "Are you hungry?"

"Always," he replied.

It felt good to have everyone back together, although my dad didn't last long at dinner, quickly excusing himself to head to his office and work. We all knew what he was like after a bad game; we'd only been graced with his presence at dinner because Max was here.

Eventually, Tessa took the girls to get ready for bed, Max switched a game on the TV, and I snuck off to my room before

I got recruited to help with Daisy and Skye's bath. It usually ended in an all-out war between the two of them.

My room was sparse; just a bed and the suitcase I'd arrived here with. I was still waiting for all my moving boxes to get here. The only color in the room was on the wall opposite my bed where I was painting my mural. It was going to be a wintry lake scene once it was done, with a thick pine forest and snow-capped mountains beyond. So far I'd done the background and big color blocks, and I was hoping to build up the shadows and midtones this weekend. Maybe even add some linework.

My cat Mitts hissed at me from her position on my bed as I entered the room. It was her standard greeting. She hated everyone—even me.

"I've been thinking we should get a dog," I told her.

Mitts gave me a judgmental glare before she repositioned herself so all I could see was her fluffy black back and curling tail. She then proceeded to calmly lick her bright white paws.

Just then the door behind me burst open. Daisy stood in the entrance, holding a Barbie in her tiny hands. Her eyes were big and filling with tears.

"Skye. Cut. All. Barbie's. Hair. Off," she blubbered, before darting into the room and throwing herself into my arms.

I instinctively pulled her in close. "I'm sorry, Daisy," I murmured. "You know Skye's only little. She doesn't understand."

"That's. What. Mom. Said."

Apparently, it was also the last thing my sister wanted to hear right now.

I gently took the doll from her hands and inspected the

damage. This was the end of the world for my sister; I wished my problems were as simple as a broken doll.

"I actually kind of like her new haircut," I said.

"You—you do?" Daisy blinked her big tear-stained eyes up at me.

"Yeah. She looks so cool. Like she's about to join a punk-rock band."

"A band?"

"Yeah. You know what, I might have a blue marker in my pencil case somewhere. We could color her hair, if you want?"

She blinked at me several more times as she thought it over. "Could we dress her up like she's in a band too?"

"Yeah." I laughed. "We can do that."

The two of us spent the next twenty minutes fixing Barbie. I loved spending time with my sister, but it also made me a little sad. When I was her age, there hadn't been anyone to color a Barbie's hair with me. My mom was gone, and my dad hadn't really been present. It often felt like it was just Max and me. And Max would be more likely to test how far a doll could fly than try to do its hair.

But our lives changed for the better when Tessa started dating my dad. And then when Daisy and then Skye were born. The love and joy they brought into the house felt like it filled a hole inside me.

When we were done with Daisy's doll, I was actually quite pleased with the result.

"Thanks, Kenzie!" Daisy beamed, hugging her doll tightly to her chest. "I love her."

"She looks great, doesn't she?"

"Yeah, she does. I'm going to go put on a concert in my bed." Daisy hurried from the room, happy once more. Although I'm sure it wouldn't be long until Skye fixed that.

I changed into my pajamas, crawled into bed, and succumbed to the urge to check my phone one last time. Then immediately wished I hadn't.

The algorithm must have been laughing at me—I only followed a few people from Ransom on social media, yet the first thing in my feed was a picture of Parker in all his naked glory. I almost dropped my phone. Thankfully the image had been captured from behind, and had been edited to cover Parker's butt with a large peach emoji.

I should have felt victorious. But instead, my act of vengeance only seemed to have inflated the guy's ego further. There wasn't one negative comment on the post. Just floods of heart and fire emojis, some skull emojis too, and countless flattering compliments from desperate admirers. It was like witnessing a digital standing ovation. Even Parker had commented with a winky face of his own. He wasn't just unaffected by what I'd done; he was enjoying the attention.

Parker walked through life as easily as he'd strolled across that foyer today. The rules the rest of us mere mortals had to abide by just didn't apply to him.

I threw my phone down on my bed, narrowly missing Mitts, who hissed at me again. Our classmates could worship him all they wanted. I was committed to doing the exact opposite.

Chapter 10
PARKER

Considering how bad our loss was on Friday night, I felt like quite the celebrity come Monday. I'd be lying if I said I didn't like the attention. The smiles, the giggles, the way girls went out of their way to brush past me in the corridor. It was great. I'd only had a few classes so far today, and I already had five new numbers in my phone.

"Maybe I should walk around naked more often," I said to Seth as I followed him onto the school bus. We had a science excursion to some museum, and I was lucky Seth had asked the bus to wait for me because art class had run way over.

"Please don't," he groaned. "I've seen enough videos of your ass this weekend to last me a lifetime."

"I can't help that my ass went viral."

"No part of you should ever go viral. Your ego can't handle it."

"I don't know what you're talking about; my ego is loving it." As I made my way down the aisle to find a seat, a girl wiggled her fingers at me flirtatiously. I couldn't remember her name, but she was cute, so I flashed her a smile.

Seth groaned again and I glanced over my shoulder at him. "What?"

"You're just proving my point," he said. "But at least everyone's distracted from the game."

That knocked my ego down a few pegs. Did he really have

to bring up the game? With Reed and Grayson visiting, I'd also been forced to finally tell them I was yet to be named captain, and probably never would be. I just wanted to forget the whole evening. Hell, I'd even give up my ass's new celebrity status if I could go back in time and get another shot at that terrible game.

Unfortunately, I had little reason to believe the next one would be any better.

"Did you see this?" Seth asked as we took a seat at the back of the bus.

I shook my head as he handed me a poster. It was enthusiastically advertising hockey tryouts for tomorrow night—Coach Foster was looking for an additional goaltender.

"I know it says *additional*," Seth continued. "But I think we all know this means Coach won't be letting us suffer another week with Anderson. He wants a new starter until Elliot is back."

"I guess so," I agreed, placing the poster on the empty seat next to me. The bus rumbled to life and took off from the curb.

"Who do you think they'll pick?" Seth asked.

"No idea. We already had tryouts and apparently, other than Elliot, Anderson was the best we could find." Coach Foster had missed the start of preseason, so I assumed he was hoping some hidden talent might have been overlooked during the previous tryouts. Or maybe he was banking on someone who played another position stepping into the role. Neither felt likely to happen.

"Maybe we'll get lucky," Seth said optimistically.

"It's going to take more than luck to find someone good

enough," I replied. "These tryouts are really going to be scraping the bottom of the barrel. We need a miracle or we're screwed."

"We're not screwed yet. I'm sure Coach will figure something out."

I pointed at the poster. "If this is his solution, then I'm quickly losing the little faith I had left in him. Maybe it's up to us to do something." I couldn't just sit by and watch my senior year season go down the drain. Even if I wasn't going to be named captain, I still wanted to win.

"If you're about to suggest strapping on the pads and taking up the challenge, I don't think losing our best offensive player is the answer here."

"Obviously not. That would be stupid. We just need . . ." My voice trailed off, as some students started shouting and laughing from the seats in front of us. A few of them were cheering and pointing out the window of the bus.

"Mackenzie?" Seth suggested.

"What?" I turned to him to check I'd heard right.

"Mackenzie," he repeated.

Had he lost his mind? "Uh, that's not quite what I was thinking . . ."

"No," he continued, nodding at the window. "That's Mackenzie. Everyone's heckling her. She missed the bus."

Kids were streaming into the aisle to peer outside, and I leaned over to get a look too. Mackenzie was sprinting down the sidewalk after the bus. She was surprisingly fast, and I was impressed to see she was actually keeping up. Most kids would have given up a long time ago or not bothered to run at all. No surprise that Mackenzie was too stubborn to let our school bus get the better of her.

Finally the bus driver started to slow down, then pulled over. Disappointment rumbled through the crowd of students who'd been excitedly watching Mackenzie's pursuit. The show was over though, and everyone started returning to their seats.

Mackenzie clambered onto the bus, her chest heaving. The way she was scowling at the bus driver, I half expected him to catch on fire. She muttered a few things to the science teacher at the front, then went in search of a seat.

As she started down the aisle, her gaze went straight to mine. Her expression only darkened, as though she had somehow decided this was all my fault. A part of me wished it was. I still owed her a little payback after Friday night. Unfortunately though, I couldn't take credit for this one.

Despite the lethal look in her eyes, I smiled and lifted a hand to wave. Not for the first time in my life, I wondered if I'd been born without any proper defensive instincts. When someone looked at you that way you were supposed to freeze, hide, or flee. I just smiled and waved.

She scowled at me before slumping into the nearest seat. The girl had serious issues with me—clearly. Yet I was still smiling. And now, I was thinking, which was even more dangerous. I knew Seth hadn't genuinely been suggesting Mackenzie was the answer to our goalie problem. But what if that idea wasn't as crazy as I'd initially thought?

She was a loose cannon. She couldn't be trusted. She'd likely torch the entire school just to see me burn. But that wasn't what I was thinking about right now. Instead, I was remembering how she'd played at her dad's summer camp.

She'd been incredibly fast, fiercely competitive, and she knew how to guard the net.

"We need to find someone who hasn't already tried out," I said, turning to Seth once more.

"Yeah, except hasn't every guy who can play already tried out?"

"Every *guy* who can play . . ." I nodded over to where Mackenzie was sitting. "We haven't tried out every girl."

Seth looked confused. "You know I wasn't suggesting we recruit her for the team, right?"

"I know, but it's not the worst idea. I've seen her play. She's good."

"You're serious?"

"Maybe."

"You want the girl who stole your clothes playing alongside you?" He spoke slowly, as if he was worried I wouldn't be able to fully grasp the concept.

"Well, I'm hoping that won't happen during a game," I joked, though Seth didn't laugh. No, he was still staring at me like I'd been slammed into the boards a little too hard.

"She'll never go for it. She'd say no just to spite you."

"Then we convince her. She already told me she wouldn't be sitting on the sidelines if she had a choice."

I was suddenly wishing she'd told me more about why she didn't play anymore when she'd brought it up in the locker room.

"Perhaps," Seth continued. "But even if she agrees, you know she'll have to try out. And it's her dad, not you, who decides who joins the team."

I waved his concern away. "If she's the best person for the job, there's no way her dad will say no."

"Because Coach Foster is such an open-minded guy. You don't even know if she's still a good player. That camp was three years ago."

His arguments were starting to stack up, but I didn't let it derail me. It felt like I was onto something. "She just managed to chase down a bus. She's clearly fit. And determined."

"Okay..."

"And we know she doesn't back away from a fight. I'm still recovering from her killer right hook."

"Yeah, but can she still stop a puck?"

That was the million-dollar question. And the only one that truly mattered. "No idea. Guess we'll just have to find out."

"You're going to get yourself punched again, aren't you?"

"No. Well, maybe. But if my instincts are right, it'll be worth it."

When we arrived at the museum and everyone filed off the bus, my mind was still racing. I couldn't shake the idea that Mackenzie, the girl I thought was my biggest problem, suddenly seemed like my only solution. Once we were off the bus, everyone gathered in front of the museum entrance, and a teacher started rattling off instructions. I wasn't listening though. My eyes were on Mackenzie.

I needed to put her goalie skills to the test; needed to know if she still had the lightning-fast reflexes I'd seen three years ago. I could hardly ask her to strap on a pair of skates and let me shoot pucks at her. I was going to have to be more covert. But how could I test her skills without her realizing? And even if that succeeded, how the hell was I going to convince her to try out for the team? When she turned and caught me watching, she grimaced in disgust. Not a great start.

The teacher stopped talking and everyone started for the museum entrance. I pushed through the crowd toward where Mackenzie was walking next to Jaz.

"Hey, Parker." Vanessa's alluring voice sounded beside me, and I turned to find her and Britt smiling brightly.

"Ness. Britt."

The two girls giggled and batted their eyelashes up at me. Now *this* was how girls were supposed to respond to me. I wasn't used to them turning their nose up like I was something that got stuck on the bottom of their shoe. Still, I kept making my way toward Mackenzie. When I reached her, she sighed.

"Jaz," I said. "Melancholy."

"That's not even a name," Mackenzie hissed.

"You should probably take that up with your parents," I agreed. "Oh, how's my outfit today?" I held out my arms and looked down at myself. "Sorry, I know you prefer me without clothes..."

"I prefer when you leave me alone."

"Leave you alone? Be honest, you'd miss me."

Her eyes were flaring with irritation once again, and she quickly dragged Jaz away. It only seemed to make my heart pulse faster. I enjoyed messing with her, and I was smiling to myself as I continued inside the museum.

"I kind of thought you were going to start playing nice," Seth said under his breath as he joined me.

"Don't know what gave you that impression."

"She'll never agree to what you want if you keep annoying her."

Since when was Seth the sensible one? It was becoming harder to argue with him, but I just wasn't sure I had it in me to play nice. Especially not with Mackenzie Foster. Every time she looked my way, some deep instinctual part of me wanted to growl. Who was I to deny my inner wolf?

Although I hadn't heard a word of our teacher's introduction, I soon gathered that we had time to explore the museum before some sort of presentation, so Seth and I wandered through the exhibits. Most of them were interactive and probably would have been enjoyable if we were five. The place buzzed with energy as kids' laughter mixed with the sounds of beeps, whooshes, and rushing water. Lights blinked and flashed on different displays and demonstrations. It felt like it was all trying a little too hard to make science fun.

I kept one eye on Mackenzie, from a safe distance, as I waited for inspiration to strike. When I left this place, I knew I wouldn't remember a single exhibit. I *would* remember that after chasing the bus, several strands of Mackenzie's blonde hair had come loose from her ponytail. That her eyes lit with a sense of interest and amusement as she took in each display. That she laughed easily whenever Jaz leaned in close to talk to her. But her relaxed expression turned to irritation whenever she caught me watching.

"You're being weird," Seth said as we skirted to the side to make way for a couple of kids who were racing toward a station of vibrating strings.

"Don't know what you're talking about." I feigned interest

in the nearest display—a barrel filled with foam balls and a tube pumping out a stream of air. I had no idea what it was supposed to be representing and couldn't be bothered to read the description card beside it. This was why I stuck to hockey and art.

Seth waved a hand in Mackenzie's direction. "You haven't taken your eyes off her since we got here. You're stalking her like a lion hunting his prey."

"That girl is no one's prey. *She's* the lion. Well, the lioness. And we all know they're the true killers in the pack."

He raised an eyebrow at me.

"What?"

"Mackenzie's hot. It's not surprising you're attracted to her."

"I am *not* attracted to her"

"You kissed her the first time you met her."

"She kissed me!"

He scoffed and shook his head with disbelief.

"It's true," I continued. "Besides, I would have kissed anyone who was willing back then. In fact, I'd still kiss pretty much anyone who's willing—anyone *except her*."

"I don't buy it."

I grunted my frustration. "This is all about hockey, trust me. I'm just waiting for the perfect moment to test her reflexes."

"Here? Now?" Seth looked around at the packed exhibition. It wasn't exactly a subtle place to execute my plan. Not that I really had one yet.

"Why not? Tryouts are tomorrow, and we've got another game this weekend. We haven't got time to waste."

I looked back down at the activity in front of me before

slowly picking up one of the foam balls. I tossed it up and down in my hand a few times, as an idea formed. "In fact, why don't we check her reflexes right now . . ."

"Uh, what do you—"

I pulled back my arm and then launched the ball toward Mackenzie before Seth could convince me otherwise. Almost instantly, I regretted the decision. I'd thrown the ball just a little too enthusiastically, and she wasn't even looking this way. My aim was too good. It was flying straight toward her head. There was no way she'd see it coming and this time she really would kill me.

As the moment of impact approached, I wanted to turn, run from the museum, pack my bags and find a new town to live in. Maybe a new country? But then Mackenzie's arm darted out, and she snatched the ball from the air. She'd caught it. My mouth dropped open.

"Whoa," Seth whispered in awe. "That was some real *Spider-Man* shit."

I felt a little awed, too. But it quickly dissipated as her eyes flashed in my direction. I was dead. *So dead.* All I could think as she stormed across the room toward us was that I'd messed with the wrong girl. But I also knew I'd found the right one . . .

"What is the *matter* with you?" she fumed.

I was asking myself the same question. She emphasized her point by launching the ball directly at me from close range. I didn't even try to deflect it, letting it bounce off my forehead and onto the floor.

"You've still got it," I said, not taking my eyes off her.

"Uh, I think what he means to say is, sorry," Seth added.

I ignored him. I wasn't sorry in the slightest. "Was that a lucky catch? Or are you really that good?"

"You're a psycho, you know that, right?"

"And you're fast," I continued. "Really fast. You can catch a ball without even looking, and you don't back down. *Ever*. We need you."

She started to frown. "Did I hit you too hard with the ball just now?" Turning to Seth she asked, "Is he okay? Should we call a teacher over?"

Seth smirked. "Just hear him out."

"Fine, I'll play along." She slowly returned her gaze to mine. "Need me for what?"

I suddenly felt nervous. I didn't think she'd listen to me even for a second. But now I had a chance. What if she said no?

"We need you to be the Ransom Devils' new goalie."

She stared at me for several moments, remaining silent and still, but confusion was clearly swirling in her eyes. Doubt gathered in my gut. She was going to refuse.

"Look, I know we've had our differences..." I said.

"Is that what we're calling it? Differences?"

"But our team needs someone who can defend the net, and I think you might just be the only person at our school who's capable. The way you caught that ball... You're perfect."

"Perfect?" she scoffed. "You know I'm a girl, right?"

"Right."

"And you play for a boys' team."

"Yes, and?"

She crossed her arms. "I'd say no just to ruin your day."

"This isn't just about me, though," I pointed out. "This is

about the whole team. You saw the game on Friday. We can't win this season without you."

Her expression was impossible to decipher as she considered me, but then she started to smile. "Well, I guess you're going to lose."

And with that, she walked away, taking all my hopes of a successful season with her.

Chapter 11

MACKENZIE

I didn't know whether to laugh or cry. Parker wanted me to be the Ransom Devils' new goaltender. Fate had a messed-up sense of humor, considering he was a big part of the reason I was banned from playing hockey in the first place.

The idea was still circling endlessly in my head when I got home that afternoon. It was crazy, right? The thought of me playing for a boys' team. Max had always told me I could have held my own on his teams. And he knew better than anyone, seeing as I'd practiced with him for countless hours over the years. But suiting up for the reigning state champions in a competitive game was a little different than one-on-one pond hockey with your older brother.

I knew if I told Max about Parker's suggestion, he'd tell me to go for it. But unfortunately, even if I wanted to consider it, I couldn't. Not when my dad refused to let me play, and he was the one running the team.

Maybe that was for the best. It would make it easier to forget the whole thing. It didn't matter what I wanted; it could never happen.

"Tessa, I'm home," I called at our front door. Despite my traumatic experience with school transport before the science trip today, I'd taken the bus home.

"Hi, Kenzie. How was school?"

I followed my stepmom's voice to the living room and

found her peeking out from inside a blanket fort she'd built with my little sisters.

"Boring," I said with a laugh. "You've clearly been having much more fun here." I dropped my bag on the floor and knelt to look inside the fort. Both my sisters were huddled together under the blanket, along with almost every doll and stuffed toy they'd brought with us to Ransom.

"We're hiding from the dragon," Skye said in her most serious tone.

"It tried to eat my toes," Daisy cried.

"See, it hasn't been all fun and games," Tessa added with a smile. "I need to start dinner. Can you take over for me? I'm guarding the entrance."

I laughed and nodded before taking her place just inside the makeshift door of the fort.

"Be careful!" Daisy squealed at her mom.

"I will!" she called back.

I made myself as comfortable as I could on one of the cushions under the tent-like structure, which was pretty much just a blanket stretched over two chairs. It sagged in the middle, so I had to crouch low to stop my head from hitting the roof. One wrong move and I was sure it would all come crashing down.

"Did you see the dragon out there, Kenzie?" Skye asked.

"No, but perhaps he's hiding somewhere else. Like his lair."

"What about at school?" Skye continued. "Is there a dragon there?"

"Kind of." I leaned in close. "His name is Parker. He's big and scary and breathes fire if you look at him the wrong way."

My sisters both gasped, their mouths hanging open, and I wondered if I'd scared them too much.

"Was he there today?"

"He was."

"And did you run away from him?"

"No." As if I'd give him the satisfaction.

"Why not?"

"Because being brave means standing your ground and refusing to let the dragon scare you off. Besides, I'm a Foster, and we're not afraid of anything. The dragons should be scared of us."

The girls' eyes lit up, like they were little soldiers and I'd just delivered a rousing battle cry.

"You're right." Skye nodded firmly. "Fosters aren't afraid!"

Together, my little sisters jumped up and charged out from under the tent, shouting as loudly as they could.

"Roar!" they both bellowed as they ran across the living room and disappeared into the hallway. They returned a few moments later and started to shout, "We did it! The dragons are scared of *us*."

I played with my sisters for a while longer as Tessa prepared dinner. When my dad got home, he stuck his head into the living room to say a quick hello before he went into the kitchen to help. I could overhear him and Tessa talking and my ears pricked up when I caught mention of the Devils.

"It hasn't been the best start," my dad was saying. "I'm not sure what we're going to do if tryouts don't go well tomorrow."

"Is the current goalie really that bad?"

I didn't hear my dad's response, so I had to assume he was

simply nodding his head.

"What about the boy who got injured? Will he be able to play again soon?"

"Ford's out for at least six weeks. That might be enough time to improve Anderson a little, but we can't afford to lose many more games if we're going to make the playoffs."

They both fell silent for a few moments before Tessa said, "I'm sure it'll all work out. You always seem to find a way."

She only got a grunt in response. I couldn't work out how to feel after what I'd heard. My dad was desperately searching for a solution to his problem and was running out of options, yet he remained oblivious to the fact there was a perfectly good one sitting in the next room. Okay, maybe I wasn't a *perfect* option, but I was an option. At least, I would be if he was able to stomach the idea of me in hockey gear.

"Kenzie, you're not playing," Daisy whined, nudging me from my thoughts.

I didn't hear any more hockey talk coming from the kitchen after that, and there was none at dinner, but I was still eager to get to my room once I'd finished eating. Mitts was lying on my bed as I entered, licking one of her bright white paws. I smiled at how cute she looked but only received an irritated huff in reply.

"I'm sorry, did I interrupt you?"

Her judgmental side-eye told me everything I needed to know.

There was a loud *tink* as something hit my window, making Mitts scamper out the door. It was probably just the wind or the branch of a tree. I dismissed the sound and went to grab my paints. My mural still wasn't finished, and all I wanted to do tonight was block out the rest of the world and work on it.

But the *tink* came again, louder this time, and not so easily ignored. I slowly approached the window to investigate, trying not to feel like the first victim in a trashy horror movie. It was dark outside, and when I reached the glass, it took a moment for my eyes to adjust. When they did, I was almost disappointed to see it wasn't a serial killer standing on my front lawn. It was Parker Darling, with his arm lifted as though he was about to throw something.

I quickly opened my window. "What are you doing?"

"Throwing stones at your window."

"*Why?*"

"Because we need to talk. Can you come out here?" He whispered the last bit and glanced around the lawn cautiously.

"No," I hissed. "Go away."

"Just for a minute?"

"Not going to happen."

"Please?"

"Go home, Parker."

He grinned up at me, then disappeared from view. I leaned out the window and looked down to see him grabbing the latticework that ran up the front of the house.

"Now what are you doing?"

It only took him a few seconds to scale the wall and reach my window. And his grin had only grown on the way up. "I said I want to talk to you," he repeated, one hand now on the windowsill.

"Well, I don't want to talk to you." I slid the window firmly shut and stepped away.

"You know I'll wait out here all night—" Suddenly he swore under his breath. "Shit, I might actually need some help here." I darted back to the window to see Parker was now gripping my windowsill with both hands and there was a concerned look on his face.

"What is it?"

"I think the trellis is breaking," he grunted in reply. "Let me in, quick."

I hesitated.

"By all means, take your time, but I can hear the wood cracking and it's a pretty long way down."

"Ugh, fine." I quickly lifted the window again, and Parker hoisted himself inside.

He smiled brightly as he stood tall, looking far too relaxed for someone who had just survived a near-death experience. I felt the urge to look out the window and double-check whether the trellis genuinely was close to breaking, but instead, I hurried over to my door and eased it shut. I could only imagine how angry my dad would be if he found a boy in my room, especially if that boy was Parker Darling. The only consolation was that Parker would get in trouble too. The thought almost had me calling out to my dad just to see what would happen.

"So, this is your bedroom," Parker said. "It's got a bed, at least . . ."

I watched as he carefully inspected his surroundings. His presence filled my mostly empty room, and even though we were standing on opposite sides of the space, my skin reacted like we were only inches apart.

"What did you expect? That I sleep in a dumpster like a raccoon?"

"I hadn't ruled it out."

"Can you please just explain why you've broken into my house?"

"I didn't break in. You let me in. Besides, I thought having a hot guy climb up to your bedroom window was every girl's dream? It's very Romeo and Juliet."

"You know they both die at the end, right?"

His eyes glinted with amusement.

"I like your painting." He nodded toward the half-finished mural that covered the far wall. "It's peaceful."

Had Parker just given me a genuine compliment? I didn't like how it warmed my chest, and I folded my arms to try and dampen the sensation. "Just tell me what you want, Parker?"

He sighed and faced me once more. "To talk."

"There's nothing to talk about."

"Just hear me out," he said, stepping across the room toward me. "I risked a lot coming here. I nearly died scaling your wall, and I can guarantee your dad will bench me for eternity if he finds me in here."

"Then you better get out before he does."

"I can't do that. This is too important. The team needs you. You have to reconsider."

"This again?" I almost laughed out loud. "Don't you think this is all a little ironic?"

"What do you mean?"

"You asking me to play hockey when you're the reason I can't."

He stared blankly at me. "Seriously, what are you talking about?"

I didn't owe him an explanation; didn't need to bring up the past, argue with him, or even have him apologize. But I did need to get him out of my room and put a stop to his ridiculous ideas of me playing hockey, so I could just go back to painting my mural in peace.

"My dad has never liked the idea of me playing hockey," I began. "He thinks it's too dangerous for girls."

"Well, that's just stupid."

Apparently, there was one thing Parker and I could agree on. "Yeah, it is. But freshman year, I convinced him to let me join his summer camp. It was my one shot to show him I deserved to play. To prove I belonged out there. But when he caught you kissing me—"

"Uh, you mean, when he caught *you* kissing *me*."

I took a deep breath and tried to remember I was revealing all this to get rid of Parker and it would all be over soon.

"When my dad caught *us* kissing," I continued, "he decided I wasn't serious about hockey and used it as an excuse to ban me for life."

"For life?" Parker looked disgusted. "Are you serious?"

"Yes."

"That's bullshit."

"Of course it is." I shrugged. "But it doesn't matter. The point is, even if I wanted to try out for the Devils, there's no way my dad would ever allow me to play."

Parker's blue eyes watched me closely, and he shook his head. "I didn't realize. I thought I was the only one to get in trouble."

"I wish."

"If I'd known, I . . ." His voice was surprisingly soft, and as he stared into my eyes a myriad of thoughts flashed across his gaze. "I guess we both kind of screwed each other that day."

It was probably as close to an apology as I'd ever get from him.

"But now we've got a chance to fix it." He stepped closer and the energy in his voice returned. "I can help you get back on the ice, and you can help me stop my senior year of hockey going to shit. Once we've both got what we want, we can go straight back to hating each other."

"You think I can just stop hating you?"

He rolled his eyes. "If it means you get to play hockey again, I'm sure you can suck it up. We'll just call a truce for a while."

"You're forgetting there's still the issue of my dad, Parker."

"We desperately need a new goalie. If he could see you play, I know he'll change his mind. He'll have to."

"*You* haven't even seen me play."

"I saw enough at camp to know you're good. To know you've got more potential than any other goalie at Ransom High. Or was that a fluke?"

"Well, you did tell me you missed a shot on purpose that day."

"I say a lot of things." He grinned at the memory and my glare intensified.

"No," I said firmly. "It wasn't a fluke."

"Then what are we waiting for?"

"I'm *not* interested."

His smile grew and his blue eyes started to sparkle, like he sensed victory was close. Like he could see right through me. "Look, I know we got off to a rocky start."

"That's putting it mildly."

"And two days ago, I could not have imagined we'd be having this conversation. But you're talented. We just need your dad to see it too. Don't you *want* to play again?"

I hated how his words struck at something deep inside me. I'd spent my whole life dreaming of playing for a real hockey team, but I'd given up hope these last few years. Parker was making it all feel possible again.

"You don't know my dad. I'd need to try out for the team, and if he sees my name on the list, he'll probably cancel the whole thing. I'm sorry, Parker, this just isn't going to happen—"

"Parker?" The door opened and my sisters both squealed from behind me. I hadn't even realized they were there.

"We're not afraid of you!" Skye shouted.

"Go away, dragon!" screamed Daisy.

I had to smother a laugh when I saw Parker's shocked expression. He even took a slight step back as my sisters growled and glared at him.

"It's okay," I said, turning to the girls. "You guys go and play. I'll get rid of the evil dragon."

Daisy and Skye both gave Parker one more stern look before they turned and ran off down the hallway, giggling as they went.

"Does your *whole* family hate me?" he asked, once I'd closed the door.

"I mean, you haven't met my stepmom or my cat yet, but Tessa's a softy, so she doesn't count, and Mitts hates everyone, so I wouldn't take that personally."

"I take it Mitts is the cat?" he asked.

"Of course she's the cat."

"Why am I not surprised you have a cat that hates every—"

"A dragon?" My dad's voice sounded in the corridor making my heart all but stop.

"Yes!" my sisters cried together. "In Kenzie's room! Come and see, Daddy."

There was a firm knock at the door and Parker's eyes widened when my dad's voice called from the other side. "Uh, Mackenzie, can we come in?"

Parker didn't hesitate as he dove toward my closet, tore open the door and leaped inside. It might have been funny to watch him cram his huge frame inside the tiny space and try to squeeze the door shut if we weren't both totally screwed if we got caught. I motioned for him to hurry, but I'd only recently filled the closet with clothes, and he could barely fit.

"Just a minute," I called to my dad, desperately trying to think of a way to stall him. "I'm, uh, I'm naked."

Parker was still doing his best to disappear amongst my coats and dresses, but he instantly stopped and turned to me. A smirk pulled at his lips and a familiar twinkle returned to his gaze. "Naked?"

I stepped toward the closet and gave him a hard shove, pushing him far enough inside that I could force the door closed. Was this boy capable of taking *anything* seriously?

"Kenzie?" Dad called. "You all good?"

I grabbed my bathrobe from the bed and quickly wrapped myself in it to keep up the ruse. "Uh, yep, I'm decent. You can come in."

My bedroom door opened, and my dad peeked his head through the gap with an awkward smile. "I hear you've got a dragon problem."

My sisters burst into the room from behind him.

"He was right there, Daddy." Skye pointed to the empty space beside me.

"Where did he go?" Daisy asked, her eyes a little more calculating as she scanned the room. I swallowed nervously as her gaze drifted past the closet that contained the missing dragon.

Dad chuckled to himself. "Should we try to find him?"

"No!" I shouted, my heart racing. "Uh, I mean, no need. The dragon is gone now. I think he realized he should never have come here in the first place."

"Because we're so scary?" Daisy asked.

"Yep, that's right, terrifying."

My sister nodded firmly. "Good. I didn't like the Parker dragon."

"The what dragon?" My dad let out an uncertain laugh.

I shrugged at him, as though I was just as confused as he was.

"I should probably get started on my homework," I said, hoping my dad would get the hint.

"Sure." He nodded and started ushering my sisters from the room. "Come on, girls."

The tightness in my chest only relented when the door clicked shut behind them. I waited until I heard their footsteps on the stairs before I stalked over to my closet door and wrenched it open.

Parker grinned happily as he stepped out. "Your clothes smell nice."

"I—" I shook my head. "My dad came *this* close to catching you here and that's all you have to say? My clothes smell nice?"

"*Real* nice," he added. "Like roses or something."

"You need to go!" Did he really not understand the urgency of this?

Parker leaned against the closet door and tucked one hand in his pocket, like there was no reason to rush. "I'm not leaving until I've got a new goaltender."

"I already explained why that's not going to happen."

"You gave me some excuses, sure. But are you really not willing to even try?"

"What's the point when I know it'll end badly?"

"I'm not convinced." His eyes narrowed thoughtfully. "There has to be something else that's holding you back. Unless..."

I knew I shouldn't encourage him. That whatever he was getting at I wasn't going to like. Yet, for some reason, I couldn't stop myself. "Unless what?"

"It's the tension between us, isn't it?"

"If you've only just realized how much I hate being around you, then you haven't been listening."

"I'm not talking about that kind of tension." He pushed off the doorframe and walked toward me, and my heart seemed to beat faster with every step he took. It had to be the adrenaline still coursing through my veins from nearly being caught, right?

I wanted nothing more than to back away as he came close,

but I resolutely stood my ground. "There is no other kind of tension."

"No?" His eyes glinted with mischief. "Look, I know resisting me is hard. Especially since we kissed and you probably want to do it again, but surely that's not going to stop you joining the team."

"I'm not refusing to join the team because we kissed!"

"What other reason could there be?"

"Uh, I've given you a few, and I can think of plenty more."

"You're really saying you haven't thought about kissing me once since that summer?"

"Not once."

"I find that hard to believe. It was a pretty good kiss."

He was standing so close to me now, I had to tilt my head back to look up at him as he towered over me.

"I don't remember."

His eyes glittered. God, I hated when they did that. "If it would help, I can remind you. Maybe it'll release a bit of that tension."

I hesitated, but only for a moment before I tore my eyes away from him and stepped back. Was he serious or just that desperate for a new goalie?

"You're really pimping your lips out to get me on the team?" I asked.

"Hmm, that's not a no to my offer . . ."

"That's a *hell* no to your offer."

He grinned, as though he was completely unbothered by my rejection.

"Tell me you'll think about the goalie tryouts, and I'll

leave," Parker said. "They're tomorrow night. And if you want another chance to prove your dad wrong, I'll figure out a way to make it happen."

"Fine, I'll *think* about it."

Parker beamed.

"But only to get you out of my room."

There was far too much satisfaction in his gaze for my liking. "I guess that means my work here is done."

He pulled a yellow piece of paper from his pocket, unfolded it and placed it on my bed. It was one of the posters advertising the tryouts. Then he turned and opened the window. I didn't even have a chance to ask him what he was doing, because the next moment he was crawling through it and easing his way onto the broken trellis. Then he dropped from view.

I rushed to the window to check on him, but he was already on the ground.

"Are you crazy?" I whispered down at him. "You could have killed yourself." But when I took a closer look at the trellis, there didn't seem to be anything wrong with it.

"Didn't know you cared," he called up, his voice just above a whisper.

"I don't."

He chuckled softly as he walked off across my front lawn, into the darkness. "Goodnight, Mackenzie."

I slammed my window shut. I think I preferred it when he couldn't remember my name.

Chapter 12

PARKER

"Do you think she's coming?" Seth asked before immediately answering his own question. "I don't think she's coming."

The two of us were waiting in the ice arena parking lot. It was close to four o'clock, and we were due on the ice any minute now for practice. The goalie tryouts were tonight, and while Mackenzie hadn't made me any promises she'd be here, I was still hopeful she'd show.

As much as she might try to deny it, I knew she loved this sport just as much as the rest of us. I'd seen it in her eyes when she'd told me she was banned from playing. It was something I still couldn't quite wrap my mind around. I knew Coach Foster was strict, but banning his kid from a sport they loved was shitty, even for him. I'd been trying my best not to think about my own involvement in her ban; to ignore the guilt that had flared in my chest when she told me it was because of our kiss. Perhaps offering to kiss her again immediately after hadn't been the smartest move. It had somehow gotten her to think about trying out, though.

"She'll come," I replied, because I honestly didn't want to think about the future of this team if she didn't. There had been a small group of wannabe goaltenders getting ready inside. Some had already tried out for the position and failed, and there were a few new faces too, but they all looked like they'd only recently hit puberty. I already knew none of them would be good enough.

"You heard what she said yesterday," Seth continued. "She won't come, just to piss you off."

"Yeah, well, I'm hoping I convinced her to reconsider last night."

"You saw her last night?"

"Uh, yeah." I coughed, wondering if perhaps I should have kept that detail to myself. "I may have gone to her house to try and talk her into it."

"Wait, what? Was Coach Foster there? What did he say?"

"He didn't see me." The knowing grin that was already spreading across Seth's face convinced me to skip the explanation of how I'd climbed into Mackenzie's bedroom.

He shook his head at me. "You really *are* desperate."

"I just don't want to lose again. You should feel the same."

"Yeah, losing like that did suck. But I think you're reaching if you believe Mackenzie cares about it as much as you do."

"Don't speak too soon," I said, as Jasmine Cleaver's car pulled into the lot. Seth turned to follow my gaze, just as Mackenzie climbed out of the car and started toward us. For a moment it felt like the world stilled. She'd come. She'd actually come.

"Well, well," Seth said, sounding as shocked as I felt.

Mackenzie wore a frown as she approached with her large sports bag slung over her shoulder. She looked as though this was the last place she wanted to be, yet I had never been happier to see her.

"You're here," I said, struggling to hold in my smile as she dropped her bag in front of us.

"Yes, I'm here," she grumbled. "But only to prove I'm right; this whole idea is ridiculous. You won't even be able to get me on the ice without my dad flipping out."

"You need to have a little faith."

"Yeah, Parker's got a plan," Seth added.

She looked between the two of us. "Well, what is it?"

"A disguise," I answered quickly, although now I'd said it out loud, it sounded a little stupid. "Well, it's not exactly a disguise, but we've got some goalie gear stashed inside the refs' locker room. We'll sneak you in, you'll get suited up in secret, and as long as you keep your helmet on, no one will know it's you. Simple."

"That's your grand plan? Wear goalie gear to the goalie tryouts. *Genius*."

"It'll be fine," I continued, ignoring the look of concern on her face. "Your dad has been trying to play down the importance of these tryouts, so Coach Rainer is taking the lead while Coach Foster runs the team's practice as normal. By the time we get in there, everyone will be warming up already, and you'll be able to join in without anyone asking any questions."

"What if someone asks me my name?"

"I've thought of that. You're on the tryouts list as Ken Manly."

Seth spluttered out a laugh. I nudged him with my elbow but a smile escaped my lips too. Mackenzie scowled at us.

"Don't worry," I continued, before she could pick any more holes in the plan. "I even got you one of my practice jerseys. You'll fit right in." I pulled the jersey from my bag and handed it to her. She immediately scrunched up her nose.

"Ew, no thanks."

"What? It's clean."

"I don't want to wear any jersey that belongs to you."

"Must be the first girl to tell you that," Seth said under his breath.

I ignored him and thrust the jersey toward Mackenzie again. "Do you want to play or not?"

She gave a small nod.

"Then you've got to do what I say."

She shook her head but muttered, "Okay, fine."

"Great. Just tuck your hair in, keep your helmet on, lower your voice when you talk, and then play better than you've ever played before."

"Oh, that's all, is it?" She bit her lip, clearly still uncertain.

"It'll work, trust me, *Ken*."

She glared at me, but her gaze quickly softened and she released a breath. "You're not exactly trustworthy, but what have I got to lose, right?"

"That's the spirit." I grinned. "Come on. Let's get inside."

Seth headed for the boys' locker room, while I ushered Mackenzie into the referees' room so she could change. We needed to make sure no one saw her, so even the girls' locker room was too risky.

"These pads are going to be too big for me," she said, grimacing as she got a look at the gear I'd taken from the school's storage room. It was the smallest I could find.

"You'll just have to make do," I said. "You won't be the only one out there today in gear that doesn't fit perfectly. I'm sure your dad will get you the right size when you make the team."

"I think you mean *if* I make the team."

"You will."

I left her to get my own gear on. I was running late, and the locker room was empty by the time I arrived. Despite what I'd told Mackenzie, I really had no idea if our plan would work, but it was worth a try. Like she'd said, we had nothing to lose, and I knew we had everything to gain.

"You're late, Twelve," Foster barked as I stepped out onto the ice. The number sixteen was literally printed on my jersey, but clearly I was still some cocky immature kid to him, and he couldn't seem to see past that to the player I'd become.

I itched to correct him, but I knew that if I wanted to stay on the team and have any chance of becoming captain, I needed to keep trying to win him over.

"Sorry, Coach."

I hurriedly joined the team warm-up and glanced over to where the goalies were gathered at the other end of the rink. I smiled when I saw Mackenzie. Her hair was tucked totally out of sight and with the helmet on it was difficult to tell it was her. She was right about the pads being too big. It should have made them hard to maneuver in, but she was warming up as if they weren't bothering her at all.

There were six hopefuls in total, but to me she was the only contender. She moved across the ice so naturally, despite the bulky goalie equipment, and held herself like she was born to be out here. I didn't need to see her stop a puck to know she was the best goaltender we had.

"Worry about your own warm-up, Twelve!"

Two warnings in just a few minutes. It seemed I was only

taking steps backward when it came to winning over Coach Foster. I waved a hand at him and did my best to focus, but it was hard to keep my attention where it should be when so much was riding on what was happening elsewhere on the ice.

For the first part of the tryouts, the goalies were kept separate, as Coach Rainer ran them through some basic drills. But as the session progressed, our two groups were combined so we could test them under game-like situations.

It was only now that Coach Foster seemed to be taking more of an interest in the goaltenders. He began eyeing them closely, analyzing how they handled different plays. My palms were literally sweating. Mackenzie was well hidden under her helmet, but surely it wouldn't take much for Foster to recognize his own daughter. The longer the session went on, the more closely he watched her, and I prayed it was only because she was playing so well.

For someone who had never played competitive hockey, Mackenzie handled pretty much everything the coaches threw at her. Her positioning and movement were good, and she looked confident and focused— her stick-handling was a little weaker, especially when it came to recovering from rebounds and clearing the puck, but there was one skill that made her really stand out: her reflexes. She was incredibly fast. Every time she reached out a glove to catch the puck or dropped to the ice to save a shot with her pads, she did it so quickly and gracefully I felt the urge to cheer.

We were all given a chance to shoot against each of the potential goalies. One by one, they stood in front of the net. And one by one I scored on them. Some of their attempted saves were so poor they made Anderson look like a superstar.

Finally, it was my turn to face Mackenzie. Part of me wondered whether I should give her a simple shot so Coach Foster could see her make yet another save. But I knew I couldn't do that. If she was going to make the team, I needed to show she could compete with the best of us. Plus, she'd probably punch me again if she found out I'd gone easy on her.

She gave me a subtle nod in challenge. I gathered the puck and raced toward her. She tracked me intently, slightly adjusting her position to match every move I made. I couldn't shake the memory of the last time we'd done this together, three years ago, and I found myself firing the puck at the top-left corner, just like I had that day at camp.

And just like that day at camp, her arm snapped out like lightning and the puck slapped against her glove. I stared in shock. As much as I'd wanted her to save it and impress her dad, I hadn't been sure she actually could. Since the last time we'd faced off, I'd become one of the best high school hockey players in the state, and the best goal scorer in the league. Yet she'd made the save. And she'd done it with ease.

She tossed the puck back to the ice, and I grinned as I scooped it up. There was no way Coach Foster could pick anyone but her.

A few minutes later, Foster brought the session to an end with a loud whistle blast, and we all gathered round. Mackenzie kept to the back of the group, her head ducked as she avoided her father's gaze.

"Good work tonight," he said. "Thank you to everyone who came to try out for our open goaltending position. I'm pleased to announce that Assistant Coach Rainer and I are both in agreement on who will be joining the team. Everyone, I would like to welcome . . ." He paused as he went to check his clipboard and frowned when he read the name. "Uh, Ken Manly."

My teammates applauded, and Seth cheered loudly, as I turned to smile at Mackenzie. I wasn't surprised. She was clearly better than the others; hell, she'd have given Ford a run for his money if he'd been here tonight. I was just glad Coach Foster had noticed it too. As the applause died down, excited murmurs filled the room. Everyone was clearly relieved we'd somehow managed to find a solution to our goaltender crisis.

But there was still one little problem ahead of us. And apparently Mackenzie wasn't going to wait to tackle it. She pulled her helmet from her head and stepped forward. "Actually, it's Mackenzie Foster."

Chapter 13

MACKENZIE

Everyone was quiet. You could have heard a puck drop from the locker room. The only noise was from my own shallow breaths in and out. This was it. The moment of truth. I'd felt confident throughout the tryouts, and excited when I heard I'd been selected, but revealing my identity had made my blood turn cold.

Every person in the room was watching me. The cool air in the rink felt thick with their surprise. But there was only one person I was watching—my dad. His eyes were wide with shock, but it didn't take long for that to turn to anger.

"Woo-hoo, Mackenzie!" Seth cheered. But his echoing claps slowly petered out when no one joined him. You'd think the guys on the team had never seen a girl in hockey gear before. I gave Seth a grateful smile and he shrugged at me. At least he'd tried.

"What are you doing?" my dad thundered. I'd thought the tension in the air was unbearable before, but his fierce tone had the whole team shifting with discomfort. When he remembered he had an audience, he lowered his voice. "Go and get changed. We'll talk about this at home."

"I'm not going anywhere," I said. "You just selected me as your new goalie."

"No, I didn't. This is a boys' team, playing in a boys' division."

"I know that," I replied. "But does it really matter if I'm good enough?"

I was met, once again, by silence. This wasn't looking good. I knew my dad would never agree. Why had I put myself through this? Why had I stupidly dared to hope?

My dad looked as though he was about to respond, but then Parker stepped forward.

"She's right, Coach." All eyes turned to him. "Mackenzie was the best player to try out, and we all know it. Even you." I knew Parker wanted me on the team, but I was still surprised he'd spoken up for me. Especially considering my dad looked close to exploding. But that didn't stop the Devils' star player.

"There's nothing prohibiting a girl from playing in our division," he went on. "Especially when the high school doesn't have a girls' team."

There were a few murmurs and whispers from the other players, who had all been stunned into complete silence until now. The boys looked to Parker and then to me, and a few began to nod in agreement, as though Parker's words had released them from their initial shock.

I suspected if Parker jumped off a cliff, most of his teammates would fight over who got the privilege of following him over the edge first. But even with Parker's approval, I never expected others to start speaking up.

"Yeah, Mackenzie was awesome," Seth shouted.

"She's got hands like glue," Owen said.

"Some of those other kids couldn't even skate," another guy added. "No offense, Brent."

"Screw you, Cullen!"

"She is a girl . . ." Someone sounded unsure.

"So's your mom!"

A few of the guys laughed.

"Who cares if she's a girl?"

"It'll make us a laughing stock."

"Not if we start winning some games."

The chatter and debate grew louder, but the person who mattered most was still quiet.

My dad's arms were firmly folded, and he was glaring at his players. I stepped to the front of the group and moved toward him. "Please, Dad. Just give me a chance."

He glanced down at me, and then back at his team, who were still debating amongst themselves. My dad was hard to read, because he almost always had the same stern crease across his brow. But right now, he looked defeated.

He let out a heavy breath. "Fine."

"Really?"

"You haven't given me much choice, have you?" he gritted out. "You'll join the team on a trial basis. You've got three games to prove you can keep up."

I swallowed as I nodded. "I'll keep up. You can count on it."

He turned to the players once more and raised his voice to address them. "Mackenzie will join the team, but she's on probation. Anyone have any issues with my decision, you know where my office is." Without another word, he turned and stalked off the ice.

Coach Rainer clapped to get our attention, then started wrapping up the session. But I was still focused on my dad's retreating figure. I'd never seen him this angry before. Didn't he realize he was the one who betrayed me first?

Only after the team was dismissed and I was walking out through the tunnel did what I'd achieved start to sink in. I'd made the team—even if I was on thin ice. After spending my entire life longing to play for a real hockey team, I was finally going to get that chance. And it never would have happened if not for Parker.

As I followed the other players back to the locker rooms, a few of the guys congratulated me or gave me encouraging slaps on the back. Plenty of frowns and concerned glances were also directed my way, but I supposed I had to expect some resistance.

I peeled off from the rest of the team to go change, but when I entered the small referees' room, I was surprised to find Parker waiting there. I quickly closed the door behind me. The last thing I needed was for my dad to see us together.

"What are you doing here?"

"You did it," he said with a genuine smile. "Congratulations."

He closed the small distance between us and my stomach dipped. Was he going to hug me? If so, was I going to let him? I imagined his strong arms pulling me close and the thought sent adrenaline pulsing through me. It was probably just a natural fight or flight response. He must have had a similar reaction, because he suddenly stopped, a brief look of confusion appearing on his face, before giving me an awkward pat on the shoulder.

"Uh, thanks," I replied, just as awkwardly.

"I can't believe we actually pulled it off."

"You don't have to sound so surprised. I thought you said

this plan was perfect."

His eyes glittered in reply. "Well, it wasn't. But you were. Your dad didn't have a choice but to pick you."

I felt my cheeks grow warm at his compliment, so I quickly moved past him to get to my bag. With Parker in here, the room felt far too small. It wasn't just his body that seemed to take up all the space, it was his energy too. I felt jittery because of it. He was being nice enough, but that was almost more unsettling than the mischievous smirk I'd become so used to seeing since arriving in Ransom.

"Maybe." I rummaged through my bag. "But you heard him—it's only on a trial basis."

He nodded. "The next three games are against some of the best teams in the division. And the third one? That'll be the homecoming game against our biggest rivals, the Sunshine Hills Saints."

"Great, so I'm doomed."

"I wouldn't go that far."

"My dad will be looking for any reason he can find to kick me off the team. The first time I slip up, I'll be gone."

I glanced up at Parker, suddenly panicked. He'd gotten me this far, but what was I supposed to do now?

"Parker, I've never even played in a real game."

My vulnerability surprised both of us, and I immediately wished I could take the words back. I didn't want Parker doubting my skills or my confidence.

"I'm sure you'll be fine," he replied. "Just play like you did tonight."

I nodded, somewhat grateful he had shrugged my worries

off so easily, but not so sure I could do the same.

"Well, whatever happens, I wouldn't have made it this far without you," I said. "So, thank you, Parker."

A flicker of pride crossed his eyes, but it was instantly replaced by mischief. "Wait, did you just *thank* me?"

Ugh. "Yes, but don't get used to it. It was a one-time thing."

"Good," he said, still smirking, as he started for the door. "I'm not sure I liked it. Then again, you *are* my biggest fan, so I guess I'll take it."

And then he was gone. He truly had a talent for making me not totally hate him one moment to wanting to throw him out the closest window the next. I guessed now that I was on the team, our little truce was over. It was probably for the best.

I changed out of my gear and made my way to the parking lot where Jaz was waiting for me. She was picking up Owen and had offered to give me a ride too. After the way my dad had reacted today, I was grateful to avoid an uncomfortable car trip home with him.

Jaz was looking down at her phone, but the moment she spotted me she pushed off the car and rushed toward me. "How did it go?"

I couldn't stop the smile from forming on my lips. "I made the team."

"I knew it!" she squealed with excitement and pulled me in for a hug.

I laughed as she squeezed me. "Don't breathe in while you're hugging me, I smell."

"I have two hockey-playing brothers." She laughed too as she stepped back. "I think I'm immune to the smell now."

"Well done, Mackenize." Owen appeared beside us. "You were brilliant out there. I'm still getting over the shock of you removing your helmet, though."

"Oh, I wish I'd been there to see it," Jaz said.

"It was very dramatic," Owen told her. "The whole team forgot how to speak. The coaches did too."

"It wasn't *that* dramatic," I said. "And my dad did have a few things to say. I'm on the team, but only on trial."

"I'm sure you were incredible," Jaz gushed as she unlocked her car. It was old, small, and a bright shade of pink, but I was beyond jealous. My parents let me borrow my stepmom's car when they needed me to drive somewhere. But it wasn't the same as having my own wheels. "You'll have to tell me all about it over dinner."

"Dinner?" I asked.

"We need to go out and celebrate, obviously," she explained as Owen and I loaded our bags in her trunk. "How do you feel about pizza?"

I knew I should probably go home and face my dad, but I was somewhat terrified by the prospect. It didn't sound nearly as fun as dinner with my friend.

"I love pizza," I said.

"Excellent. We know the perfect place."

I smiled. My dad could be mad at me later.

Jaz and Owen took me to a pizza bar called Nino's. The food was amazing, and I was glad she'd convinced me to celebrate a little. It was also a good opportunity to spend time with Owen. He seemed like a really sweet guy, and now that I was semi-officially a Ransom Devil, it couldn't hurt to get to know some players on the team other than Seth and Parker.

After a couple of hours loading up on pizza and ice cream and laughing with Jaz and her brother, my worries felt like a distant memory. Until the moment I got home.

As soon as I opened the front door and stepped inside, my dad looked out into the hallway from his office. "Get in here, Mackenzie. Now."

I grimaced and quietly shut the door behind me, slowly making my way down the hallway. My sisters were already in bed, and Tessa was nowhere to be seen. There was no one to save me. Not even Mitts. But I'd got myself into this mess. With a deep breath, I stepped into the office.

My dad stood up from his desk when I entered the room, pressing his fists onto the tabletop as he leaned toward me. "What the hell were you thinking, Mackenzie? You deliberately deceived me, in front of all my players and the assistant coach. Don't you understand the difficult position you've put me in?"

"I'm sorry, Dad, but—"

"You're *sorry*? You know this isn't what I want for you," he continued. "You gave me no choice but to allow you onto the team."

"What about what I want?" I'd never really understood his reasons for being so resolutely against me playing hockey, and maybe I never would. But he was sorely mistaken if he thought I was just going to roll over and quit the team.

"It's not about what you want, or what I want, it's . . ." My dad paused, and his eyes fell to the desk as he shook his head. "You just shouldn't have been out there today."

"Why not?" I released a humorless laugh. "Seriously, what

is so wrong with me playing hockey?"

His eyes still avoided mine. "I'm just trying to protect you."

"I'm not afraid of getting injured."

"That's not..." His voice trailed off.

"That's not, what?" I demanded. When he stayed silent, I carried on. "You have three daughters, Dad. I would've thought you'd want the best for us. That you'd think we could do anything."

"You *can* do anything. Anything but hockey."

"Well, it's too late. I'm on the team now. You've given me three games to prove myself and that's what I plan to do. I'm not fourteen anymore. I won't let you take this away from me again."

I turned to the door.

"We're not done here, Mackenzie—"

But I'd already heard enough. I left without another word, my insides taut with frustration, disappointment, and anger. My dad had never been this annoyed with me before. Yet he still hadn't told me I couldn't play. He probably thought I'd drop out after one game, but I was ready to prove him wrong. Playing today had been everything I'd ever wanted, and now that I'd had a taste of being on a team, he'd have to drag me away from it kicking and screaming.

Chapter 14

MACKENZIE

I had one practice with the Ransom Devils before my first game. *One.* And it didn't go well. I hadn't played with my brother since last winter, so I was noticeably rusty. The guys on the team did little to help me shake off the cobwebs. Most of them seemed hesitant to shoot against me, which was a stark contrast from the way they had played in tryouts, before they knew I was a girl. Between that and the fact that I was the head coach's daughter, I understood why they were acting that way. But it was incredibly frustrating.

On top of everything, my dad was refusing to talk to me. At practice he pretended like I wasn't there. I'd been hoping to get just a little bit of direction; maybe some tips on how to improve or "keep up" as he had demanded. But the few words of advice I did receive were from Coach Rainer, and even he seemed more focused on Anderson. It was like they wanted me to fail.

I was actually shocked to hear my name when my dad announced the starting lineup for the game on Saturday night. A part of me had assumed he'd just let Anderson play. But then I wondered, was he genuinely giving me an opportunity to prove myself, or throwing me in at the deep end to watch me drown?

Our away game against the Suffolk High Sharks was a short bus ride from Ransom, at a rink a few towns over. The boys blasted music on the bus and the energy was high, but I was a nervous mess by the time we arrived, struggling to ignore the deep-seeded feeling that I wasn't ready. That I needed more time. Training this week had left my body aching in places I didn't know existed. And I'd tossed and turned the whole night before, picturing today's game and the group of angry boys with hockey sticks who would be skating toward me hellbent on taking me down.

Unfortunately, it wasn't a nightmare; it was the reality of what I'd gone and signed myself up for. And as we warmed up for the game, I kept glancing at the opposition. The Sharks players were huge. Even at a distance, they looked double the size of my Devils teammates. I knew that wasn't true, and I kept trying to tell myself it was all in my head, but our opponents seemed to grow a few inches each time I looked at them.

I felt like I was going to be sick as my dad called us together and delivered his pregame pep talk. I didn't hear a word. The ground seemed to be swaying beneath me, and I could almost sense my skin turning green.

Dad probably thought it would only take one game to make me realize what an idiot I was for thinking I could handle this. He probably figured I wouldn't even make it to the rink today. That I'd quit before I even left the house.

The surest sign of his lack of faith was the jersey I'd been assigned. It was an old practice jersey, and while I looked the same as all my teammates in our white road uniforms with the red Devils logo on the front, I was the only one without a name on the back. Just the same number Ford had worn: one. It was as if I was keeping it warm for him.

Parker kept shooting me worried glances. It was the only thing keeping my stomach in check. The last thing I wanted to do was throw up in front of *him*.

He came over once my dad had finally finished his speech. "What's wrong?"

"Nothing."

"You look whiter than my ass in the middle of winter."

"That image isn't helping my nausea."

"Oh, God, you're not seriously going to be sick, are you?"

"No," I replied. "At least, I don't think so. It's just some pregame jitters." He continued to frown at me, as though I'd failed to reassure him, but I didn't have the energy to argue right now.

"Fine, I'm a little scared, okay?"

"*Scared*?" He said it like he'd never even heard of the concept before.

"Those guys out there are twice my size, and they all want to eviscerate me." I was beginning to see why perhaps my dad had some reservations about me playing hockey. Girls could do anything—yes. But what kind of damage would I suffer if a full-grown boy slammed into me? I was putting a whole lot of trust in my pads and helmet.

"You're only just realizing that now?" Parker asked. "You know you're playing on a guys' team, right?"

"Of course I do. It's just a little different to playing one-on-one with my brother. These guys couldn't care less if I end up in the back of an ambulance." I swallowed. What if I *did* end up needing an ambulance?

Parker rubbed a hand against his forehead. "Look, you

don't need to be scared. Goalies rarely end up in hospital."

"*Rarely?*"

"Nothing is going to happen to you."

"But—"

"Just focus on defending the net. I'll take care of the rest."

"What is that supposed to mean?"

He didn't respond, just stared out at the ice.

"Parker?"

He snapped round to face me. "It means, no one touches my goalie."

His goalie? I wanted to laugh—I wasn't his anything—but Parker's expression was deadly serious. It made me feel safer, like I wasn't going to be alone out there.

He turned and stalked away, erupting through the gate and onto the ice. As I followed, I noticed a few smirking faces watching me from the Sharks' bench.

"Hey look, it's goaltender Barbie," one player laughed. "This should be fun."

"Don't break a nail out there, princess," another mocked.

Their words struck me harder than I expected, and anger pulsed hot in my veins. I wanted to turn, skate toward them and show them exactly what this princess's nails could do. But I couldn't allow myself to be distracted, not when there was already so much anxiety churning in my gut.

Parker was just finishing a lap. I could hear the Sharks players still laughing from the bench and saw Parker's eyes narrow. He started skating toward me, but I quickly held out a hand to stop him.

"Don't," I said. "I can handle it."

He glanced between me and our snickering opponents. Judging by the look in his eyes, it was taking all his willpower not to ignore my request, jump over the boards, and beat the two guys to a pulp.

"But—"

"No, Parker. I told you, I can handle it."

He skated away with a disappointed sigh, as though I'd stopped him from playing with his favorite toy.

As I took up my position in front of the net, my nerves only increased. The arena felt much larger when you were right in the middle of it, with rows of seats looking down at you, all filled with cheering Suffolk High fans willing you to fail. Music blared from the speakers surrounding the rink so I could barely hear the familiar sound of skates scraping the ice, and the arena somehow felt colder than Ransom's. Not for the first time, I tried to convince myself this was all in my head, but before I knew it the game started. There was no turning back now.

I'd watched countless hours of ice hockey from the stands and on TV over the years, but it felt like an entirely different game from where I now stood. The players seemed faster, the collisions bigger. The puck flashed across the ice so quickly I was struggling to keep track of it. I soon realized I couldn't afford to lose focus for even a second because the Sharks forwards were relentless, firing off shots whenever they had half a chance. I managed to save the first few, but that didn't dent their resolve, and they continued to test me, with both their slapshots and their verbal blows.

"Try not to cry when I score."

"Don't worry, baby, I'll take you out after we've won."

"You know we're going easy on you, right?"

The patronizing comments kept coming, and I did my best not to let them put me off. But there was only so much I could ignore before my jaw started to twitch and my anger started to build.

Unfortunately, my lack of fitness wasn't helping my performance. Each save I made felt a little harder than the last. I kept waiting for my dad to notice and replace me with Anderson, but the call never came. Eventually, my exhaustion got the better of me. I saved a shot but the puck fell at the feet of a particularly mean-looking Sharks forward. I was too slow to react to the rebound, and he scored the first goal of the game, less than a minute before the end of the period.

As my dad barked instructions at us during the intermission, I could tell Anderson was itching to take over. But there was no way I was going to ask my dad to pull me out. Besides, I'd only let one goal in so far. We could still win this game. I was just going to have to ignore the way my body was screaming for a rest.

As we took to the ice for the second period, the Sharks forward who had scored earlier slid up alongside me. He was easily their most intimidating player, and he towered over me. His mouthguard was hanging from his lips as he leered through the grill on his helmet, revealing a couple of missing teeth.

"Damn, I thought for sure they'd have sent you back to the kitchen by now." He let out a low menacing laugh. "Not that I'm complaining. I could do with another goal or two."

"Is there a problem here?" Parker skidded to a stop next to us, putting his body between the guy and me. They were inches from each other, and I knew I needed to deescalate the situation quickly.

"There's no problem," I replied, tugging Parker away. "Let's play."

Once again, he reluctantly obeyed, like it went against every instinct in his body to skate away from a fight. Was he always this desperate to throw down in a game? I didn't see him squaring up with Sharks players on behalf of his other teammates.

"You know," Parker said, "I could easily knock a couple more of that dude's teeth out for you, if you like."

"I'd much prefer you even the score instead."

"Okay, okay," he said. "I'll leave you to it. Just don't let these idiots get in your head, yeah?"

I waved him away, but things only got worse when the game started again. The Devils pushed hard for a goal but couldn't find one. Parker was an unbelievably skilled player, but it was almost as if he was trying to win the game on his own. I couldn't really blame him, as the rest of our teammates looked as tired and frustrated as I felt. They were constantly making mistakes, missing passes, and giving the puck right back to our opponents.

Suddenly, after yet another turnover, the Sharks had a breakaway. The toothless forward was tearing straight toward me with the puck, skating so fast it was like he was going downhill. I wanted to move forward to close the angle, but his size and speed were overwhelming. I instinctively felt myself retreat to the goal line as he bore down on me and he easily scored his second goal. My confidence shattered.

I'd never flinched like that while playing against my brother. In fact, I didn't think I'd ever shrunk away from a challenge that way, on or off the ice, in my life.

"You okay, Foster?" Seth asked, as I clambered back to my feet.

"Fine." I nodded. "I'll get the next one."

I had to believe it was a one-time mistake; that I wouldn't let it happen again. Seth seemed convinced, but as he skated back into position, I saw Parker pull him aside. The other defenseman, Marc Jansen, joined them. The junior was so tall and broad he could easily have been mistaken for a college senior. The three of them huddled together and Parker appeared to be issuing strict instructions to each of them. From the way they kept shooting glances over their shoulders at me, I had to assume I was the root of their problem.

It didn't take long to figure out Parker's solution. Seth and Marc began shadowing me so closely it was like I had my own private security detail. They seemed primed and ready to throw themselves in front of any player or puck that came my way, and they kept drifting close to my crease and blocking my view.

"Hey, there," Seth said as he hovered in front of me. His voice was cheery, like we'd just randomly bumped into each other at a coffee shop. "Having fun?"

"Move, Seth! I don't need a babysitter!"

Marc was just as close, and I panicked when I lost sight of the puck behind his massive frame.

"Jansen!" I yelled. "Get out of the way!"

"Can't," he called back. "Just doing my job."

"Well, *I* can't do *my* job if I can't see!"

I could hear my dad yelling something similar from the bench, but the two defensemen completely ignored him. A few minutes later, I'd let in another two goals. One skidded through Marc's legs and into the net before I even saw it. And I had even less chance of saving the second shot, which bounced off Seth's back as he dived to make a block.

This was Parker's doing; I was sure of it. He must have told the guys I needed help. Or at least made them so worried about my skills they felt like they had no other choice. Did he not trust me?

I got some respite when Parker finally managed to pull a goal back, but the Sharks weren't finished. I let in yet another goal before the final siren sounded, this time from a shot that deflected off Jansen's ass. Apparently, he thought it more capable of stopping the puck than I was.

I left the ice exhausted and feeling like a total failure. We'd lost by five goals to one. Another L for the Devils. We'd barely done better than the previous game.

My dad gave the team a brief speech focusing mostly on how hard we were going to have to work at practice next week if we wanted to reach the level he expected from us. Judging by the silence after he finished speaking, everyone agreed. I was relieved not to be singled out, but I felt certain the rest of the team blamed me for the loss.

I hadn't played well, and I was just as angry and disappointed at myself as they were. But I was equally annoyed at Parker. Annoyed, and a little hurt. It was like he gave up on me in the final period, pretty much ordering Seth and Marc to fill in for me because I couldn't do the job myself.

I wanted to confront him, but I didn't get a chance before we boarded the bus, and the mood on the return trip was so somber I didn't want to make it worse. When we got back to Ransom, I was relieved to find Jaz waiting to give me a ride. Her gloomy expression told me the game hadn't looked any better from where she'd been seated in the crowd.

"I know, I know," I said, as I dumped my gear in the back of her car. "I sucked."

"You didn't suck," she replied softly. "That was a tough game. And you made a lot of good saves."

"I made a lot of mistakes, too." I sighed. "I got tired. Struggled with my focus. Missed too many shots." I didn't want to go into much more detail than that, so I just shook my head. "They would have been better off with Anderson."

"They would not have!" Jaz exclaimed. "Don't be so hard on yourself. It was incredibly brave to even go out there. Besides, it was your first game. You'll do better next time."

I nodded, but only because I didn't have a choice. I *had* to be better next time. I was running out of chances.

"I just want to forget that game ever happened," I said.

"Well, I have the perfect way." Jaz started to smile. "There's a party tonight."

"A party?"

"Yep, there's almost always a party after Devils games."

"Even when they lose?"

She looked thoughtful for a moment, then shrugged. "They don't usually lose."

Now I definitely didn't feel like partying. Plus—

"My dad will say no," I said.

"What about your stepmom?"

I went quiet as I considered whether it was worth the trouble. While I might not want to go to a party, maybe Jaz was right, and it would take my mind off things.

"Tessa might be okay with it," I said. "And my dad's not speaking to me, so I couldn't ask him even if I wanted to."

"It sounds like you should ask her." She was practically bouncing up and down on the spot with anticipation.

"Okay, fine, it's worth a try." I pulled out my phone to type the message as we climbed in the car. Tessa responded before Jaz even started the engine. I grinned when I saw her reply. "Looks like we're going to a party."

"Yes!" Jaz threw her arms up in the air, dancing in her seat. "She really said it's okay? That didn't take much convincing."

"Tessa's cool. She still feels guilty about starting me at a new school senior year. Plus, I think she's secretly on team Mackenzie in my current showdown with my dad."

"Will he be mad?"

"That's tomorrow's problem," I replied. We weren't even at the party yet, but already I felt a weight lifting from my shoulders. Tonight, I was determined to forget all about that nightmare of a game and try to have a little fun.

Chapter 15

PARKER

"Well, that was a disaster," Seth said as we headed back to the locker room. "I wonder," he continued. "Could it have had anything to do with the fact *some* of our players were distracted trying to protect our new goalie?"

I wasn't in the mood to take shit from him right now. I was already well aware I'd made a bad call telling him and Marc to shadow Mackenzie during the third period, but there hadn't been any other choice.

"She needed us," I grunted.

"Did she?"

"Yes." I didn't explain to Seth how Mackenzie had confided in me that she was scared before the game. I didn't bring up the fear I'd seen in her eyes when that Sharks player had come flying toward her. Between Mackenzie's apprehension, her exhaustion, and the fact our opponents were having a field day taunting her, I'd thought a little extra support from our defensemen would help her regain her confidence, especially as she constantly refused my other offers to lend a hand. Unfortunately, it had backfired.

"She was pretty pissed."

"Yeah, I noticed."

A smile slowly crept onto Seth's lips as he watched me. "Are you sure you're not into her?"

I gave him my most disapproving look.

"Don't look at me like I've grown a second head," he said. "You pretty much threw the game for this girl, and you wouldn't throw a game for your own mother."

"I didn't throw the game. Whatever I did, I did it for the team."

"Uh-huh."

I quickened my pace to get away from him and pushed through the locker room door.

Seth was being ridiculous, but for some reason his words left me questioning myself. Had my actions really been for the good of the team? I wanted to believe I'd done it to give Mackenzie the support she needed to get through the game. That I was just doing my part to ensure she didn't quit the team and we got stuck with Anderson and Elliot for the rest of the season. But the truth was, my chest tightened whenever I pictured the look on her face when that Sharks forward had rushed her.

My thoughts were interrupted as Coach Foster entered the locker room. He'd already spoken briefly to the team, but now his attention was zeroed in on me. "Parker, a word, now."

I couldn't work out whether the fact he was using my name instead of my number was bad news, or really bad news. I drew in a breath, and Seth patted me on the shoulder. "It was nice knowing you."

It did feel a little like a death march, following Foster out into the corridor. I already knew what I was going to get slammed for, and I braced myself for a verbal bashing. I hadn't been thinking straight, but I could hardly tell him why.

"Care to explain your actions today?"

"Actions, coach?" I did my best to play dumb.

"You know exactly what I'm talking about."

"The goal I scored?"

"No, the fact that you convinced our defensemen to crowd our goaltender. It cost us three goals."

It was hopeless trying to deny it. This guy saw everything that happened out on the ice. And lying to him was only going to bury his opinion of me under a few more tons of dirt.

"Yeah, okay, maybe. I just thought she needed a little extra support."

"That's not your call to make. We were only two goals down. Had you focused more on your job instead of hers, we might have achieved a better result."

For once my mouth did exactly what my brain told it, instead of digging me into an even deeper hole.

"You're right," I agreed. "It won't happen again."

He nodded. "Make sure it doesn't. Clearly your teammates listen to you, for better or worse. But if you want to be a real leader, then you need to put the team first. Not any one individual."

"Understood."

I thought we were done, but Foster stepped a little closer and seemed to stand even taller. "And Twelve," he said. "I don't know what you're playing at with Mackenzie, but I've told you twice now to stay away from my daughter. Do not make me say it again."

He emphasized his threat by pointing two fingers toward his dark eyes and then turning them to face me. I swallowed. Didn't people only do shit like that in the movies? If it was anyone else, I might have laughed. But in real life, coming from Coach Foster, it was intimidating as hell.

I gave him a brief nod, but as he marched back into the locker room, I felt my frustration grow. Mackenzie wouldn't have needed help today if Coach Foster hadn't left her completely high and dry at practice this week and during today's game. He'd given her zero encouragement or support, and she'd been completely unprepared. Whatever I thought about Mackenzie, I couldn't deny she was a good player. Didn't Foster realize that, given the right guidance, she could be a *great* player?

But his warnings were clear. I couldn't afford to help her anymore. Not unless I wanted to screw myself out of everything I'd been working toward. There was nothing I could do. Mackenzie was on her own.

The last thing I felt like doing after such a terrible loss was going to a party at Elliot Ford's house. He had become a regular party host this year, because his parents were "cool parents". At least, that's what they told us as Seth and I entered through the front door. I'd never cringed so hard in my life.

I'd expected the atmosphere to be mellow after our loss, but people appeared to be enjoying themselves as much as they usually did. There was music pumping, drinks being passed around, and a large group of people glued to a hockey game that was lighting up Ford's massive TV.

The Raiders were playing, and Reed scored a goal only a few moments after I set eyes on the screen. The room erupted in cheers, and my heart clenched as Reed and Grayson gathered each other in a celebratory hug.

"The amount of ice time your brothers get is amazing considering they're freshmen," Seth said from beside me. "And the camera loves them."

Seth was right; my brothers were taking the league by storm. And, while it had only been a few games, it seemed like they were the most talked-about players in college hockey right now.

I was ridiculously proud of Reed and Grayson, but it kind of sucked to see them killing it at college when nothing was going according to plan for me here. I should be creating my own legacy this season, becoming the Devils' shining star. But it felt more like I was falling fast, destined to crash down to earth with a bang. We needed to start winning or I was never going to make captain or repeat last season's championship. And then it would always feel like I couldn't succeed without my brothers.

But all I said to Seth was, "Yeah, well, it will be my ugly freshman mug taking up your screen this time next year."

"Not if you keep sacrificing our games for cute goalies."

My eyes narrowed. "I don't know any cute goalies."

Seth laughed. "Okay, maybe you're right. She's a little more than cute." He nodded across the room.

I turned to see Owen and Jaz walking through the front door, Mackenzie trailing behind them. I felt a flash of heat in my chest. She looked different tonight with her hair tumbled down her back in soft curls and dark eye shadow making her green eyes shine.

Jaz and Mackenzie were laughing about something and

judging by the way they kept glancing back to the front door, I had to assume they'd also met Elliot's "cool" parents. Her laugh fascinated me. I didn't think I'd really heard it before. At least, not like this. It was easy, and unrestrained, making her eyes crinkle at the corners. And I stood there, staring like an idiot.

As if she'd felt my stare, she glanced across the room and caught my eye. I couldn't look away. Couldn't even raise a knowing smile. She held my gaze just a heartbeat too long before her jaw tightened with irritation and she hurried further into the house. It was only once she was gone I could think clearly again.

"I'm going to get some fresh air," I murmured to Seth. But I didn't get very far. As I entered the kitchen, a hand reached out to grab me.

"Where have you been?" Vanessa tutted.

I let out a sigh and turned to face her. Vanessa was hot, and we both knew it. We'd made out a few times at parties over the summer, but I'd stopped paying her any attention when I saw her laughing at something Paige was wearing. Insulting my brother's girlfriend was as bad as insulting me. Plus, I happened to like the multi-colored, hand-knitted scarf Paige always wore.

"Hey, Vanessa."

She pouted up at me. "You look sad. I'm sorry you guys lost. Is there anything I can do to make it up to you?"

Her voice was thick with suggestion, and she trailed a finger across my chest.

"I think I'm good."

"Really? Because Elliot has a jacuzzi outside..."

"Huh." There was an expectant look on her face, so I quickly added, "I didn't bring a swimsuit."

"Neither did I." She leaned in close. "Then again, I wasn't planning on wearing one..."

I swallowed and tried to convince myself I was a good guy. That somewhere deep inside I was more than the infamous playboy the rumors made me out to be. But the longer Vanessa smiled up at me, the more I seemed to forget. The more I wondered whether jumping in the hot tub with her would really be such a bad idea. Perhaps Vanessa deserved a second chance. Why couldn't I let one of the hottest girls in school help me take my mind off a disappointing game?

"That sounds..." I didn't finish the thought, as someone moved past the kitchen door and caught my attention. Mackenzie. She looked between Vanessa and me, rolled her eyes, and walked on. The sight of her disdain was a splash of cold water, and suddenly the jacuzzi with Vanessa didn't seem so appealing.

Was there something wrong with me, or was that just the Mackenzie Foster effect? Wasn't she already causing me enough problems?

"That sounds..." Vanessa prompted me hopefully.

"Like a bad idea," I said. "It's freezing out. I wouldn't want you to catch a cold."

She laughed lightly. "I won't if you're there keeping me warm."

Nope, I still wasn't feeling it. Damn Mackenzie and her judgmental eyes.

"No thanks."

"But Parker—"

"Maybe ask someone else." I glanced up and noticed Owen innocently peering into the kitchen from the other side of the room. When he saw me, he waved cheerfully.

"Like Cleaver," I continued. "He loves a good hot tub. And I hear he also gives great massages."

"Owen?" Vanessa turned her attention to my friend. "Really?"

"Yep," I said, wiggling my eyebrows when she glanced back at me. "People say he has magic fingers."

"Interesting . . ." Vanessa only considered the idea for a moment, before fixing her hair, adjusting her top and ditching me to slink across the kitchen floor toward Owen.

I gave him a subtle thumbs up, but his expression morphed from confusion to horror when he realized Vanessa was making a beeline for him. A second later she was hanging off his shoulder and whispering something in his ear. His eyes only grew wider.

Poor kid. I'd really thrown him to the wolves. He clearly thought the same, because when Vanessa was done with her whispering, Owen stammered something in reply and then practically sprinted away.

It wasn't a bad strategy. I followed suit by making an equally quick exit from the kitchen and heading outside. It was much calmer out here. There were a few people hanging out on the back porch, but my eyes were drawn beyond them, down to the garden, where a blonde girl was standing alone, staring up at the maple tree.

Of course Mackenzie was out here. I couldn't escape her.

The girl who was to blame for my coach hating me, who stole my clothes and gave me a black eye. The girl I'd been specifically ordered to stay away from yet still seemed to cause me trouble at every turn.

But as I looked at her, I was struck by the sorrow in her eyes. It hit me even harder than the look of fear I'd seen on her face before the game today, because, this time, I knew I was to blame.

My feet were moving before I could stop them. I guess I had always liked a little trouble.

Chapter 16

MACKENZIE

Five minutes at my first Ransom High party, and already I was counting down the seconds until I could leave. I wasn't particularly excited about socializing after the game. The aches and pains in my muscles had already started to set in, each time I moved my legs a reminder of how badly I'd failed today.

I'd been hoping the party might provide a much-needed distraction. But so far it had only been a disappointment. The music was so loud I could barely think, our injured goalie and party host Elliot had taken a break from downing tequila shots to corner me in the hallway and gloat, and I'd lost my friends in the crowd. I probably should have searched for them, but instead I chose escape.

It was freezing outside tonight, but as I wandered into Elliot's backyard I found the night's cold air far more comforting than the throng of bodies inside. It felt like the entire school was here. The opportunity to drink and party was clearly enough to make most people forget the Devils had lost today. I wished I could forget so easily.

"You know, the party's supposed to be inside."

I spun to see Parker standing behind me. I must have been really lost in thought for him to sneak up on me like that, especially when the air around me seemed to vibrate at his very presence. I was just glad it wasn't Elliot returning to revel in my failure once more.

"Then what are you doing out here?" I asked. "I saw you inside with Vanessa. Looked like you were having a good time."

"You say that like it's a crime."

I cursed myself for admitting I'd been watching him. Who was I to judge Parker for cuddling up close with girls at parties? Why should I even care?

He stepped closer, leaves crunching underfoot. He was near enough now that I could smell him. I kept waiting to be hit by some off-putting aroma, like stale beer or a suffocatingly intense cologne. Instead, Parker's scent was subtle, familiar. It was the smell of fresh laundry and sun-warmed cotton. I decided to breathe through my mouth.

"So, today didn't go well . . ." he started.

"Yeah, thanks to you."

"What's that supposed to mean?"

"Seth and Jansen were trying to do my job for me in the third period, and I know it was because of whatever *you* said to them. All they did was get in my way."

"You looked like you needed the help."

"Well, that *didn't* help."

"What else was I supposed to do?"

"How about you trust me?" I shook my head. "I don't need protecting. I get enough of that from my dad."

He straightened his back and a serious look entered his eyes. I knew he must regret asking me to join the team. But I was the one who had been let down—and not just because of what he'd done in the game today.

Parker had convinced me to try out, smuggled me in, gave my dad no choice but to pick me and then, in the middle of our first game, decided I couldn't hack it. Now he was blaming me. Screw this.

I started moving back toward the house, but when I brushed past him, I felt his hand on my arm.

"I do," he mumbled.

"What?"

"I trust you."

There was something so sincere in his expression, it took me a moment to regroup. My voice held a little less edge as I replied, "Then why did you send your little sidekicks to stand guard at my side during the final period?"

Parker paused, a frown crossing his features. He usually spat out the first thing that came to mind, and I couldn't work out what was different right now.

"I wasn't thinking," he said. "Is that what you want to hear?"

He hesitated, and I realized I was holding my breath as I waited for him to continue.

"Before the game, when you told me how scared you were, I didn't blame you." He suddenly realized his hand was still resting gently on my arm and he pulled it back. "I harassed you into joining the team. And then you only got one practice. I didn't want you to have such a bad experience that you decided to quit after one game." He was looking at the ground, but then his blue eyes darted up and locked with mine. "I need you."

I swallowed, my mouth suddenly dry.

"*We*," he quickly corrected himself, shaking his head. "The team, I mean. You're good, Mackenzie. Really good. We've got no chance without you. I messed up today, and I'm sorry, but we've still got two more games."

His eyes were soft and his expression unguarded. Like he meant every word he said.

"Well, I don't see the next two games being any better. I'm not getting the coaching I need at practice, and even if I was, I'm never going to succeed when my own teammates are undermining me. Thanks to you, everyone now thinks I need Jansen's oversized ass to save shots for me."

He blew out a long breath as he ran a hand through his hair. "Okay, fine."

"Okay, fine, what?"

"You've made your point." His lips started curving with the return of his famous mischievous smile. "I'll make it up to you."

I already didn't like where this was going. "What? How?"

"I'll help you." He said it like it was the most obvious thing in the world.

"Isn't that the reason we're in this mess in the first place?"

"Maybe." He laughed. "But now I know exactly what needs to be done—I'm going to train you."

I frowned and my mouth fell open slightly in shock as he continued.

"You know how to stop a puck, but there's more to being a great goaltender than that. Your dad's not giving you the support you need at practice, and the guys are all too worried about pissing him off to shoot against you properly during drills. Either that, or they're being nice to try and get in your pants."

"Lovely," I muttered.

"Come on," he said, holding out his arms. "Let me train you, and we'll prove everyone wrong."

I wanted nothing more than to prove my dad wrong. But could I really commit to practicing with Parker? Almost every interaction we'd ever had seemed to end badly for at least one of us.

"We've only got a week before the next game," I said. "You can't expect a miracle."

"Now that you've got me? Sure, I can."

I let out a groan, mainly because I knew I didn't have a choice. Maybe this could work. If we didn't kill each other before the week was out. "Fine." I sighed. "But just so we're clear, I'm not going to enjoy a single second of this."

"Likewise." He grinned at me in a way that made my pulse flicker. "Go for a light recovery jog tomorrow. Do some stretching and maybe add in some core work. Then meet me at the rink when it opens on Monday morning for our first session."

I watched as he turned and headed back toward the house, wondering what the hell I'd just signed myself up for.

"Kenzie!" Jaz and Isaac were waving at me from the deck. "What are you doing out here? It's freezing!"

"Questioning my sanity," I muttered as I went to join my friends.

Had Parker really just agreed to help me train? And had I really just accepted? It all felt like some cruel joke, though neither of us would be laughing if we lost the next game like we had today's.

But apparently I was going to find out how serious Parker was when I joined him at the rink bright and early on Monday morning.

Chapter 17

PARKER

"You need to learn how to drive," Cammie said. She was sitting in the passenger seat of my truck, her eyes glued to her phone. I had no idea how she could judge my driving when she wasn't even looking at the road.

"I can drive just fine."

"Tell that to the old lady who had to jump out of the way as you swerved round the corner back there."

"There was no old lady!"

"Well, we were lucky then, because you would have taken her out for sure." She lifted one disapproving eyebrow before returning her attention to her phone. "I miss Reed and Grayson. They were much more sensible behind the wheel."

All I could do was grunt. I was so sick of everyone missing my older brothers and being constantly reminded of how I'd never live up to them. I thought this year would be different. But even in the comfort of my own car, I was still being compared to them.

"Yeah, well, they're not here. And if you're going to complain so much, next time you can walk to the rink."

"Or maybe I'll just get my license," she replied smugly.

I wasn't going to hold my breath. Cammie was too used to being a passenger princess. It was probably better than her being able to drive though. I dreaded the day I had to share this truck with her.

"You're not going to get your license," I replied. "You don't have the time."

"Yes, well, if you keep this up, I'll make time." Her focus fell back to her phone, but she wasn't quiet for long. "So, tell me more about your new girlfriend."

"Mackenzie's not my girlfriend." I knew my sister was just trying to annoy me. She wasn't even being subtle about it. But it was still working.

"You don't get out of bed early for anyone."

"I'm helping her train. That's it." To be honest, I was almost as surprised as Cammie that this was happening. Heading to the rink first thing on a Monday morning to give our new goalie some extra practice was the last thing I wanted to do. And yet here I was.

"I don't see you getting up before sunrise to train with any other players. You must *really* like her."

"I'm not doing it for her." I was doing it for the team.

"I didn't say you were doing it for her. You're doing it for a hook up."

"I could think of nothing worse."

"Reed and Grayson agree with me."

"What?" I turned to her, and she wiggled her phone in the air. "Tell me you're not messaging them."

"Of course I am," she said with a wicked smirk. "We've been talking about you for days. Grayson even changed the name of our group chat, see?"

She held the phone in front of my face, and I took my eyes off the road just long enough to check the screen. The group chat was named *Parker's dating coaches,* and the profile picture was a cute little monkey.

"I wonder how long it took Grayson to come up with that," I scoffed.

"It's changed a few times," Cammie said. "This is my favorite though. Especially the picture. We all know how much you love Mom's nickname for you, *monkey*."

I let out a long sigh. It was too early for this shit.

"So, the boys think going after the coach's daughter is a really bad idea," Cammie continued. "But I say, a few red flags never stopped you chasing a girl before."

"I don't go after girls with red flags."

"You're like a bull, Parker. You see a red flag and charge."

"Not with Mackenzie," I replied. "Her dad pretty much told me he'd kill me if I even looked at her that way."

"Oh, so she's forbidden? That must be even more enticing for you." Cammie's eyes were sparkling with glee. She only got this much joy out of two things: skating and teasing her brothers.

Thankfully, we'd finally arrived at the rink, and I didn't have to spend long looking for a parking spot because there was barely anyone else here.

"You guys all need to mind your own business," I said.

"Wow, touchy," she gasped, but then she nodded. "You must really be a goner for this girl." Before I could respond, she jumped out of the truck and slammed the door shut.

"I don't like her!" I yelled from the driver's seat, but Cammie was already opening the doors to the arena and disappearing inside.

With a sigh, I gathered my stuff. Cammie was training

with her pairs skating partner this morning. They had the rink booked so the place was otherwise empty. I'd managed to talk her into letting Mackenzie and I practice down the far end of the ice.

I began to reconsider the whole thing though when I found Mackenzie waiting for me.

"You're late."

"Good morning to you too." I set my bag down and started to take out my gear.

"I've been waiting for twenty minutes."

We were definitely off to a bad start. "Well, you must be nice and warmed up then."

I got the feeling she wanted to throw her stick at my head.

"You said to meet when the rink opened. My parents think I'm working out with Jaz this morning. I don't have long."

"I had to drive my sister, and she was taking forever to get ready." I shrugged. "We'll just have to make do with the time we have."

"You're blaming your sister?"

"Yeah, and she's right over there if you want to take it up with her." I nodded to the other side of the rink where Cammie was talking to her coach. She looked like she was apologizing for being late. I wasn't sure I'd ever seen her say sorry to anyone for anything. Her coach might just be the one person Cammie respected, perhaps even liked.

"That's your sister?" Mackenzie was looking between us like she was trying to spot the family resemblance. It can't have been hard. My siblings and I all had dark hair and the same blue eyes as our dad. I supposed Cammie had taken after Mom in the height department, though she more than made up for her short stature with a big attitude.

"Yep, that's Cammie."

"She looks too nice to be related to you."

"Ha!" I spluttered and shook my head. "Out of me and Cammie, I'm *definitely* the nice one."

"Yeah, right."

"I am. Although you might disagree with me after we start training together."

"Weren't you listening? I disagree with you *now*."

"All I heard was you stalling. We've got work to do. Start with five hard laps. No coasting."

I steeled myself for another cutting comeback or, worse, for her to launch her stick at me and storm off. But to my surprise, she set off, skating hard as she made her way around the perimeter of the rink.

I could have joined her, but I was still waking up. I'd never been a morning person, plus I was still a little sore from the game. My ego wasn't the only thing that suffered. I'd taken a couple of hard hits from the Sharks' defensemen, and I probably should have spent Saturday night in a freezing ice bath instead of going out.

Mackenzie finished her laps without complaint before she started stretching in front of the net. I'd been thinking a lot about how I could help her improve, and I'd picked out a couple of problem areas. Fitness was an obvious one. She'd been exhausted by the end of the first period, and we'd need to build up her stamina over the next few weeks. But there was one issue in particular I wanted to work on today.

"Okay" I skated over to her. "We're going to work on cleaning up your rebounds. You stopped most shots no problem against the Sharks, but you didn't clear the puck well enough. That's why our toothless friend scored his first goal on Saturday."

I was being brutally honest, and I expected to see Mackenzie glaring at me through her helmet. She wasn't exactly the kind of girl who liked being told what to do. Especially not by me. But I was surprised to find her listening intently, so I powered on.

"Don't just stop the puck; control it and redirect it away from the slot."

Again, I was shocked when she didn't tell me to go to hell and nodded instead. "Okay, let's try it."

She continued to surprise me as the session went on. She was intently focused on clearing the puck after each save and, before long, Mackenzie was effectively using her stick to push the puck away from the net before instantly readying herself to face the next shot. She was a fast learner. Either that, or I was a miracle worker. Probably the latter.

This might have been the longest period of time we'd ever spent in each other's presence without an argument breaking out or tension boiling over. It didn't feel right. It wasn't us.

It also wasn't very reflective of how intense the game against the Sharks was. Mackenzie wasn't used to the emotional rollercoaster of anxiety, frustration and adrenaline that flowed through you during a chaotic battle on the ice. But those things were hard to replicate during an early morning practice. The roar of the crowd, the proximity of other players, the snarky comments from opposing forwards.

An idea sparked in my mind, and I fought to withhold a smirk. Maybe there was one thing about the game I could replicate after all. God, she was going to kill me.

After the next save Mackenzie made, I swooped in to pounce on the rebound and scored before she could stop me.

"That was sloppy," I said. "I know pretty girls think they can get away with anything, but you're not *that* pretty."

"What did you say?!" Her glare was back as she shot to her feet. Oh, how I'd missed it.

"I said you're pretty, but not *so* pretty I'm going to pass up an opportunity to score such an easy rebound."

"Don't talk to me like that."

"It's okay, you make up for it in other areas." I paused, bracing myself for the lasers she was about to shoot my way. "Like your ass. Have I ever told you how great it looks? Even in your goalie gear."

She stiffened, and I could almost hear her teeth clenching from where I hovered at a safe distance.

"Yep, that thing is the stuff of legend," I said as I gathered the puck again. She was stunned into silence and stood frozen in the net, so when I took my shot, it sailed right past her. "It's the kind of ass that break hearts and ruins men's lives."

"Talk like that again and I'll ruin *your* life."

I grinned. I think I preferred this Mackenzie to the one who nodded and followed instructions. She looked like she wanted to murder me, and the way she scowled daggers in my direction made my whole body light up. It was like Christmas, if your tree was on fire and you were a pyromaniac.

"I'm serious," I continued as I took another shot. "An ass like yours could start a war." She was still distracted and let the puck hit the net once more. "Shame you can't stop a puck to save your life."

Mackenzie looked like her head was about to explode, but when she suddenly seemed to realize I'd just scored on her twice she readjusted her position in front of the net. "Do you have a death wish?"

Probably, but I continued.

"Shakespeare would have written sonnets about it." I took shot after shot as I teased her, and she soon started making saves like I knew she could. "It makes guys forget what they're talking about."

"You're going to regret this, Parker."

"They even forget their name."

"I knew training with you wouldn't work."

"All they know is that they've seen perfection, and they'll never experience anything like it ever again."

She finally yanked her catch glove off, pulled her helmet from her head and stormed toward me. "Are you trying to piss me off?"

I skated to meet her, grinning. She was pink in the face, covered in sweat, and her hair was as wild as her eyes. It was a seriously good look on her.

"Yes, I am."

"Huh?"

"I'm trying to piss you off. Just like those guys from the game on Saturday. I doubt they'll be the only jerks you encounter out here."

"I'm looking at one right now."

"Fair." I smirked. "But you can't afford to let stuff like that disrupt your game."

Her eyes slowly started to dawn with realization. "All that was to teach me a lesson?"

"Obviously." I shrugged. "Although, it was kind of fun."

"Wait, so, you don't think I've got a great butt?"

"Oh, no, I totally do. I just let my inside thoughts out."

She whacked me on the arm with her blocker, but my resulting laughter only seemed to evoke more frustration in her eyes. But then there was a slight crack in her expression, and a moment later she started laughing too.

Something about her expression hit me square in the chest. She never smiled or laughed when I was around. The way her eyes were sparkling right now felt like discovering a rare hidden treasure. The thought stopped me short. Did I actually like making her laugh?

She shook her head at me but was still smiling. "You're the worst."

"I know. But you wouldn't have me any other way, right?"

"I'd prefer you literally any other way."

From her sharp tone to her piercing glare, there was no doubt in my mind this girl couldn't stand me. So, why did her words make me smile? And why when our eyes met did everything else seem to fade away?

"You dropped me on purpose!" Reality came quickly hurtling back as we both turned to the sound of my sister shouting from the other side of the ice. She went up to her partner and shoved him in the chest.

He stumbled back slightly but then folded his arms and stood his ground. "Maybe you fell on purpose."

"Ugh!" Cammie screeched before turning to skate off. Her coach was yelling after her.

"Told you I'm the nice one," I said. "I think that might be her third partner this year."

"I mean, I'd be pissed if a guy dropped me, too."

"Maybe, but it doesn't take much to piss you off."

"Not when it comes to you."

We decided to end our session there because we still needed to get ready for school. As we went to leave the ice, Mackenzie turned to me. "Thanks for today. I feel like I've still got a lot of work to do, but it's good to have something I can focus on."

"Just calling it how I see it."

"Max never said anything about my rebounds. I think he was just happy to have someone to shoot at."

"Your brother?" I guessed.

She nodded. "He's the reason I started playing hockey. Dad didn't let me practice with a team or play in games, but Max used to practice against me all the time, right up until he went to college. He's a forward; one of the best players in the state."

"He plays for the Raiders with my brothers, right?"

"Yeah, that's right. If you can stop one of his shots, you can stop anyone's."

As she looked up at me, I could see she was genuinely grateful. It was another emotion I'd never seen her feel when it came to me. Another one I liked.

"Yeah, well." I coughed to try and dislodge the tightness in my chest. "We've still got a lot of work to do. We'll pick up where we left off tomorrow morning."

"Sure." She nodded. "But you might need to rethink your coaching methods. No more checking out my ass."

"I'm not making any promises," I called after her as she turned and skated away.

Without glancing back, she stuck her middle finger up over her shoulder. All I could think was that I actually had a good feeling about getting out of bed early tomorrow.

Chapter 18

MACKENZIE

"I already knew Parker hated me, but I didn't realize he hated me *this* much." I groaned as I lowered myself into the passenger seat of Jaz's car. Every part of my body was complaining. I'd practiced with Parker the last four mornings in a row, and today's session had been particularly brutal. It started with sprints and ended with Seth and Owen joining us to simulate game plays, which felt like a much more effective way of training than having Parker compliment my ass while shooting pucks at me. That on top of our daily team practices had left me exhausted.

Today we had the afternoon off. Only, instead of resting like I should have been, I was on the way to a hoop dance class, because Jaz convinced me I needed to loosen up. I wasn't even sure what hoop dance was. All I knew was Jaz loved it, and apparently the class instructor was ridiculously hot.

It also meant I could spend a few extra hours away from my house and, more importantly, my dad.

"Remind me again why I agreed to this?"

"Because when your parents asked where you were going every morning before school you panicked and used me as a cover story for all your secret rendezvous with Parker."

"But I don't need a cover story for today. And I told them I was working out with you, not that I was hoop dancing..."

"Well, now it's time to work out with me for real." She

grinned. "Don't worry. It'll be fun. Great for your core strength. And, if you get tired, you can always just sit back and enjoy the view. That's what I do."

I shook my head. "Is the instructor really that hot?"

"Dominic is *super* dreamy. He graduated from Ransom a couple of years ago. I like guys who are a little older."

"Really?"

"Of course," she replied innocently. "Boys our age suck. They have no idea how to treat girls, and I swear half the guys in our year forget to shower most days. I can't wait for college."

"What about Isaac?"

"What about Isaac?" Her cheeks flushed slightly.

"Does he suck?"

"Well, no. But he doesn't count, obviously."

"Obviously," I repeated.

"I heard Vanessa talking to Britt this morning," Jaz said, quickly changing the subject. "She was wondering if she should try out for the hockey team too."

"Why on earth would she do that?"

"Probably jealous, now that everyone's talking about you being the first girl ever to play for the Ransom Devils. Maybe she thinks Parker would pay her more attention if she was on the team."

I didn't like the idea of people talking about me at school. But I guessed it was a more positive thing to be known for than assaulting the star hockey player or having to wear lost and found clothes on my first day.

"I wouldn't wish his attention on anyone," I replied. "Not even her."

Jaz shrugged. "They had a bit of a thing over the summer. But I think he got bored of her once school started back up."

"Is she really surprised? I've known enough guys like Parker; they all seem to tire of girls quickly."

"Until they find the right one."

"Oh, *please*." I rolled my eyes. "You must read too many rom-coms. We all know that doesn't happen in real life."

"Don't be so pessimistic." Jaz wagged a finger at me. "My brother Matt was always dating different girls in high school. But he met someone the first day of college this year and they've been inseparable ever since. I *never* thought he was the kind of guy who'd get a girlfriend in college, but he's already planning on bringing her home for Thanksgiving."

"I guess there's an exception to every rule."

She smiled and shook her head at me. "Just how bad were the guys at your old school?"

"I mean, not *all* of them were bad. But it's not something I really worried about."

"Why's that?"

"Because my sparkly personality scares most guys off," I said, batting my eyelashes.

Jaz smiled. "I'm sure that's not true. And even if it were, it says more about the guys than it does about you. Look at Parker; he's not scared of you. Even after you punched him."

"Yeah, well, that's Parker. If he's the yardstick we're using to judge all men then we're in big trouble."

Jaz laughed and nodded in agreement. "Well, I happen to love your *sparkly* personality."

"You also love some strange sport called hoop dance..."

She scrunched her nose at me, and I smiled back. I hadn't been in Ransom long, but already I felt close with Jaz. She could be a little odd sometimes, but that was probably my favorite thing about her. She was sweet and sincere, and there weren't nearly enough people like her in the world.

The car slowed as Jaz pulled into a free space, and she nodded out the window at the old red-brick building in front of us. "We're here. I hope you're ready to swoon—I mean, hoop."

I gave an awkward laugh. "It's too late to back out, right?"

"Absolutely. Let's go." Jaz jumped from the car and practically dragged me toward the entrance.

A faded sign above the doors read, 'ansom Community Center.' The place looked like it might be missing a piece of its soul, along with the first letter on its sign. But I was pleasantly surprised as I followed Jaz inside. It was light and bright and a little chaotic. Between squealing toddlers darting through the foyer, music pumping from the back of the building, the smell of fresh coffee, and all sorts of different people mingling throughout the space, the center felt alive with activity.

Jaz guided me to a room at the back of the building that overlooked the park behind. Colorful hoops were spread out on the floor. And standing in the middle of it all, dressed in bright orange spandex, was Dominic.

"Oh, my God." I lifted a hand to my mouth to hide my laughter. He must have been about twenty, yet he was being swarmed by a group of women who were at least my stepmom's age. Dominic didn't seem to mind though. In fact, given the flirtatious smile he was flashing around the room, I suspected he wore the oh-so-tight spandex on purpose.

"Hot, right?" Jaz said, fanning her face. "This is the best part of my week."

"Looks like it's the best part of a lot of people's weeks." I nodded at the women again. But Jaz turned to me and frowned.

"You're supposed to be swooning. Why aren't you swooning?"

"Oh, I'm swooning on the inside," I replied, laughing at her disappointment. I guessed the guy was quite good-looking, but the tight one-piece really didn't do it for me.

"You better be." She glanced at Dominic and gave an appreciative sigh. "Come on, we need to get hoops at the front before they all get taken."

Jaz hurried across the room to a hoop right in the center of the front row, mere inches from where I imagined Dominic would be demonstrating for the class. I reluctantly took my place at the hoop next to her.

When the class started, I was surprised by how much fun it was. For the first time in a while, I wasn't thinking too seriously about what I was doing. It also became clear very quickly why the women in the class where fighting tooth and nail for positions in the front row. You got a total eyeful of Dominic hooping in his spandex, but personally, after forty-five minutes, I wanted the sight firmly scrubbed from my mind.

By the time class was over, I was struggling to catch my breath, and my body was covered in sweat.

"That was great, wasn't it?" Jaz said, puffing too.

"Yeah, it was fun. But..."

"But?"

I glanced around and lowered my voice. "I think Dominic stuffs his pants."

"He *what*? Why?"

"To make his, you know, *package* look bigger."

Jaz gasped. "No way!"

We both glanced over to where a group of women were once again encircling our instructor. Even from here, you could clearly see that Dominic's sock, or whatever he'd stuffed down there, had come dislodged and was now stationed up near his hip. Jaz turned to look at me in horror but then burst out laughing.

I quickly ushered her from the room before anyone noticed.

"Told you," I said, when her laughter quietened a little.

"Why were you looking down there?"

"I had no choice! You put me in the front row. He's been thrusting his hips in our faces for the last hour."

She collapsed into fits of laughter again.

"It's not funny," I protested.

"It definitely is. So, you'll come next week?" Her voice was hopeful.

"I'm not sure. I think I've seen enough of Dominic to last me a while."

"Understandable," she agreed. "Don't worry, I'll keep you updated on the wanderings of his spare pair of socks."

"Please don't."

She started laughing again.

The escape to hoop dance class had been fun, but it was over way too fast, and my mood soured as Jaz drove me home.

I'd rather spend another hour with Dominic and his thrusting hips than face my dad again.

I turned to Jaz as she pulled up outside my house. "Do you think I'm crazy playing hockey when it makes my dad so mad? And when I'm clearly not cut out for it?"

Jaz was frowning deeply as she turned to me. "I think you're the only person who can answer those questions, Kenzie. You love hockey, right?"

"More than anything."

"Then it sounds like you don't have a choice. You've got to follow your heart."

"Even if I suck?"

She smiled at me. "You had one rough game. I'm no hockey expert, but Parker Darling is. He went out of his way to get you on the team and now he's spending all his free time making sure you stay there. He wouldn't do that for just anyone."

As much as I wanted to discount her words, they still caused an unusual warmth to flood my chest.

"Maybe." I stared down into my hands. "I'm just worried it will all be for nothing. My dad might kick me off the team either way."

She reached across the center console and squeezed my hand. "Then enjoy every minute of the time you get to play."

I smiled at her and nodded. "You're pretty wise, Jaz."

"Oh, I can be. Usually only happens on a full moon."

I glanced out the window and laughed when I saw a bright, perfectly full moon in the sky above us. "I better get inside. Thanks for taking my mind off things tonight."

"Don't thank me. Thank Dominic," she replied with a grin.

"I'll see you at school tomorrow."

"Yep, I'll be the one hobbling through the halls with hips that no longer remember how to move from side to side."

I waved as I got out of the car and Jaz drove away. Glancing up at the moon again, I wished a little of its wisdom could rub off on my dad too. When I got inside, I headed straight to my room, making sure to stay quiet as I made my way past his office.

Our moving boxes had finally arrived this week, but mine were still piled in the corner of my room. I didn't feel ready to unpack them yet, and the room looked more like a storage shed than a bedroom. I hadn't made much progress on my mural since I'd started playing hockey either. But the mountains were almost done and the soft shade of blue I'd chosen for them made me smile every time I saw it.

As soon as I slumped my bag on the floor, Tessa appeared at the door.

"How was hula hooping?" she asked.

"Fun, but I'm pretty tired."

"I'm not surprised; you've barely been home this week."

A part of me wanted to confide in my stepmom. She was such a good listener, and I knew she'd be supportive. But I couldn't risk my dad finding out what I was doing each morning.

"I just really need to get in better shape for hockey," I said. "It's hard work, but I like hanging out with Jaz too."

Tessa smiled. "Seems like you two are getting along well."

I rolled my eyes. "Is it really that difficult to imagine I made a friend?"

"No, not at all. I'm just happy you're settling in here. I know how tough moving can be."

I simply gave her a tight smile in response.

"Do you want some dinner?" she continued. "I made grilled cheese and tomato soup."

"No, I'm okay, thanks. I'm not that hungry."

Tessa sighed. "You're going to have to talk to your dad eventually."

Apparently, she could see right through my excuses. "Maybe you should tell *him* that. He's the one that's angry."

"He's just worried about you."

"Yeah, well, I'm old enough that I don't need my dad worrying about me anymore."

"I know," she said quietly. After a small pause she added, "I'll bring you a tray, in case you get hungry."

When she left the room, I grabbed my headphones and my paints. I knew I should be resting, but I wanted to work on my mural. There was something uniquely comforting about music blaring in your ears so loudly it blocked out the rest of the world. Tessa always said she could feel the teenage angst radiating from me whenever she overheard what I was listening to. I much preferred my angsty music to the boppy stuff she always insisted on playing in the car.

I caught movement from the corner of my eye and started to wave Tessa away. "It's okay, I'm not—" I stopped when I realized it was my dad standing in the door.

Guess I couldn't avoid him, after all. This was the first time he'd sought me out in days. Could there be a chance he was finally willing to make peace?

I swallowed and removed my headphones.

"It's looking good," Dad said, nodding at the art on my wall. "But wouldn't you be better working on your portfolio pieces? Can't exactly submit a wall to art schools..."

Why was it that whenever my father took an interest in what I was doing, he always found something to criticize?

"Can I help you with something?" I asked, hoping he'd keep his visit as short as possible.

"Max is playing tonight. I thought you might like to come watch the game with Tess and me."

"I can watch it up here."

He nodded but stepped further into the room. His invitation to watch the game must have just been an excuse to come up here.

"You know, Mackenzie," he started. "We've got another big game this weekend."

"Yeah, I know."

"The Chargers are one of the best teams in our division."

"Okay..."

"Well, I just wanted to let you know that no one will think less of you if you decide to sit this one out."

And there it was; the real reason my dad was here. I carefully put down my paintbrush as I turned to glare at him. "You're trying to make me quit hockey again?"

"You're not ready, Mackenzie. You've never played competitive games like this before."

"And whose fault is that?"

He let out a short sigh but otherwise ignored my comment. "I know how much you and Max played together. But this is different. Surely you realize that."

"What I realize is that you don't support me. That you probably never will. You pretend you're giving me a chance, but you're setting me up to fail all so you can say you gave the girl a shot, but she simply wasn't good enough."

"Mackenzie, I'm just—"

"Just what? Just trying to protect me?" I was getting so tired of that argument.

He paused, and for a moment I thought he might try a different approach, give me another tenuous explanation for why hockey was off limits for me and me alone. But eventually he just nodded.

"I might not be as big or as strong as the boys," I continued. "But that doesn't mean I don't have as much potential. You need to stop thinking about me as your daughter and start treating me like one of your players."

"But you are my daughter, and it's—"

I didn't want to hear any more, so I cut him off.

"You gave me three games to prove myself. If you want to go back on your word, fine, you can cut me. But I'm not quitting. I still have two games left. Until then, perhaps you should go back to giving me the silent treatment."

Returning to my mural, I pulled my headphones over my ears. I turned the volume up even louder than before and allowed the music to scream into the void for me.

Chapter 19

MACKENZIE

"You're extra snarky this morning," Parker said. "Did you wake up on the wrong side of bed?"

We'd started training at six and I'd been feeling like crap all morning. Obviously, I wasn't doing a very good job of hiding it. I'd slept badly, going over the latest argument with my dad all night, and now I struggled to focus. I was slow and sluggish, and it felt like every time a shot got past me, I was only proving my father right. Still, I pasted on a smile for Parker.

"I don't know what you're talking about. I don't have a wrong side of bed."

"Right." He slapped a hand against his forehead. "I forgot, raccoons sleep in dumpsters."

"I'm not a raccoon!"

"You're scrappy and you leave a trail of chaos wherever you go. It's very raccoon-like."

It was too early to be arguing about raccoons with Parker. And while he probably thought being called scrappy and chaotic was an insult, I actually took it as a compliment.

"Can you just keep shooting?"

"I've scored five in a row," he said. "You're not concentrating. Are you too tired for this?"

I was exhausted, but that didn't matter. "I don't have time to be tired. I need to get ready for the weekend."

"Well, playing like this isn't going to get you ready. It's going to get you injured."

"I'll be fine."

"You won't be if you keep going. You're clearly stiff and hurting. That last save attempt was agonizing to watch. My grandma could have gotten off the floor quicker than you did."

"Your grandma must be a beast."

He smirked. "She's in a nursing home, Mackenzie."

I swallowed as he said my name. Only a few days ago he'd been deliberately getting my name wrong just to piss me off. Now suddenly he was worried about me hurting myself and getting enough sleep. I quickly dismissed the thought. He didn't really care about me. All he cared about was winning, and for some reason, right now, he thought I was his best chance of achieving that.

"I didn't sleep well, that's all. Keep shooting, I'll save the next one."

"No, I think that's enough for this morning. We'd be better off spending some time stretching."

"Stretching?"

"Yep. We've got practice tonight with the rest of the team. You need to save your energy for that."

"So, we're done?"

"Out here? Sure."

Grumbling under my breath, I started skating for the boards. I wasn't sure why we'd even bothered with training this morning; it had been a complete waste of time. As I left the ice and started for the locker room, Parker called after me.

"I'll meet you in the warm-up room."

I sighed. He was serious about the stretching? I almost

considered bailing, but I couldn't deny how stiff and sore I was.

There were a few figure skaters heading out of the warm-up room as I arrived, so it was just Parker left when I stepped inside. He was in the back corner, already stretching, and the corner of his mouth started to lift as I walked toward him. Parker's smile always made me feel like I'd missed a joke. Either that, or he just found my mere existence highly amusing.

"You made it," he said. "Thought you might make like a raccoon and scurry out of here."

My exasperated expression only made him chuckle. I hated that sound. It was deep and rumbly, and it lit up his eyes, making them impossibly blue. Maybe I was just jealous of how cheery he seemed to be, considering the sun wasn't even up yet and I was already wishing I could crawl back into my dumpster.

I sat on the floor beside him and stretched one leg out in front of me, reaching my hands down to grip my foot.

"Let's just get this over with," I said. The sooner we finished stretching, the sooner we could go our separate ways for the day.

"So, does your dad hate all women playing sports, or does he just have special rules for his daughter?" Apparently, Parker hadn't understood I'd been planning to stretch in silence.

"I thought you wanted my bad mood gone," I replied.

"I never said that. I don't mind you being in a bad mood. It's like a challenge; can I make it worse?"

"There's something wrong with you. You know that, right?"

"What?" he protested. "I happen to think raccoons are cute when they're angry."

"Sounds like a good way to get bitten."

He raised one eyebrow. "I mean, a guy can always hope." There was something wolfish about the way he grinned at me, and the air between us seemed to crackle in response. I firmly ignored the sensation, even though it sent goosebumps down my arms.

"Sorry to disappoint, but my teeth aren't going anywhere near you."

"Bummer." He didn't look too disappointed. "Guess I'll just have to be satisfied with your *biting* words."

I ignored his jab as I adjusted my position. "You know, with all the gossip that goes around about you, I'm surprised I never heard how irritating you are."

Parker shuffled around until his stretch matched mine. He made it look simple, while my muscles were screaming and begging for me to stop.

"So, you've been listening to gossip about me?" He looked delighted by the idea.

"It's a little hard to avoid."

"And what have you heard?"

"Oh, just the usual. Parker Darling, playboy party animal. Deadly to his opponents on the ice, devastating to girls' hearts off it."

"Sounds about right." He smiled proudly.

"Is it true you started a cult?"

He leaned in close and smirked at me. "What if I did? You want to join?"

"I think there's already more than enough people worshipping you around here."

He was still grinning as he leaned back. "Sounds like you

already know all my deep dark secrets. Stop avoiding yours. What's your dad's problem?"

Parker didn't know when to give up. Why did he even care about my whole pathetic story?

"He's always been protective when it comes to me. He thinks if I play, I'll get hurt, and he doesn't want me taking the risk."

"So, he just bans you from the sport for life? Seems a bit extreme."

"I guess he has his reasons."

"Like what?"

I hesitated. Was I really about to open up to Parker Darling? Surprisingly, the thought didn't horrify me. In fact, I found I actually wanted to share more, and the words spilled from my lips. "My mom died when I was little..."

"Oh." His voice was soft and shock filled his eyes. "I'm sorry."

"It's okay," I replied. "I was so young, I barely remember her." I must have said the same thing a thousand times before. People didn't want a complicated answer when they found out about my mom. It was far easier to pretend I felt nothing at all.

He sat in silence watching me, waiting for me to continue. I knew it would have been okay if I didn't, but still, I found I wanted to. Maybe Parker could handle a little complication.

"My dad doesn't say it, but sometimes I wonder if he worries about me a little more—well, a lot more—because he lost my mom. Don't get me wrong, he's totally overreacting, but I think it comes from a good place."

"I'm sorry," Parker said again. "That really sucks." He paused and looked down at the ground before returning his gaze to mine. "He really doesn't know how strong you are, though."

The way he was looking at me made my breath catch. I managed to reply with a small shrug. "It doesn't matter. He's still never going to believe girls are as fast or as strong as boys. And they are pretty useful skills for hockey."

"Clearly your dad hasn't been on the end of your right hook."

"Ha, ha."

"And physicality aside, he's missing the kind of strength that counts."

"Which is?"

"Mental strength. I think most girls have got guys outmatched in that department. And that's one of the most important attributes of a great hockey player. Especially a goalie."

"Is that a compliment, Parker Darling?"

"I said, *most* girls. Clearly, I wasn't talking about you."

"Clearly." I shook my head at him but couldn't stop myself from smiling.

We held each other's gaze a little longer than I expected and something in his expression shifted. The way the air charged between us took me totally off guard. I'd always thought looking into Parker's eyes was a little dangerous, like boarding a dinghy in the middle of a stormy ocean. It was wild and unpredictable, and all you could do was allow the waves to toss you about and pray you survived. I was simply trying my best not to get swept away.

I needed an excuse to pull my eyes from his, so I shifted

positions to stretch out my other leg. But, as I did, I felt a jolt of pain in my hamstring. I inhaled sharply and reached my hand to the back of my leg.

"Are you okay?" Parker asked.

"Yeah, I'm fine." I tried to massage the spot that was hurting but winced as the muscle cramped.

"Lie down," Parker responded. "I'll help you stretch it out."

"I said, I'm fine."

"Has anyone ever told you how stubborn you are?"

I squinted at him through the pain shooting up my leg. "Has anyone told you how persistent you are?"

"Frequently. I like to think it's one of my greatest strengths. So, you should probably just let me help."

"But I don't need your help." Despite my words, I knew my face was still visibly contorted in pain.

"Fine. Don't blame me when you're limping your way through our next game."

I huffed and lay back on the mat. "Okay, you win."

Parker wore a satisfied smirk as he knelt beside me. He took my ankle in one hand and rested his other hand on my thigh just above my knee. I swallowed as a shiver danced up my leg all the way to the back of my neck. His strong hands were firm but gentle as he eased me into the stretch. When my leg tensed, I let out a hiss, making me realize I'd been holding my breath.

Parker paused, a serious look on his face. "Am I hurting you?"

"No, no. It's good."

The sparkle instantly returned to his eyes. "How good?"

"Not *that* good," I quickly corrected myself. "In fact, I hate this. It's worse than the cramp." It was a blatant lie. I didn't want him to stop, and every place on my body his hands touched was tingling.

Parker smirked with delight, and when his hands shifted so he could deepen the stretch, the slight movement left a trail of fire across my leg. We were totally alone in here and the silence seemed heavy around us, like the room was holding its breath in anticipation.

Parker's gaze didn't move from mine, and I was too damn stubborn to look away first. I was determined to ride out the storm, but I felt dangerously close to capsizing. There was so much intensity in his eyes, it was like he knew exactly how he was affecting me. Whatever he was thinking, I hoped he kept it to himself.

"See, if I didn't know any better, I'd say you're enjoying this." Parker's voice was low and hit me somewhere in my core. Yes, I definitely hadn't wanted to know what he was thinking.

"I literally just told you I'm hating it."

"No, you hate *me*. You can hate me and not hate this."

"I hate this too."

"Are you sure?"

"Yes." It was partly true. I hated the way my body was craving his touch. And I hated the way I was apparently incapable of resisting him.

"Can I let you in on a little secret?" Parker continued.

"No."

But he grinned and told me anyway. "I don't hate this either."

When he slightly shifted his hands once again, the heat

trailing across my skin where he gripped me flared bolder and brighter. His touch didn't just spark, it ignited like a wildfire, burning hot and spreading quickly. If he kept this up, I was going to do something stupid, and I knew the only thing that could douse the sensation was distance.

"I think I'm good now." I quickly dropped my leg from his grasp and got to my feet. But before I could move toward the door, Parker reached out to stop me.

"We're going to be late for school," I told him.

"I think we have a much bigger problem than that."

"I told you my leg's good."

"I'm not talking about your leg."

"Then what are you talking about?"

"This." He gestured at the space between us.

"What's 'this'?" I waved at the space too.

"Us." He took a step nearer. "You're telling me you don't feel something when we're this close?"

"Uh, I don't know, disgust?"

"No." He edged toward me again, making me back up.

"Anger, then."

"You're really saying that when I touched you just now, you didn't feel sparks?" I backed up another step and bumped against the wall. Parker stopped mere inches away.

"I don't know what you're talking about."

It was another lie. Of course I'd felt sparks, and they only grew stronger when I realized he was feeling them too. I couldn't work out when the energy surging between us had suddenly changed from anger to attraction. When the desire to pull him close had started to challenge the urge to push him away. I could have kneed him in the balls and left three questions ago. I should just move past him and storm from the room. And yet I didn't do either.

"There's a way to stop all this," Parker said.

"And that is?"

He leaned his head down toward me. "We get it out of our system."

My chest rose and fell with shallow breaths as I looked up into his impossibly blue eyes.

"My offer still stands," he murmured.

His gaze fell to my lips and my heart pounded wildly in reply. He'd joked about us kissing again the night he climbed into my bedroom, and I'd quickly shrugged it off. But, right now, he looked serious, and I wasn't finding it quite so easy to argue with him.

"That didn't work out so well for either of us last time."

"There's no one here this time," he replied. "Just you and me, and whatever this is between us."

"There is nothing between us." Yet my heart continued to beat hard against my chest like it was trying to cross the short distance that separated us.

"Prove it," he dared. "Kiss me so we can go back to simply hating each other. Kiss me, so I can stop feeling this way whenever you walk into a room."

One kiss.

It sounded so simple. So tempting. But what if that one kiss only proved there *was* something between us?

"You can't deny this tension," he continued. "And I don't like it any more than you do. Don't you want to get rid of it?"

I did. *More than anything*. But I held firm.

"You can't get rid of something that's not there."

Finally, my body listened to me; I ducked past him and made for the door.

"I guess that means you'll think about it," he called after me.

Except as far as I was concerned, there was nothing to think about. Tension or not, kissing Parker Darling again was definitely not an option.

Chapter 20

PARKER

I was beginning to think I'd lost my touch. Mackenzie had turned me down. Although, I suppose it wasn't all that surprising. One moment she'd been telling me about her mom, the next she was struck by a painful cramp, and then I'd started begging her to kiss me. Not exactly my smoothest move. But the sparks that had been flying between us were undeniable, so it had seemed like a solid strategy at the time.

That was half the problem though. When I was around Mackenzie, any ounce of rational thought seemed to escape me—and I didn't have much rational thought to begin with.

Maybe Cammie was right about me. Mackenzie was forbidden, and I'd always liked a challenge. She was an itch that couldn't be scratched. It had started as a slight inconvenience, but the longer I resisted it, the more it was slowly driving me insane. I'd been joking when I suggested we kiss in her bedroom, but I wasn't laughing when she turned me down today.

Despite this latest rejection, I was certain it wasn't all one-sided. Fireworks didn't just appear in the sky for no reason. There was a rocket and a flame, so an explosion was inevitable. The fuse just needed lighting.

Unfortunately, for now, the itch remained. All day, I'd struggled to get Mackenzie off my mind. Even in art class, while working on my comic strip, my head wasn't clear. I'd even started sketching characters that looked a little too much like her.

As I got ready for practice that night with the rest of the team, Elliot hobbled into the locker room. A few guys bumped fists with him as he slowly ambled past. My greeting wasn't quite so friendly.

"What are you doing here, Ford?"

"Just caught up with the athletic trainer," he replied.

"And?"

Elliot grinned. "Want to know when I'll be back playing again, huh? Makes sense. I'd be missing me too after the last two games."

I got the feeling he was about to give me his thoughts on Mackenzie's performance, so I raised an eyebrow, daring him to continue. I didn't want to have to give him another injury.

"Don't worry," he said as he carried on past me, giving me a firm pat on the shoulder. "Trainer says the boot might be off sooner than he first thought, and I can rescue this season from disaster."

I struggled to hide my disappointment. I knew if Mackenzie had enough time to show everyone what she could do, Elliot would never get the starting goaltender spot back.

"Oh," he continued. "The Raiders game last night was crazy. Your brothers are on fire." It was probably the hundredth time I'd heard someone praise Reed and Grayson today. I was happy for them, but I was a little over talking about it now.

"That goal Reed scored . . ." Elliot let out a low whistle. "You've got some big shoes to fill. Though Coach hasn't even made you captain, has he? Maybe your feet just aren't big enough."

His words were flippant, but the way his eyes lit with silent victory showed he knew exactly how hard that blow had landed. My hands tensed to fists, and I had to remind myself I was supposed to be staying out of trouble.

I leaned forward in my seat and nodded at his boot. "Just worry about your own foot, Elliot. And maybe give the shower stretching a rest, yeah?"

The guys around me sniggered as Elliot's cheeks grew hot, but I stood and left the room before he could say anything else.

I hated the fact there was even a possibility he might say something in response. Ford never would have taken a swipe at me if my brothers were still on the team. No one dared mess with any of us when we were together. When we were the infamous Darling Devils. But everything was different now.

I didn't *want* to need my brothers' support. I wanted my team to follow me because I was a great leader. I wanted idiots like Ford to keep their thoughts to themselves—or never have them in the first place—because they respected me. But that wasn't going to happen until I figured out how to become a captain like my brother.

Unfortunately, Ford's words followed me onto the ice and messed with my focus. I knew I was putting a lot of pressure on myself to perform, but there was still no sign of Coach Foster changing his mind about me. I wished I didn't need his approval, but I couldn't help feeling like no matter how hard I tried, I'd never get it.

As practice finished up for the evening and I made my

way off the ice, Mackenzie caught my eye only to glance away instantly. Was this how it was going to be between us now? *Awkward*? I didn't do awkward. Mostly because I didn't usually care. But Mackenzie and I still had a hockey game to win this weekend. I couldn't have her avoiding me. Before I could work out how to fix it, she had disappeared to the girls' locker room.

"What was up with you tonight?" Seth asked as we walked out to the parking lot.

"Nothing was up with me."

"You barely said a word to anyone all night."

"Aw, Walker, you keeping tabs on me?"

"Someone's got to," he replied with a smirk. "Mackenzie did well."

I shrugged.

"Don't pretend you didn't notice. I saw you watching her."

"We both know I'm her *real* coach. Of course, I was watching her." It had nothing to do with this morning. Absolutely nothing.

"Well, I think your hard work is paying off."

"I hope so. I guess we'll find out tomorrow."

When we reached my truck and started loading our bags in the trailer, I caught sight of Mackenzie in the distance. She was lugging all her gear toward the road.

Seth paused at my side and followed my gaze. "She usually catches a ride home with Owen and his sister, right?"

"No idea," I grunted, despite the fact I was well aware she always climbed into Jaz's waiting car once practice was over. But Owen had missed today's session because he was sick, and that meant Jaz wasn't here to drive Mackenzie home. She wasn't actually planning on walking with all that stuff, was she?

I tossed my keys to Seth. "Want to take my truck for the night?"

A knowing smile started to form. "Nice night for a walk, huh?"

Hardly. It was freezing.

"Yep."

He released a breathy laugh, like he didn't have it in him to question my decisions anymore. "Okay, I'll take your truck home. I can swing by yours in the morning and drop it off."

"Thanks, man." I was already jogging after Mackenzie.

I probably could have offered her a ride with me and Seth, but I kind of preferred the idea of walking with her. I hoped a little time together might help dispel any awkwardness still lingering from this morning. I needed us to be good, especially with a game tomorrow.

As I caught up with her, she glanced up and pulled the headphones from her ears, leaving them hanging around her neck. "Parker?"

"What are we doing?" I asked, tucking my hands into my pockets as though I was out for a casual stroll.

"I'm walking home. I've no idea what *you're* doing."

"That's a long way to go with all your gear."

"It's not that far. I've been walking here for our morning sessions all week."

"*You what*?"

She rolled her eyes. "No need to overreact. It's fine."

It wasn't even close to fine. "Why didn't you ask me for a ride?"

"Because I didn't need one. Besides, I think we spend

enough time together."

"I'm sure we could survive an extra couple of minutes in the truck."

"I'm not sure that I could." She frowned and peered around. "Where *is* your truck?"

"Uh, Cammie borrowed it."

"And your gear?"

"With Seth. I'm not stupid enough to carry it home."

Her eyes flashed with annoyance, but instead of responding she quickened her pace. "Okay, well, have a nice night."

I didn't let her get very far as I quickly stole her gear bag off her shoulder and heaved it on to my back. Damn, it was even heavier than my own crap.

"Hey!"

"Lucky for you, your house is on my way home."

She tried to grab her bag back, but I didn't let her.

"I don't need you to carry my things for me."

"And I don't *need* to drink coffee when I wake up, but it's better for everyone if I do."

"That's completely different."

"Can you stop being stubborn for five minutes?"

She hesitated. Surely she realized I wasn't going to give up. That she was up against someone just as hard-headed as her.

"I'm walking you home," I added. "What's the worst that can happen?"

She lifted an eyebrow at me. "Have you met yourself?"

"I'll be on my best behavior."

"You don't know the meaning of the word."

She glared at me, then suddenly seemed to accept the fact

it was pointless. "Fine." She groaned and continued walking.

Feeling very pleased with myself, I fell into step beside her. I was struck by the scent of roses as we walked. And glancing at her, I noticed her hair was wet.

"You had time to shower before leaving?"

"Not all of us enjoy being sweaty."

"Well, *some* of us have a trauma relationship with the locker room showers."

She chuckled softly. It was so cute, it was almost worth losing my clothes for.

The corner of her mouth was tipping upward, and there was a sparkle in her eye as she stared at the path ahead. With her wet hair piled on top of her head and her cheeks still flushed from practice, I started to wonder why I was being so hard on myself for wanting to kiss her again. Mackenzie was beautiful. My stomach clenched and I quickly focused back on the sidewalk. I was supposed to be making things *less* awkward between us.

I gritted my teeth, trying my best to remind myself that Mackenzie Foster wasn't interested in me. That her father would bench me if he caught me so much as glancing her way. Mackenzie was completely out of bounds for me. *Forbidden*. Unfortunately, the more that word echoed in my thoughts, the more it only seemed to be heightening the appeal. Why couldn't I be the kind of guy who ran from danger, instead of charging straight into it?

I found my attention drifting toward her again, and this time she caught me. "Is there something on my face?"

"No."

"Then why do you keep looking at me?"

Instead of answering, I reached out and pulled her headphones off her neck. "I'm wondering what kind of music you like."

Surprisingly, she didn't try to fight me. "Has anyone ever told you that you don't understand personal space?"

"Yep." I placed her headphones over my ears. Her music was still playing, but the moment I heard the song she was listening to I jerked the headphones off. "Who hurt you?"

She rolled her eyes and took her headphones back, returning them to her neck. "Some of my music might be a little dark."

"A *little* dark? Listening to two seconds of that gave me an irrational urge to paint my nails black and steal my sister's eyeliner."

"That might be a good look for you."

"Everything's a good look for me."

She fought a smile, and I found myself a little mesmerized as I silently willed her to let it spread wider. Yeah, it couldn't just be the fact she was forbidden. I would give just about anything to turn that subtle curving of her lips into a full-blown laugh.

When we reached Mackenzie's house, I walked her to the front door and placed her bag down by the step.

"You can feel free to thank me at any time."

"Thank you for stealing my bag, or thank you for annoying me the whole way home?"

"Either or." She really hated it when I did something nice for her. It kind of made me want to do it more. "I usually accept verbal or written thank yous, but I'll also accept a bunch of flowers. Kisses work, too . . ."

She reached down, grabbed her bag, and pulled out her

house key. "Good night, Parker."

I grinned and started to back away. "See you tomorrow, Mackenzie."

She disappeared inside and I was surprised to find a flash of disappointment shoot through me. Already it felt like the space at my side was too empty. Did I miss her? I didn't *want* to miss her. I didn't want to *like* her. But if I didn't, then why did I ditch my truck tonight? Why did I carry her things? And why did I walk her home when she lived on the opposite side of town? I had a long trek home to consider all three questions.

Chapter 21

MACKENZIE

"There's a cute boy at the front door." It was Saturday afternoon, and Tessa had just entered my room. I was scattered and flustered as I'd been racing around the house trying to get my things together for today's game, so the last thing I cared about was who was at our door.

"It's probably just a delivery guy," I said.

"A delivery guy in a Ransom Devils sweatshirt?" Tessa smirked. "He was asking for you."

"What?"

"He said his name was Parker."

"Parker's downstairs? What's *he* doing here?"

Tessa's smile was wider now. "I think he wants to give you a ride to the game."

"I don't need a ride! The rink's only a few minutes away. I'm walking."

"Well, now you don't have to."

Why was my stepmom pushing this? I was surprised she was even okay with it.

"You're really encouraging me to hop in a truck with Parker Darling, the bad boy of Ransom High?"

Tessa waved away my concern. "He seems like a very sweet young man. And like you said, it's just a few minutes away. I'm sure you'll be fine."

Clearly my stepmom knew nothing about Parker.

"You know Dad would kill me for getting in that truck, right?"

But Tessa just smiled. "Dad's not here, Kenzie."

"As my parent, you're supposed to be the cautious one, not me."

"I think your dad is cautious enough for all of us when it comes to you. I've told him he needs to loosen up a little."

"Yeah, good luck with *that*," I muttered.

"It's just a ride down the road in a cute boy's car."

I shook my head at her. *Cute. Sweet.* Where was she getting this from? I guess it wasn't surprising that Parker had managed to hide his true self during the thirty seconds of conversation he and Tessa probably had at the front door.

"*Go*," she ordered, pointing down the hallway. I let out a frustrated sigh.

"And good luck with your game today," she called as I trudged out of the room, mumbling curses under my breath.

When I got downstairs, I found Parker waiting in the entranceway. Not only was he in my house, he also had my cat in his arms.

"I wouldn't touch her. She bites everyone," I warned. "Then again, you'd probably like that."

But as Parker looked up, I realized Mitts was perfectly content in his arms. *Little traitor.* That cat didn't like anyone. Not even me. Apparently, Parker was the exception.

"She seems happy enough," he said as he scratched Mitts behind the ears and she purred loudly. His grin was a combination of cheeky and innocent all at once, offering only the smallest glimpse of the devil he was inside. When he smiled that way it was easy to see why so many girls at school adored him.

"What are you doing here, Parker?"

He gently placed Mitts down on the ground, but instead of darting off like she normally would, she started rubbing herself against Parker's leg. Even my cat couldn't resist him.

"It's good to see you, too."

"It won't be good if my dad sees you here."

He looked totally unconcerned. "I know he gets to the rink early before games. But I can climb up to your bedroom window again, if you prefer."

I responded quickly to avoid my cheeks flushing. "Seriously, Parker, what are you doing here?"

"I'm driving you to the game. I figured given how stubborn you are, you'd be planning to walk again."

"Well, I'm sorry you came out of your way, but I don't need a ride."

"Oh, so you're not playing against the Chargers today?"

"No, I'm playing."

"Someone's picking you up then? Your stepmom giving you a ride?"

"Well, no."

"Walking," he scoffed. "I knew it. You realize, it's freezing outside, right?"

"I don't mind a little cold weather."

"A *little* cold weather? The lake behind my house is already frozen over. Not great for your muscles right before a game."

"My muscles will be fine."

He grabbed my gear bag from just inside the entrance and

started outside. "Come on, Mackenzie, let's go."

"Hey!" I chased after him, but he was already halfway to his truck. Damn his stupidly long legs.

"I didn't ask for this," I called as I raced to catch him up.

"I know." He dumped my bag on the bed of his truck. "But I like winning. Picking you up helps me achieve that. I don't need you wasting energy walking to the rink."

I kept my feet rooted to the spot. It was bad enough I'd accepted so much of his help with hockey. I didn't want to owe him any more than I already did.

"Also, I kind of like how much it pisses you off when I help you." Parker pulled open the door of his truck for me and nodded at the passenger seat. "Just get in. We've got a game to get to."

As much as I wanted to keep refusing, I was already nervous about the game and knew how tough it was going to be. Conserving my energy was probably a good idea.

"Fine. But no more surprise visits to my house. You don't just show up at people's doors unannounced, enthrall their cat, steal their gear, and force them into your truck."

He was grinning again as I climbed in. "I'm just working on winning you Fosters over one at a time."

I slammed the door shut and could hear his chuckles as he walked around to the driver's side. He was still smiling as he got in and started the engine. It rumbled to life with a deep hum before music started drifting from the speakers.

"My cat clearly has no taste," I said as he pulled away from the curb.

He laughed, flashing me that smirk again. "*Clearly* she's the one member of your family who has *any* taste."

"My stepmom seems to think you're okay." I was still pissed at her about that.

"Does she now?"

"Don't get excited. She literally only just met you."

"Too late. It's already gone to my head."

I despised my lips for tilting upward, and quickly kept them moving to stop an actual smile from forming. "Tessa also has the worst taste in men. She likes my dad after all."

"Yeah, that's true," Parker agreed. "How's it going, with your dad?"

Just the mere mention of him made my heart feel heavy. "Not great. He still hasn't changed his mind about me."

"A Foster being stubborn?" He feigned a look of shock. "No way."

"I'm not nearly as bad as him."

"Sure."

"I'm not!"

"I guess you did eventually agree to get in the truck."

"And I'm starting to wish I was walking." It was nice and warm in Parker's truck though. And we were already turning into the rink parking lot. Perhaps spending an extra few minutes with him wasn't the worst thing in the world.

"You know, for someone who makes out like they don't want to be around me a whole lot, you're around me a *whole* lot." He pulled into a parking space close to the entrance. But I didn't get out of the car right away. Neither did he.

"I'm just using you for your wheels and your hockey skills."

But he leaned across the console. "Admit it, you don't

totally hate me."

"I-I do." The feeling was still there, somewhere deep inside, I was sure of it.

"I don't believe you."

"You want me to be more convincing?"

He laughed softly. "I mean, you can try."

"Fine. I loathe you."

"You can do better than that."

"I'd happily walk ten times the distance from my house to the rink in a blizzard, with no shoes, wearing nothing but a bikini just to avoid you."

"Now that I'd like to see."

"Ugh!" I threw my hands in the air. "Is there any way to shut you up?"

"I can think of one way..."

In the small confines of the truck, he felt so close, and I couldn't stop my eyes dropping to his lips. My breathing all but stopped. Thoughts of what it might be like to kiss Parker again invaded my head, and I held onto them for a little too long. Just one kiss. The idea was both tantalizing and terrifying.

The sound of Parker's door opening brought me back to reality. "Let's go, we're going to be late," he said as he jumped from the truck.

I felt a little unsteady as I opened my door. Maybe I'd been holding my breath too long. My brain was clearly deprived of oxygen if I was contemplating a kiss with Parker.

By the time I'd found my feet, he was already behind the truck with both our bags. I quickly took mine from him. Thankfully, he released it without a fight this time, and as we made our way inside, I kept my gaze looking straight ahead. I didn't know why I was being so awkward. So what if I'd considered kissing him for a fraction of a second? Intrusive thoughts happened to everyone.

When we reached the girls' locker room, I was glad to be able to escape inside, while Parker went to join the rest of the team. The moment I was alone though, all my nerves and doubts about the game came flooding back.

I got ready and went to meet the team, but my nerves reached another level the moment I stepped onto the ice and made my way to the net. After a week of training with Parker, I should have been feeling more confident than our last game. But seeing our opposition made me want to run and hide. Were those guys all taking steroids? They were even bigger than the Sharks players. That couldn't be natural.

Get your shit together, Mackenzie. It's just a game.

A game where if I take a hit I might literally end up in the bleachers.

"You, okay?" Parker asked as he skated past.

"Fine."

"We're going to win this one," he said. "I can feel it."

I nodded silently, fearing his optimism was seriously misplaced.

"And don't worry," he added. "I trust you."

He flashed me one last smile before skating over to center ice. All I had to do now was trust myself.

"Don't let me down," I murmured to my posts as I readied myself for the faceoff.

The referee dropped the puck between Parker and the

Chargers center, and it almost seemed to fall in slow motion. All I could think was *please don't come down here.* It hit the ice, and Parker swept in, winning the puck. Game on.

It quickly became clear that Parker wasn't messing around today. He was relentless in the first period, and it felt like he'd somehow heard my internal mumblings, because he did a good job of keeping the puck in the offensive zone. On the few occasions the Chargers crossed the blue line, Seth and Jansen defended well, without crowding my crease, but I still couldn't relax. Not even when Parker scored the opening goal of the game.

Another faceoff, a line change, and suddenly the puck was coming my way. An opposing forward streaked toward me. He was fast and skillful, and he fired off a powerful shot. My legs flared, my chest squared, and I dropped into a butterfly instinctively. *Thud*. The puck hit my pad. I managed to control the rebound and flick the puck away to Seth.

"Nice one, Foster!" He gathered the puck and took off down the ice.

My heart was racing. One save down. But how many more to go?

As the period went on, I grew in confidence. The sessions with Parker must have been helping. I even managed to shrug off the condescending comments that Chargers players threw at me. I just kept telling myself that none of them would ever come close to being as annoying as Parker Darling.

The second period, however, wasn't so good. I was starting to tire, and it began to feel like I was wading through quicksand as I moved in front of the net. My legs were heavy, and every movement felt slower than it should have been. The Chargers scored their first goal after I failed to clear a rebound, and then the forward with the powerful shot scored another. There wasn't much I could do to stop it. He was seriously good. Maybe even close to Parker.

Now that the Chargers were ahead by one, time seemed to fly by. I could sense the crowd getting nervous, my father's temper growing, and my teammates becoming more desperate as we tried to find a goal. All of us knew the Devils couldn't afford to lose another game. It seemed like *one* loss was unheard of at this school. Three in a row would be catastrophic. And for me, it could mean I never got to play another game again.

With only a few minutes left in the third period, Parker drove past the Chargers' blue line and streaked around the back of their net, his stick guiding the puck as though it was part of him. One moment he was behind the goalie, the next he was tucking the puck just inside the post. A perfect wraparound goal.

The arena erupted. My teammates cheered. And my heart filled with relief. The game was tied.

"And that's how it's done," I said to my posts. Parker caught my gaze as he skated back to center ice and flashed me a cocky grin. It was no wonder he had such a big ego; he had the moves on the ice to back up every inch of it. I only wished I could stop myself from smiling back at him.

All we had to do now was score once more. But we were running out of time. And the Chargers had the exact same ambition. After a poor pass from Jansen to Owen, suddenly the Chargers had the puck. Their forward was thundering toward me like an out-of-control train. My eyes were on the puck as he drew close. I held my ground. He took aim and fired. The puck hit my blocker and dropped right in front of me. I'd made the save, but the puck landed in the perfect spot for a rebound. The Chargers player lunged. I dropped fast and my glove clamped down on the puck. The whistle blew and play stopped. I could breathe a little easier.

Wham.

A body collided with mine and I was thrown against the post. My head knocked hard against the metal, and I'd never been more grateful for my helmet. But then a knee jabbed my rib, and a stick was forced under my glove. The Chargers' forward was scrambling for the puck as if it was still live.

"Get off me!" I snapped.

Then his leering face was hanging over mine. "If you can't handle the heat, get off the ice."

I didn't have a chance to respond as he was yanked away. I pulled myself up, breathing hard. Everything hurt, but adrenaline propelled me forward. Seth was already squaring up to the guy.

"She can handle the heat just fine," he shouted.

"Yeah, back off," Owen added, shouldering in beside him.

But then Parker appeared, like an unexpected bolt of lightning. He grabbed the guy's jersey and drove him into the boards. Their sticks clattered to the ice as the two of them grappled. Parker was out for blood. And he was too strong for the guy, despite their equally impressive heights. He practically lifted him off the ice and sent him sprawling to the ground.

Whistles blared. The refs rushed in. Every player on both

benches was standing, and Owen and Seth dragged Parker off the guy before any other Chargers players decided to get involved. When the chaos settled, Parker was sent to the penalty box; two minutes for roughing. But the Chargers' forward was only given a warning.

For a moment we all stared in stunned silence. Then the place exploded again. The crowd was booing. Several Devils players were protesting to the refs, and I could hear my dad yelling from the bench. I couldn't believe they hadn't penalized the Chargers player; had the refs forgotten he'd totally taken me out? Did they think it was an accident?

The refs refused to listen to our complaints, though, even when my dad pulled one of them aside to make his feelings clear.

I looked to the penalty box where Parker was sitting stone-faced, his jaw clenched. What had possessed him? There was no need to go after the player like that. And with less than two minutes left in the game, when we were still searching for a goal, it felt like any chance we had of winning was stuck in the box with him.

By the time play restarted, the atmosphere in the arena had shifted. Moments ago, we'd been celebrating a goal, and now we were shorthanded. I felt rattled, angry and hurt—both physically and mentally. And as much as I wanted to get my head back in the game, I was struggling. I wasn't the only one. The whole team seemed on edge, more frantic, as we desperately tried to hold off a relentless onslaught from a fired-up Chargers team. Eventually, their extra player proved too much for us, and they scored the winning goal just before the final siren sounded.

Defeat rang through me, cold and hard. I'd done my best, but it still wasn't enough. That was strike number two for me, and the look my dad gave me as I came off the ice only confirmed it. I needed to pull off something truly special in my last game if I wanted to stay on the team.

We gathered in the boys' locker room to listen to my father's post-game speech. He pretty much told us, in as many ways he could think of, how disappointed he was. But his most cutting criticisms were reserved for Parker.

"Your time in the penalty box cost us the game, Twelve, it's as simple as that. You need to start thinking about the team, not your own personal battles. Scoring two goals doesn't mean anything if you're not there in the last two minutes when your teammates need you."

Parker didn't respond. He simply nodded, taking each verbal blow. He'd been on fire until the final minutes, and I knew my dad was being unfair.

The moment my dad left the room, Parker slammed his gloves down on the bench beside him. I was sure everyone felt like doing the same. The nightmare of suffering a third straight loss had become a reality. And my dad's rant seemed to have shattered the little confidence my teammates had left.

"We'll do better next game," Owen said hopefully. "We've got the whole season ahead of us."

Parker didn't respond. His eyes lifted to meet mine, and as they connected, I knew exactly what he was thinking. We didn't all have the whole season ahead of us. For some of us, there was only one game left.

Chapter 22

PARKER

"You guys lost *again*?"

I woke to find Reed standing over me. I hadn't realized he was coming home today, and the disappointment in his eyes was the last thing I wanted to see. Sometimes I wished Ryker was just a little bit further away.

"Nice to see you too, Reed." I slowly pushed myself up. "What are you doing here so early?"

"Early? It's eleven a.m."

I groaned and rubbed a hand down my face. It had been a rough night. Sleep had eluded me as I replayed the loss repeatedly in my mind. The final score might have been closer than the previous games, but I was still far from happy with the way we played. Missed passes, poor line changes, no communication, no intensity. This wasn't how the Ransom Devils were supposed to play. We'd been floundering long before the refs made that terrible call. But despite all that, I knew I was the one who'd cost the team because I'd left us shorthanded with two minutes to go.

"Why are you so tired? Were you partying last night?" Reed asked.

"Sure." If by partying, he meant disappearing into my sketchbook until the early hours of the morning. I'd been inspired to go in a different direction with my comic strip, and I was just a little obsessed with my new idea. It helped that drawing had provided a small reprieve from thinking about the game.

Three defeats in a row; it had to be some kind of record for Ransom High. If this continued, we'd be lucky to make the playoffs this year, let alone win another state championship. And with Coach Foster's opinion of me probably at an all-time low, I was sure my slim chances of being named captain were now almost non-existent.

Reed, meanwhile, appeared to be doing better than ever. Was it possible he was still growing? He seemed even taller than before. I'd thought I was almost catching him in height. But apparently I'd always be chasing after him.

"Where's Grayson?"

"Where do you think?" Reed grinned.

It didn't take long for me to work out the answer. When it came to Gray, there were only three things he really cared about: hockey, food, and his girlfriend. "Paige?" I guessed.

"Yep." Reed nodded. "She drove back with us, but wanted to drop by her house. They'll be here later."

"So, they're still as loved up as ever?"

"*More* than ever."

I laughed at the way Reed rolled his eyes, because I knew he was joking. We couldn't have been happier when Paige and Grayson finally got together last year. They were perfect for each other, and we all liked Paige. She was like a sister.

"You could have told me you guys were coming back today," I said, as I grabbed a sweatshirt off my chair and put it on.

"I thought we messaged you." Reed shrugged. "Although, maybe that was Cammie."

I grunted. It still annoyed me that my brothers had a group chat with my younger sister, and its main purpose seemed to be so they could gossip about me. I sincerely hoped the group had moved on to other topics by now, and that the monkey profile picture had also been replaced.

"Is Gray feeling okay after that hit he took in your game yesterday?"

"He'll be fine," Reed said. "It's the other guy you should probably be worried about."

I laughed and nodded. Most people who went head to head with Grayson on the ice ended up regretting it.

"I hear you made a new friend at the end of your game, too," Reed continued.

"I got two for roughing, no big deal."

"Sounds like you were lucky to get away with only a two-minute penalty."

"What do you mean? The only person who got lucky was the Chargers player. He didn't get punished at all."

"True, but I heard you weren't even near the play."

"I was right there."

"Parker, you went coast-to-coast to throw down with the guy."

"Says who?"

"Uh, Cammie, Mom, Dad, our neighbor Jerry, some dude I bumped into at the gas station . . ."

"Okay, okay. I get it. Everyone saw me fight."

Reed shook his head. "No, everyone saw you sprint down the ice to defend your new goalie. I hear you've been spending a lot of one-on-one time with her . . ."

I glared at my brother, knowing exactly what he was getting at. Yes, I'd reacted poorly to seeing Mackenzie get hit and was well aware it had cost us the game. But what I wasn't sure about was *why* I'd reacted that way. One minute I was watching her make a save from the other end of the rink, the next I was wrestling the guy against the boards, throwing him to the ground and being ordered off the ice.

Something had taken over when I saw Mackenzie get hurt, and while I'd been sitting in the penalty box, I realized I'd been doing more than just defending our goalie. I'd been defending *her*. And that was what kept me awake last night the most.

"Don't start," I grumbled. Eleven a.m. or not, it was way too early for this. I hadn't even had breakfast yet.

"Why not?" Reed's grin grew wide. "It's way more fun giving you shit than receiving it."

"Yeah, well, let me wake up a little, and we'll see who's giving who shit." I slowly stumbled from my room. My stomach felt like it was eating itself. Reed followed me to the kitchen, so I changed the subject before he could keep asking about the game.

"How's Violet doing in California?"

"She's good," Reed said. "It's hard being apart from her, but she barely saw her mom last year, so I think she likes being at school close to home. She's going to try and visit when we're back for homecoming in a couple of weeks though."

"Long distance." I shook my head. "Must be tough."

"It's worth it, for the right girl." His lips twitched, and suddenly the dreamy smile he always wore around Violet was plastered on his face. I found myself wondering if I'd ever look like such an idiot when I thought about a girl.

"Besides, it's only temporary," he continued. "I just hope if I ever get drafted, I end up someplace warm. Violet seriously can't handle the cold."

"No, really?" I laughed sarcastically. I'd never seen anyone wear as many layers as Violet during winter.

He scowled at me but then slapped me on the back. "I've missed you, little bro."

I had to admit, the house had felt way too empty with Reed and Grayson gone, and I was happy to have my brothers home, too.

"Here I was thinking you're too busy being a college hockey superstar to miss me," I said.

"I don't know about the superstar stuff. But I'll never be too busy for you."

This was about as deep as Reed and I ever got, but I knew he meant it. It could be frustrating sometimes to watch Reed so easily achieve everything I wanted, while my own hopes and dreams were currently slipping through my fingers. But I could only ever be happy for him.

Mom was sitting at the kitchen counter reading a book with a half-naked man wearing a kilt on the cover, which she slammed shut when we walked through the door. Her face was glowing when she looked up at us. I certainly hoped it was because she was happy to see her sons back together, and not because she'd just discovered what was under that man's kilt.

"Have you eaten, Reed?" she asked.

"Yeah, I grabbed something on the road."

"How about you, monkey?"

No matter how many times I told my mom to stop calling me that, she couldn't let the habit die.

"I'll just get some cereal."

"Don't eat it all," Mom said. "Save some for your brothers."

She should have known by now, when it came to our pantry, it was every Darling for themselves.

"How about your friend?" Mom asked.

I turned to look at Reed as he returned her smile. "I'm sure he's fine; he ate on the road, too."

"Friend?" I asked, my words muffled by a mouthful of Cheerios.

"Yeah, one of our teammates caught a ride back with us." Reed's voice trailed off as a tall guy with blond hair entered the kitchen.

"You guys talking about me?" He was grinning from ear to ear.

I vaguely recognized him and started running through the Raiders' roster in my head, trying to recall his name.

"I'm Max," he said, holding out his hand. "Max Foster. You must be Parker."

I almost choked on a Cheerio. "There's a Foster in our house?"

I instantly regretted my comment and tried to hide it with a cough, before I quickly shook his hand. "Uh, I mean, it's great to meet you, man." The world was way too small.

Either Max hadn't heard me, or he didn't mind my awkwardness, because his genuine smile didn't falter. "Great to officially meet you too. Especially since you've got some clothes on this time."

Reed snorted and Mom shot me a look, but didn't say anything. Instead, she stood up from the bench and headed for the fridge, muttering to herself. She'd already heard about my naked trek through the ice arena and made her feelings clear. To be honest, I was surprised she'd been surprised.

"You saw that?" I asked.

"Just caught the end of the show." Somehow, Max was still smiling. This Foster seemed far more friendly than the others.

"And I saw the highlights of your game yesterday," he added.

I should have been grateful he'd changed the subject, but he'd picked pretty much the only other topic I wanted to avoid right now.

"Thanks for backing up my little sister," he continued. "You really put that guy in his place. Well worth getting two minutes in the box, if you ask me. But I can't believe the refs let the other guy off." He shook his head. "What were they thinking?"

I shrugged, unsure how else to respond. I doubted he'd be thanking me if he knew the way his little sister was currently occupying my brain space. How much I was wrestling with my reasons for leaping to Mackenzie's defense so urgently. It felt far safer to just keep my trap shut.

"We'd better go," Reed said.

"Oh, so soon?" Mom asked.

"I need to drive Max home, but I'll be back for dinner." Reed then turned to me. "I heard the lake is frozen solid and someone has already set up for pond hockey. Want to go for a skate later?"

"Sure. We can see if you've actually learned anything at college."

Reed chuckled before glancing at Max. "How about you, Foster? Want to help me school my little brother?"

"I could come for a skate." Max nodded as he looked my way. "But I'm not sure your brother needs schooling. I saw your goals yesterday. That wraparound was a beauty."

"Ah, I just got lucky."

"No way, all skill."

Maybe my plan to win these Fosters over one by one was working. If only Mackenzie and her dad were as simple to please as Max, their stepmom, and the cat.

"Guess we'll see you later then," I said.

"Looking forward to it," Max replied. "Maybe I'll see if Kenzie's up for it, too."

I swallowed as Reed and Max left the room. I wasn't sure if I was ready to face Mackenzie after yesterday. We hadn't spoken since the game, so I had no clue how she was feeling about my penalty. It didn't take a genius to know she'd be annoyed I'd got stuck in the box and cost the team. But the way I'd reacted to her getting hit? I wasn't sure I wanted to know what she thought about that.

She was probably just pissed we lost. Especially as she'd been playing a lot better than her first game. No one could blame her for letting in the goal at the end though. That was all on me. Another unfamiliar feeling entered my chest. Oh God, not guilt. This girl was really messing with my head.

"You okay?" Mom asked. I'd kind of forgotten she was still here.

"I'm fine, Mom."

She smiled. "You just looked a little startled when Max

mentioned his sister. Is there something going on there?"

"No."

"Are you sure? You did fight that player for her yesterday."

"It wasn't *for* her. It's hockey, Mom. Fights happen."

"Okay, if you say so," she said. "It's probably for the best. You are trying to stay on her dad's good side, after all."

It *was* for the best, and yet a part of me was disappointed Mom was so fast to write Mackenzie off. My mom usually leaped at any potential opportunity to play matchmaker with her kids. She must think it was a truly bad idea to risk getting close to the coach's daughter.

"Right," I agreed. "I was worried for a second you were going to pull out your wedding planning folder."

"Well, I can do that if you want, sweetie." There was a teasing tint to her voice. "I'd certainly approve. She must be a very special girl if she can put up with you and the rest of the boys on that hockey team."

"I said no, Mom."

She was smiling happily as I made a quick exit, still clutching my box of Cheerios.

"Maybe see if Mackenzie and Max want to come for family dinner?" she called after me. She really couldn't help herself.

"I'm sure they're busy!" I called back.

"Just ask them when you're finished at the lake."

I was hoping Mackenzie wouldn't show up at the lake at all. While a part of me wanted to see her, another part was terrified this thing between us was no longer just an itch that needed to be scratched. She was stubborn, determined, completely maddening. Yet all those things that had been reasons to stay clear of her, now seemed to be drawing me closer and making me do things I regretted. And getting closer to Mackenzie wasn't an option, if I wanted to stay on the team. If I wanted any chance of convincing Coach Foster I was the player I thought I was. The captain I wanted to be.

Maybe I needed her to punch me again. Though, knowing me, I'd probably end up liking that too.

Chapter 23

MACKENZIE

It was only Max's second time visiting Ransom, but he seemed totally at home. He spent most of his time in the kitchen raiding the fridge or galloping around the house with our little sisters taking turns riding his back. Something about having him here instantly made the place feel a little more like home to me too.

My parents were just as happy to see my brother as they were last time and they flooded him with questions about life at college and, of course, hockey. He seemed to be enjoying Ryker but was typically modest about how brilliantly he'd been playing with the Raiders and kept changing the subject to the Devils, something both my dad and I were keen to avoid talking about. For a moment during the game yesterday, I felt like maybe I was playing well, only for it all to come crashing down in the final few minutes. I wasn't eager to reminisce about it.

In the afternoon, Max asked if I wanted to go to the lake for a skate, and I jumped at the opportunity. I'd never turned down the chance to play hockey with my brother before, but I also wanted to avoid any more hockey chat with my dad. Apparently, I wasn't the only one.

Max breathed a sigh of relief as we drove away from the house. "Dad was seriously grilling me about my game yesterday. Apparently, two assists wasn't good enough."

It was easy to forget sometimes that my dad was hard on my brother too. His expectations when it came to Max were ridiculously high. Luckily for Max, he mostly lived up to them.

"At least he's talking to you."

"Yeah, I noticed he was still giving you the cold shoulder," Max replied. "I thought he would have come around by now."

"I'd hoped so too. The fact we're still losing hasn't helped. It's only convinced him he's right about me. I've let in far too many goals."

My brother took a moment as he considered me. "I've watched the game tapes, Kenzie. You're not the only one on the team who's made mistakes. Yeah, you let in a few goals, but these were just your first two games. You'll get stronger and more confident over the next few weeks. But the defense wasn't working effectively to get the puck out of the zone, and the forwards missed plenty of opportunities too. Reed said a lot of guys from the Devils graduated last year. Sounds like you're not the only one who needs to improve."

I stayed silent, and his fingers tapped against the wheel as he continued. "Even your friend Parker made mistakes in those games, and he's a great player. He's already committed to Ryker next year, right?"

"Parker's not my friend."

"You sure about that?"

"Positive." I cleared my throat because I realized I'd answered a little too firmly. "I mean, he's just been helping me train."

Max shrugged, like it didn't matter to him either way. I expected my brother would have a much stronger opinion on the topic if he knew Parker was the boy I'd kissed at our dad's camp three years ago.

"I'm just saying," he continued with a sigh, "you're not solely to blame for these losses. It's a team game."

I nodded, mostly just to satisfy him. It was a little hard to agree when only one member of that team was currently on probation.

After a few minutes of quiet, Max finally changed the subject. "I saw you still haven't unpacked your moving boxes."

"I just haven't had a chance yet."

Max's lips twisted as he glanced at me. "You're still not feeling at home here?"

"No, it's not that . . ."

He lifted an eyebrow.

"Seriously. I've just been crazy busy with hockey."

He nodded. "Okay, well, you know I'm here if you ever need to talk, right?"

"Yeah, Max, I know." I gave him a grateful smile. "But I really have been busy."

"If you say so."

When we arrived at the lake and got out of the car, I was instantly struck by how beautiful it was. The surface of the lake was frozen solid and there was still a dusting of white from recent snowfalls. Beyond it, tall pine trees reached up to a clear blue sky above.

The sound of laughter pulled my attention back down to the ice, and I noticed a group of people passing a puck back and forth. A pond hockey rink had been set up, with snow pushed aside to create a large rectangle of clear, smooth ice.

At each end, slabs of wood lay on the ice as the goals. It was perfect. If they played hockey in heaven, I imagined this is how they'd do it.

But then I looked closer at the people who were playing and was quickly brought back down to Earth. Parker was here. I also recognized his sister, Cammie, and two other guys who looked like his brothers, Reed and Grayson. There was also a cute brunette girl I'd never seen before.

I glared at Max. "The Darlings are here?"

"Reed's the one who invited us," Max said. "Didn't I tell you?"

"No!"

"I could have sworn I did." He shrugged. "Anyway, it looks like you're not the only girl who's playing. Their sister's here, and that's Grayson's girlfriend."

He nodded across the ice to where the brunette was skating next to one of the boys, who I assumed was Grayson. She didn't possess the natural ease of Cammie or the boys on the ice, and every so often her arm would snap out to grab hold of Grayson to steady herself. The hockey stick in her hand looked completely foreign to her.

"Has she ever played before?"

Max chuckled. "Yeah, but Paige would rather be writing about hockey than playing it. Come on."

I felt nervous as I followed my brother over to the group. I'd laughed the first time I'd heard the Darling Devils nickname, but seeing all three boys together, I could understand why everyone at Ransom High talked about Reed and Grayson with such awe and admiration. Their towering size and striking good looks were an intimidating combination. I also knew how skilled they were at hockey, and with Parker and my brother here, I was in the presence of some seriously talented players.

Unlike me, Max was totally at ease around the older Darling brothers after spending the last few months at college with them, and he gave Paige a warm hug too. But I was surprised when my brother bumped fists with Parker. When did *they* become so friendly?

All I got from Parker was a cursory nod. It was the first time I'd seen him since the game yesterday, so I wasn't sure how he'd be feeling about the way the loss unfolded, especially in those final few minutes. I still wasn't sure how to feel myself. My dad had pretty much placed the blame entirely on Parker, but I knew Max was right. The whole team could've done better.

Our reasons for losing weren't really what was bothering me right now anyway. I couldn't stop thinking about the way Parker had rushed to my defense. And why he now seemed to be avoiding me.

"Guys, this is my sister, Kenzie," Max said, introducing me to the group with a broad smile. "The Ransom Devils' new secret weapon."

I shook my head. "If I'm the secret weapon, the team's doomed."

Reed skated over to shake my hand. "I'm Reed, and this is Grayson and Paige. I'm guessing you know Cammie and Parker. We've heard a lot about you."

"Well, whatever Max has said, just know my brother likes to exaggerate."

"It wasn't from Max," Grayson muttered.

I frowned at him, but Paige quickly butted in. "It's so good to finally meet you," she said, pulling me into a tight hug. "I got so excited when I heard there was a girl playing for the Devils. We're all coming back for the homecoming game against the Saints. Will you be playing?"

We had a bye this coming week, and the game against the Saints was the following Friday. It gave me a little extra time to work on my skills before I played again, but that would be game number three for me.

"Yeah, I should be playing."

"*Should*?"

"I'm on probation. I could get cut at any time."

Paige crossed her arms, and her sunny expression was replaced with a frown. "Do *all* the new players go on probation, or just the girls?"

"Uh, I think it's just daughters of the coach."

"Our dad's a little overprotective when it comes to Kenzie," Max explained. "He'll come around."

Yeah, right.

"Are we going to play, or what?" Parker asked.

He'd been hanging back from the group, skating back and forth with a puck on the end of his stick. He didn't even look up as he spoke. I was somewhat relieved for the interruption though. Maybe playing a little casual pond hockey would take my mind off my failures in more competitive games.

We broke into two teams. Max and I joined up with Cammie, who seemed eager to face off against her brothers, while the Darling boys teamed up with Paige. At first, four on three appeared slightly unfair, but it turned out to be quite even. Paige was not a strong hockey player, and Grayson kept getting distracted as he made sure she was okay.

I was a little out of my comfort zone without my goalie gear, but my brother was in his element. Cammie was also an incredible skater, and surprisingly lethal with a stick. She was fast and nimble, if slightly abusive when it came to her older brothers.

"My grandma can defend better than you!" she yelled at Grayson, after she'd just darted around him to score.

"My grandma *is* your grandma." The deadpan look on his face was a little frightening, but Cammie just shrugged. Meanwhile, Paige was struggling not to laugh. I personally would have thought twice about laughing at a guy who was glaring like that, but Paige's eyes were shining brightly.

"It's not funny, Pidge," he grumbled.

"It kind of is," she replied.

"Stop going easy on us," Cammie demanded as she skated back to the center of the makeshift rink.

"Yeah," Max teased. "Did the Darling Devils come to play or not?"

Reed, Grayson, and Parker shared a look. And, suddenly, the teams didn't seem so fair. When the game restarted the boys attacked with a vengeance. They were so quick across the ice and skillful with the puck, and it was like they could read each other's minds. They were constantly moving and swapping positions; it felt as though we were playing against ten of them. Every pass connected with its intended target and every shot hit the small wooden goals. Maybe they did deserve their nickname, after all.

"You do have one extra player," Cammie pointed out after the three boys combined for yet another goal. "It's kind of an unfair advantage."

"Unfair advantage?" Reed scoffed. "You told us to take Paige."

"Yeah, well, I thought she'd distract Gray for a bit longer than she did."

"Nothing can truly distract me when it comes to hockey," Grayson said. "You know that."

"Whoops!" Paige yelped as her skates flew out from under her and she fell on her butt.

Grayson was by her side barely a heartbeat later, helping her back to her feet.

"You were saying?" Cammie called to him, but Grayson was too busy checking on Paige to hear her.

"We'd still beat you even without Gray," Reed said. "Hell, we'd probably still beat you with me only skating backward, Paige playing at center, and Parker with no stick."

"Let's do it," Parker called, happily ditching his stick to the side.

Max laughed. "This ought to be good."

The game descended into chaos after that. Reed did as he suggested and exclusively skated backward. Max played with his eyes shut whenever he got the puck. Cammie got bored and started elegantly spinning in circles at center ice, while Paige simply tried her best to remain upright, and Grayson stayed within inches of her at all times to make sure she did.

After a while someone suggested getting home for dinner, so Reed called out "next goal wins", and everyone suddenly focused on the game again.

"Heads up, Kenzie," Max shouted as he fired the puck down the ice toward me. I suddenly realized I was close to the goal, and when I collected Max's pass, I charged toward it. It wasn't often I got a chance to try my hand at offense.

I was just about to shoot, when Parker appeared between my target and me. He was completely blocking my path and shielding the goal as I raced closer. Should I take the shot? Or should I try and go around him?

I chose the second option and faked as though I was going to skate left. The second Parker started to shift his weight in that direction, I slid hard to the right. But he read me like a book.

I should have stopped. He should have backed down. But I guess we were both too stubborn for our own good, because just as I flicked the puck toward the goal, we collided. The two of us toppled to the ice. His arms wrapped around me. And the next thing I knew, I had landed firmly on Parker's chest.

He grunted at the impact, but a cheeky smile touched his lips as he peered up at me. My breath caught as I stared back at him. We'd been avoiding each other the entire game, but now we couldn't have been pressed closer together. His cheeks were pink with exertion, his hair was ruffled as it fell across his face, and his eyes were glittering like a summer lake struck by sunlight. All thoughts of hockey fled my mind. The only thing I could concentrate on was how close we were. And how tightly Parker was still holding me.

The cheekiness in his gaze shifted into something more powerful as he eyes dipped to my lips. For a moment, just a moment, I allowed myself to look at his lips too. My body buzzed. My heart raced. And I wondered if perhaps he was one mistake worth repeating.

But then he started talking. "Did you just fall for me, Mackenzie Foster?"

"We collided, Parker. That was gravity."

"Well, whatever it is, it feels really good."

I shoved myself off his firm chest and clambered to my feet. Tension continued to flicker between us as he also stood. I wasn't sure why he was suddenly grinning at me when it felt like he'd been keeping his distance all afternoon.

I dusted myself off and said, "I'm pretty sure that was a penalty, by the way. You know there's no physical contact in pond hockey."

"And you know I don't like to play by the rules."

"Is that what you were thinking yesterday, too?"

The mischievous look in his eyes disappeared. "No, yesterday, I—" He paused. "Yesterday, I wasn't thinking. It's becoming a bit of a problem for me when it comes to you..."

The intensity with which he held my gaze made my heart race for all the wrong reasons. What was up with me today? This was Parker. *Parker*. The guy I'd rather punch than kiss. Unfortunately, while I still wanted to punch him, I also kind of wanted to kiss him.

"You guys okay?" Reed's voice calling over to us pulled me back to reality.

"Uh, yeah, all good," Parker replied.

"Well, game's over, time to go."

"Yeah, nice goal, Kenzie." I turned to see Max clapping

his hands at me and then glanced beyond Parker to the goal behind him. The puck was nestled against it. It seemed, despite Parker's efforts, I'd scored the winning goal.

Parker and I followed the rest of the group over to the edge of the lake where we changed back into our shoes.

"You guys want to come for dinner?" Reed asked my brother. "We can watch the Wild game too."

"Yeah, we'd love that," Max said.

We would *not* love that. I shot my brother a hard look, but he ignored me.

"Great," Reed replied. "We'll meet you back at the house."

"You don't need to look so horrified." Max laughed as we headed back to our own car. "Dinner will be fine."

I nodded, but it wasn't dinner I was worried about. It was the blue-eyed, six-foot-something, playboy hockey star who I'd just been lying on top of. I couldn't seem to think straight, because despite the fact I knew going to his house was definitely a bad idea, it didn't stop me from getting in the car.

Chapter 24

MACKENZIE

Parker lived on a scenic and quiet street in a big old house that looked tired but well loved. Tall, snow-dusted trees framed the front and soft golden light spilled out from the large windows, making it look incredibly inviting. It reminded me a little of our place, with its big front porch and classic charm. Though there was no latticework—not that I planned on scaling the Darlings' house any time soon.

Inside, though, was a different world. Our house was a jarring mix of toddler-created mess and organized but unpacked moving boxes. The Darlings' home felt lived in. Coats and shoes lined the entranceway and countless family pictures covered the walls. It was warm and just the right amount of chaotic, if a little snug once all of us had squeezed into the living room to watch the hockey game.

"Dad! What the hell?" Reed, Grayson, and Parker all yelled at their father in unison when they saw what he was watching on the TV.

Their dad turned to them, his eyes wide like he'd been caught doing something illegal.

"What is this?" Parker pointed at the TV in disgust.

"Uh, just a little show I put on . . ."

The title sequence was playing, and a familiar tune filled the room. I hid my smile. Apparently, Mr. Darling liked dating shows. Tessa was obsessed with the same one.

"*Love on the Range*?" Cammie spluttered a laugh. "Have you and Mom switched bodies?"

"Dad, why are you watching this?"

"You know the Wild game is just about to start, right?"

"Something must be wrong with him. Should we call an ambulance?" Parker pressed his hand against his dad's forehead, as if to check his temperature.

His dad laughed and batted his hand away. "I'm not sick."

"Maybe not physically," Parker muttered.

"Very funny, Parker," his dad replied. "But don't worry, I'm just trying to win a bet. Your mother didn't believe I could handle watching three episodes of her show *and* miss a hockey game."

"She's probably right."

He ignored Parker as he continued. "And I may have made a little joke about your mother not being able to cook Sunday dinner tonight without ruining it. So, now we're competing to prove each other wrong."

"Bit harsh, Danny," Paige said with a chuckle.

"What will you win?" Grayson asked.

"Uh, well, I don't want to spoil it, but it's something I've wanted for a long time. Though your mother has always been hesitant to give it to me."

"Oh, God." Parker shook his head. "It's something kinky, isn't it?"

"Parker!" His siblings groaned as Grayson punched his younger brother on the arm. But Parker just grinned.

He was still smiling when his eyes landed on me, and although he barely held my gaze for half a second, my heart stuttered. I cursed myself for the reaction. The feeling in my chest was the same as when I'd been lying on top of him at the lake. What was wrong with me? How could any part of me be attracted to this guy? He was a total menace. And I wasn't sure if it made me feel better or worse that he was just as annoying around everyone else, including his poor family.

"You haven't introduced me to your friends," Mr. Darling said, looking to Max and me. "I'm Danny."

"Max and Mackenzie," Reed said, pointing us out.

"Of course." Danny smiled. "The third best rookie on the Ryker Raiders and the new star of the Ransom Devils. Great to finally meet you guys."

I blushed at his compliment and Max laughed. "You too, Mr. D," he said. "Sorry to barge in on you while you're watching your favorite show."

Danny laughed. "No problem at all. The more the merrier in this house. But if you all want to watch the hockey while you wait for dinner, you better go to the den. I might be here for a while."

"Yeah, good luck with that, Dad," Reed said.

"I'll go grab some snacks from the kitchen," Grayson added.

"Don't you even think about helping your mother in there," Danny warned him. "No cheating!"

A subtle smile hinted at Grayson's lips. "Wouldn't dream of it, Dad."

Paige joined Grayson in the kitchen while the rest of us headed to the den. Parker sat in the middle of the couch, Max snagged the armchair, and Reed sunk into a beanbag on the floor as he flicked on the TV. I hesitated in the doorway.

"Sit down, Mackenzie, you're being weird." Parker scooted across the couch, making space for me. There was plenty of room, but my skin was still buzzing from the way he had held me on the ice, and I was worried how much worse it would become if I got close to him again. Would it be awkward if I sat on the beanbag with Reed? Definitely. But right now, I felt more confident around a college hockey superstar I barely knew than the boy who had my insides twisted into knots.

Parker was watching me expectantly. After another moment of hesitation, I reluctantly took a seat beside him, keeping close to the opposite arm of the couch.

"I still can't believe you stole my bedroom, Parker," Reed said. The game hadn't started yet, with the players still taking their positions for the faceoff.

"It's bigger." Parker shrugged.

"You moved in the day I left. My bed wasn't even cold yet."

"It's the circle of life. When the older brother leaves home, the younger one gets all his shit. I don't make the rules."

Reed turned to Max. "Did Mackenzie steal your room too?"

"No, but they moved to Ransom soon after I left for college. Besides, Kenzie always had the best room. Needed the extra space for all her clothes."

"All *my* clothes?" I protested. "I'm not the one with fifty pairs of the exact same sweatpants."

Max chuckled. "It's hardly fifty, and they were on sale."

"Snacks have arrived," Paige declared as she entered the room. All she was holding was a small bag of sour gummy worms, but then Grayson followed behind her, his arms laden with popcorn, chips and more candy.

"Mind if I sit here, Mackenzie?" Paige asked.

I scooted slightly closer to Parker to make space for her.

"Room for one more?" Grayson added, making me scoot again. I was now so close to Parker I was practically in his lap.

"Isn't this nice?" Paige said as she offered me a gummy worm. "Want one?"

"Uh, sure." I wasn't a huge fan of sour candies, but I was willing to do just about anything to distract myself from the warmth of Parker's leg pressed against mine. My skin wouldn't stop tingling, and I was hyper aware of every movement he made.

Parker seemed completely oblivious, though, as he snacked and chatted with his brothers. And he was equally at ease as the game began, issuing instructions to the players on the TV like they might actually hear him. Meanwhile, next to him, I was having a meltdown, feeling like each second lasted an eternity.

"Everything okay?" Parker murmured. His voice almost made me jump. I'd thought he was too immersed in the game to notice me. "You look stiff," he added.

"This is just how I sit."

He frowned. "Really?"

"Yeah, it's a tense game."

He glanced at the screen and his brow furrowed further. It was only the first period and already Minnesota was two goals up and dominating. Thankfully, Parker didn't question my excuse further and returned his focus to the TV.

I kept my attention on the game too, but I wasn't watching. I was trying to convince myself that I wasn't affected by Parker Darling. Not one bit.

Finally, Parker's mom called out from the other room, "Dinner!"

I jumped up like I'd been electrocuted.

Parker gave a surprised laugh. "Hungry, Mackenzie?"

Paige jumped up beside me and linked her arm through mine. "Sour worms weren't quite cutting it for me either. I'm starving."

As she led me out into the hallway, she leaned in close. "Don't worry about Parker, you'll get used to him."

"What do you mean?"

"Oh, you know, he can be a little infuriating sometimes, and he has absolutely no filter, but there's a lot more to him than most people think. He's honestly one of the sweetest guys I know, in his own way. He'd do anything for the people he cares about."

I wasn't sure why she was telling me this, and when Paige noticed my confused look, she hurried to explain.

"You just seemed uncomfortable sitting next to him."

I almost laughed. "You think I was uncomfortable sitting next to him because he's a jerk?"

She shrugged. "I mean, yeah. I figured it was either that, or you like him..." Her voice trailed off before she gasped. "Wait, *do* you like him?"

"No! God, no!"

"Okay." She was smiling brightly at me, but her voice dripped with skepticism.

"I don't." I repeated. "He's the human equivalent of a pebble in my shoe."

"Impossible to ignore?"

"More like always irritating and slowly driving me insane."

Paige only looked more intrigued. "Well, I think you'd make a very cute couple."

"You do?"

"Yeah. You guys kind of looked like one on the ice today." She raised her eyebrows knowingly.

We entered the dining room before I could dispute Paige's comment, and she introduced me to Parker's mom. Mrs. Darling immediately came over and gathered my hands in hers. "It's so lovely to meet you, Mackenzie."

"You too, Mrs. Darling."

"Please, call me Amy," she replied. "I was at the game yesterday, and I just wanted to say, I think you're incredible."

"You—you do?"

She nodded. "Yes, I was completely in awe of you. I can't imagine how difficult it would be to join an all-boys team. But I can see why they wanted you; some of the saves you made were brilliant."

"I missed three," I murmured.

Amy laughed. "Well, that happens in the NHL too, you know. And when that Chargers player slammed into you?" She shook her head. "Awful. But you got back up and kept playing like it was nothing. It was very brave. I hope you're proud of yourself."

I could feel myself blinking back tears. I wished I could have heard those words from my dad, but it still meant so much hearing them from Amy.

"Thank you."

"No, thank you. You're an inspiration. There were three young girls in the row in front of me, and I heard them talking about how they wanted to try out for hockey too. Our town needs more people like you."

All I could do was nod. Amy's praise had left me totally speechless. The boys saved me from having to respond as they all barreled into the room. But their mom's words stuck with me. I just wanted to play hockey. I never dreamed I'd inspire others to want to play too.

"Who's hungry?" Amy asked, waving at everyone to find a seat at the table.

I ended up sitting between Cammie and Paige. Other than at the lake today, I'd never actually spoken to Parker's sister. She was beautiful, intimidatingly so. And like the other Darling siblings, she exuded a don't-mess-with-me energy. Her aggression on the ice, both while training with her figure skating partner and playing pond hockey, only reinforced it. But right now, she was giving me a wry smile.

"If it's too difficult to swallow, just use your napkin to spit your food out," she said.

I laughed awkwardly. "What?"

"And if you're desperate, our dog Stanley will eat just about anything."

"What are you talking about?" I whispered, leaning closer.

Cammie smirked. "Just warning you about dinner. Be prepared..."

I turned to inspect the food on my plate. The meal looked perfectly fine. But as I glanced around the table and noticed how everyone else was cautiously checking their dinner too, I had to wonder what exactly I'd gotten myself into. There was no backing out now, though, so I picked up a taco and prepared to take a bite. What was the worst that could happen?

Chapter 25

PARKER

I was beginning to wonder if I might be one of those people who enjoy pain. Whenever Mackenzie was close to me, I found myself relishing the way she tormented me and wishing she might torture me a little more. When we'd been sitting in the den, her leg brushing against mine, my skin had buzzed with electric awareness. It was like my body's defenses were kicking in and alerting me to danger. But it was a little hard to take the warning seriously when the sensation sparking between us felt so good.

"What's wrong with you?" Grayson said quietly as we made our way to dinner.

"Wrong?"

"Yeah, you haven't given me shit all afternoon. Something must be up."

"Grumps, is that your way of saying you've missed me?"

"No."

I grinned. "Because if you want me to give you a hard time, you know I don't need much encouragement . . ."

"I definitely don't want that."

I laughed. "How's college going?" I asked.

"It's going."

"Always such a talker. What about your knee? How's it holding up?" Grayson had struggled with an injury last year, but he'd been playing brilliantly so far this season. My brother was a martyr though, so it was impossible to tell if his knee was still bothering him now.

"So far, so good." The relief was evident in his eyes. "How about you? How's school? And the new coach?"

"Don't get me started on Coach Foster."

"Still on his bad side?"

"I'm not sure the man has a good side. Even his own daughter can't get his approval on the ice, and he definitely thinks I'm a waste of space."

I half expected my brother to agree or jump on the chance to give me crap, but Grayson frowned. "Just because he can't see your talent, doesn't mean it's not there."

"I haven't been playing my best," I admitted.

"You've never needed someone else's validation before; why does it matter now?"

"He's still refusing to make me captain."

"Has he made someone else captain?"

"Well, no."

"Then maybe he's just waiting for someone to step up. It's not a bad thing. It's an opportunity."

I started to frown too, wondering if maybe Grayson had a point.

We entered the dining room to find my mom had Mackenzie's hands grasped in hers. Oh, God. What was happening? It looked like they were . . . bonding.

I went a little closer so I could hear what they were saying.

Mom was gushing over Mackenzie's hockey skills and I smiled to myself as I went to find a seat. Of course Mom had noticed what a badass Mackenzie was.

When Mom was finished heaping praise on her, Mackenzie took a seat on the far side of the table to me. I had Reed on one side of me, and on the other, there was a spare seat with a plate of food laid out for Dad. I leaned back in my chair, looking out toward the living room. "Dad, you coming?"

"Can't! I'm too busy *enjoying* my show. Derek is definitely going to choose Natalie!"

I laughed and turned to my mom. "You're really going to hold him to this bet during dinner?"

She glanced around the table. "He told you about the bet?"

"Yep."

"They forced it out of me!" Dad called from the other room.

"Yeah, right." She shook her head but smiled.

When I glanced down at my plate, I was stunned. The tacos weren't charred beyond recognition. There was no smoke drifting from the kitchen. And I definitely hadn't heard the familiar beep of the alarm going off. The food looked . . . good?

I picked up a taco and took a small, cautious bite. Years of experience had taught me never to be too careful when Mom's cooking was involved. But one taste nearly left me choking with surprise.

"Mom, what *is* this?"

She raised her eyebrows, worried. "Oh no, you really don't like it?"

"No." I said. "It's . . ." I glanced at my brothers who had similar looks of surprise on their faces. "It's actually good."

"Yeah, Mom," Reed agreed, taking another bite. "This is great."

"Nailed it," Grayson added.

Cammie was shaking her head as she stared down at her plate. "I can't believe it."

Mom rolled her eyes. "I'm not *that* bad at cooking, am I?"

"You've gone through five fire-extinguishers this year," Cammie said before turning to Max and Mackenzie. "The guy at the hardware store has to order in extra stock just for her."

Mackenzie smiled at my mom and said, "It really is delicious."

"Yeah, thanks, Mrs. D," her brother added as he took another large bite.

"Are you guys messing with me?" Dad shouted from the other room. "Because you know I can't come in there to check."

"Looks like you lost the bet, Dad!" Cammie yelled back.

"I only lose if I leave this couch," he replied. "And I can't because I'm enjoying *Love on the Range* so much. Farmers need love too, you know."

Laughing, I turned to Mom. "You still win though, right?"

"I do." She smiled. "Finally, your dad has to get the faulty wires in the house fixed. He's got until the end of the week. It's been over a year now, and he's still putting it off."

"*That's* your prize?"

"Yep, and if your father manages to stay out there for the whole episode without complaint, he gets a new TV."

"Really?" I sat up a little straighter.

"Dad *still* hasn't had the wiring fixed?" Grayson asked.

"I'm a very busy man," Dad called out again. "Though never too busy to watch my *favorite* show."

Mom bit her lip as she glanced in the direction of the living room. Maybe she was starting to feel guilty Dad was missing dinner.

"I especially like the salsa," Paige said. "It's so fresh. Did you make that from scratch, Amy?"

"Uh, yes, I did."

"Made the salsa?" Dad's muttering drifted into the dining room. "Made the salsa?" A moment later he appeared in the doorway. "There's no way. I don't believe any of you. You're messing with me. You have to be."

Mom folded her arms. "You think I'd cheat?"

"Dad, what are you doing?" I yelled. "There's a new TV on the line. Get back out there!"

But his eyes were fixed on my mom as he sat in the chair beside me. "I *know* you'd cheat." He picked up a taco and took a bite, and his eyes immediately narrowed with suspicion. "This *is* good."

"Thank you," Mom replied.

"Too good."

"Dad, you have trust issues," Cammie said.

"No, I just know my wife."

Mom smirked as she looked back at him. "I won fair and square. So you'll be fixing the wiring, and since you chose to storm in here, no new TV."

My siblings and I groaned with disappointment. Dad took another annoyed bite of his taco, before clearing his throat and standing. "I'm going to need a beer to get through this meal."

He disappeared into the kitchen, but soon after we heard a triumphant shout. "Aha!"

He marched back into the room carrying a scrunched-up

brown paper bag, which he waved in the air for everyone to see. "I knew it!" There was a logo across the front of the bag that said *Guac & Roll*. "You didn't even hide the evidence. It was sitting in the trash."

For a moment Mom's face was stoic, but then she cracked. "Okay, fine, I might have had a little help with dinner tonight."

"A *little*?" Dad replied.

"Technically, you said I couldn't ruin dinner tonight. And, *technically,* I didn't. Everyone seems to be thoroughly enjoying it."

We all nodded in agreement and Dad gawked at everyone. "No—but—you—" he sputtered. "That completely goes against the spirit of the agreement!"

"Maybe, but it's not cheating," Mom replied. "I'm so looking forward to having lights that don't keep flickering."

Dad opened and shut his mouth several times as he struggled to argue back. "I think I'll take my tacos into the living room and find out who Derek chooses."

He swiped his plate off the table and stomped out of the room. We all burst out laughing as he went. Mackenzie's gaze met mine across the table, and when I saw the joy in her eyes, sparks flared in my chest again.

"It's good to be home," Reed said.

"Yeah," Gray agreed. "It is."

I found myself nodding too. Sunday nights just weren't the same without my brothers around.

When we finished our meal, my brothers and I cleared the dishes away. There wasn't much cleaning up to do because Mom hadn't actually cooked anything. When we returned to the dining room, Reed and Grayson hovered in the doorway.

"We better go if we want to get back to school at a decent hour," Reed said to Max and Paige.

"Don't you want dessert?" Mom asked. She was putting on a brave face, but I knew she found it hard having my brothers gone. Before anyone could answer, she shook her head. "I mean, you're right. I don't want you out too late. I'll put some apple pie in a to-go container."

We all went to see them off, but Max pulled me aside before we headed out the front door. "Keep an eye out for my sister, will you?"

"Yeah, of course." The answer came all too readily.

He glanced over to where she was saying goodbye to Paige.

"Our dad . . ." Max added. "Well, you know what he's like. I just don't want her to feel like she's alone on the team."

"Don't worry, she's not. She's got me."

"Glad to hear it." He smiled. "I'm looking forward to coming back and seeing you guys play the big homecoming game."

"You'll be there?"

"Wouldn't miss it."

Max gave me a firm pat on the back before he went over and hugged Mackenzie. She squeezed her brother tightly in return, like she wasn't ready to say goodbye. I felt a little like I was intruding as I watched them pull back and saw her eyes glistening. My own farewells with my brothers were far less emotional.

Reed gripped me on the shoulder. "It was fun skating with you again today."

I smiled. "Yeah, I almost forgot what it's like to play with people you're so in sync with."

"You're not clicking with your teammates?"

"It's just different, I guess. We're all still trying to find our rhythm, but we'll get there."

"You will." Reed gave me a nod, his eyes filled with confidence.

As he walked away, Grayson knocked his arm against mine. "Time to step up," he reminded me. "And try not to piss off Coach Foster too much."

I scowled as my brother followed Reed to the car, but my expression softened when Paige came to give me a hug.

"Be nice to Mackenzie," she whispered in my ear. "I like her."

"Yeah, me too." I coughed to clear my throat when I realized what I'd said. "I mean, uh—" *Crap*. "She . . ." Words. I just needed words. "I—"

"Don't hurt yourself, Parker. It's okay to like her." She laughed as she skipped over to the truck with Max and my brothers.

I was left staring after her, wondering if I'd really just admitted that out loud. I hadn't even been able to admit my feelings for Mackenzie to myself, but now that one small admission was staring me right in the face like a blinding set of headlights I couldn't ignore.

Did I really like her? No, that couldn't be right. I liked her hockey skills, and I liked the way she looked in yoga pants. That was it.

Reed honked twice as the truck pulled away, and the noise seemed to jerk me back to reality. I'd been so in my head, it felt like time had slipped away from me for a moment. My family were all waving, but I wasn't focused on my brother's car.

"Where's Mackenzie?" I muttered, looking around. Cammie snorted at my question, and I turned to her. "What?"

"You've barely taken your eyes off her all day, but didn't see her leaving?"

"She left already?"

"Yeah, she said goodbye to everyone while you were staring into the void just now."

I glanced at the street. The car she and Max had arrived in wasn't parked out front anymore. She was gone. Without even a word to me.

"Come on, let's get inside," Mom said, waving us back toward the front door. "It's freezing out here."

But I wasn't ready to go back inside just yet. I had too many questions that needed answering, but the most important one was: would this burning tension in my chest have gone away if we'd just kissed again? Shouldn't these feelings be a distant memory by now?

I walked back to the house, grabbed my keys, and headed for my truck.

"Where are you going?" Cammie called.

"There's something I need to do."

"Don't forget your boombox," she said. "You'll need one if you're going to stand outside her window and confess your love!"

I ignored my sister as I climbed in my truck and started the engine. I didn't need a boombox to get Mackenzie's attention. I had another way.

Chapter 26

MACKENZIE

My house was oddly quiet when I got home. My dad was in his office, Tessa was asleep on the couch, and my sisters were already in bed for the night. It had been fun having Max back today and already I missed his comforting presence. He had been an especially welcome distraction given how my dad was still freezing me out.

I went straight up to my room, creeping silently past Dad's office. I could hear game footage through the door. Knowing him, he'd be reviewing it for hours. Being around Parker's family tonight had only brought my dad's lack of encouragement into sharper focus. The way Amy had spoken to me... well, I would have given just about anything to have my dad show me even half that support.

As I entered my room, I released a sigh. I hated seeing my moving boxes piled in the corner. I wasn't sure why I still hadn't unpacked. It wasn't like my dad was going to change his mind about Ransom. Maybe Max was right, and I was just waiting for this place to feel like home. And today, Ransom had felt a little more like a place I could belong. I pulled a box from the pile.

I'd barely cracked it open when there was a tapping sound at my window, quickly followed by another. Nerves churned softly beneath my skin as I crept over and peered into the front garden below. Parker was staring up at me.

I quietly opened my window. "Not this again, Parker."

"Yep, this again." He went straight for the trellis. I didn't argue. What was the point? There was clearly no stopping this boy when he had his mind set on something. Instead, I stood back as he climbed through my window for a second time.

As he stood tall my body hummed with a heady rush, and I folded my arms across myself in an attempt to contain it.

He leaned against the windowsill, gripping it tightly as he watched me. He was only wearing a T-shirt, revealing just how muscular his arms were. Even his forearms rippled. "Aren't you cold?" I muttered.

He didn't immediately respond, and as my gaze lifted from his arms, my breath hitched. There was something wild about his eyes. "You didn't say goodbye." His words seemed to pulse through me.

I tried to laugh them off. "You came all the way over here for a goodbye?"

"No. Yes. I—" He shook his head as though he'd failed to find the answer he was searching for. "We didn't discuss our plans for training this week."

"Couldn't you have just texted me?"

"It's a little hard when you keep refusing to give me your number."

I rolled my eyes, but passed him my phone. "Fine. Give me your number."

When he handed it back to me, I took a look and sighed. "Coach Darling? *That's* the contact name you're going with?"

"It's true, isn't it?"

"'Parker' would have been fine. Most Annoying Human

Alive also would have worked."

He grinned as he looked at his own phone. "If it helps, I'm putting you in as, Second Favorite Foster."

"And who's your favorite?"

"Mitts, obviously."

"Obviously." Was it weird to be a little jealous of the world's most obnoxious cat? "Well, we've exchanged numbers now, I guess you can go."

"Is that what you want?" he asked cautiously. "For me to go?"

I swallowed. No, it wasn't. I didn't want him to leave at all. Having him in my room felt intoxicating and dangerous, just like the last time he'd climbed up here. Except this time, I was enjoying the risk. Maybe even wanting to risk more.

When I didn't respond, he took a step closer. My heart pounded. All I could think about was how my body had come alive when I'd fallen on him at the lake today. How my every cell had flickered with awareness while sitting next to him in the den. How my insides had fluttered whenever he'd caught my eye across the table at dinner. Suddenly the fact Parker was in my room wasn't nearly as dangerous as the way I was feeling.

I quickly turned and headed back to the box I was sorting, saying, "You're here now. I guess you may as well tell me about training." I didn't want Parker to leave, but I needed to keep my hands busy or I'd reach out to him. Seriously, what was wrong with me?

"Right." Was that disappointment in his voice? He cleared his throat before he continued. "Our homecoming game against the Saints. It's the biggest of the season, outside the playoffs. We need to win it."

"And..."

"And while there are still things you and I can work on, I've been thinking about the team a lot since our game yesterday. We all made mistakes. Me included."

I paused and glanced up from my box. "You probably shouldn't have hit that guy."

"No, I shouldn't have."

He looked like he wanted to say more, but when he stayed quiet, I uttered the question that was hanging silently between us. "So, why did you do it?"

He let out a breath, and as his blue eyes pierced mine it felt as if the tension between us might snap. "You don't want to know." His voice was deep and gravelly, and something about it had my heart pulsing fast once more.

It felt like we both wanted to avoid the answer to my question. It was one of many that were piling up, like the boxes in the corner of my room. But our silence said all the things neither of us wanted to utter aloud. Could we keep ignoring this? Did I even want to ignore it?

"It was one mistake," I said, finally. "You won't make it again."

"No." He appeared to relax a little. "I won't. But it wasn't the only thing that went wrong. We could *all* be playing better. And I think there might be something we can do about it."

"What?"

"When Reed, Grayson, and I play together, the way we communicate feels more like telepathy. I know what move they're going to make before they make it. I know where they are on the ice without even looking. I *trust* them. Skating with my brothers today made me realize that the Devils don't have that. And we need it if we want to win."

"But you've played with your brothers for years. You can't develop 'telepathy' overnight."

"True," he admitted. "But half the guys on the team have never played together before, and it shows. Sloppy mistakes were made yesterday that never would have happened if the team communicated better. If they had more confidence in each other. I think a little team bonding could help."

I glanced up at him as his words sunk in. "You want the guys to hold hands and make friendship bracelets?"

"If it gets them connected, then yeah. We've got to do something, don't we? We need to win this next game so you can stay." A look of surprise flickered across his face, as if the words had slipped from his mouth without permission.

He didn't take them back though . . .

"So, what do you think?" he said. "Could this work?"

A few weeks ago, I would have laughed Parker's suggestion off entirely. But after the time we'd spent together, after he'd helped me so much, I felt like I understood him so much better.

"It could," I said, unpacking some clothes. "What do you want us to do?"

"I'll text everyone to meet at school first thing tomorrow morning, and . . ." He stopped and began to smile as I pulled out a hockey jersey. "Nice jersey. Is it yours?"

"Oh." I frowned as I looked over the bright blue jersey, which had a large raven plastered across the chest. I'd never seen it before. "It must be one of my dad's." I took another look in the box and realized none of its contents were familiar. "I think this is all his. Must have gotten mixed up in the move."

I went to pack the jersey away, but as the material slipped through my fingers, I caught sight of the name across the back. My heart all but stopped. There, in faded white letters, was my mom's maiden name. Hollis. Below it, the number thirty-three.

"What's up?" Parker said, his voice filling with concern. He must have noticed my shaking hands.

"I-I think this was my mom's." My eyes were wide as I looked up at him, shock making my grip on the jersey unsteady.

"Your mom played hockey?"

"No. I mean, I don't think so. My dad never said anything about it."

I started searching frantically through the box. It wasn't just the jersey. There was a medal with my mom's name printed on it—Abigail Hollis. A goalie mitt. Newspaper clippings and old ticket stubs from some of my dad's NHL games. A signed puck. A photobooth strip showing smiling pictures of my mom and dad in college. But it was the last item I lifted from the box that had tears welling in my eyes. In a tarnished silver frame, there was a photo of a hockey team wearing bright blue jerseys with ravens across their chests. They were all boys, except, there, sitting front and center, wearing goalie gear just like mine, was my mom.

I was instantly struck by a feeling of betrayal. Then an overwhelming sense of loss. These were all her things, and I'd never seen them before. Never even heard about them. A whole part of my mom's life I knew nothing about. One that must have been deliberately kept from me. Why hadn't my dad said anything?

Parker came to my side. "She looks just like you."

His words relaxed me slightly, making my heart swell with pride. It wasn't the first time I'd been told my mom and I were similar, but I hadn't realized those similarities were more than skin deep.

"Are you okay?" he added.

"I'm confused." I glanced up at him and asked, "Why didn't I know about this?"

"I don't—" We both froze as a creak sounded on the stairs. Footsteps in the hallway. Parker stared at me, panicked. I nodded toward my closet and he rushed to it.

I placed the frame and the jersey back in the box and quickly closed the lid before hurrying to help Parker shut himself in.

"Mackenzie?" my dad's deep voice called softly. It was followed by a knock on the door.

Anger, annoyance, and confusion tore through me. I didn't want to face my dad right now. I wasn't sure what I would say. Probably many things I'd regret.

"Mackenzie, are you in there?"

I'd been planning to shut Parker in the closet alone. But it sounded like my dad didn't know I was here yet, so instead of answering him, I silently slid in next to Parker. There was barely enough room as it was, but he shifted his body as I closed the door behind me and pressed against him. My hands were on his chest. His were on my waist. I didn't have it in me to care.

I couldn't face my dad. I just couldn't.

"Mackenzie?" he called again.

Parker and I both stopped breathing as my bedroom door opened. His worried blue eyes stared right back into mine. My heart was racing. My body quivering. And yet, it wasn't because I thought we might get caught. Everything I'd been denying and trying to ignore was rushing to the surface.

I heard my bedroom door click shut again, then silence. My dad was gone, but neither one of us dared to move. The air between us crackled.

"I *do* want to know," I whispered.

"Know what?"

"Why you reacted the way you did after I got hit. Tell me it was the heat of the game. That fights happen. That you would have done it for any other teammate."

"You want me to lie."

His words struck my chest like a check against the boards.

"You know why I did it, Mackenzie. I did it because when I look at you, I can't think clearly. I no longer care that you're off-limits. That you despise me. That wanting you could send my entire future up in flames. You drive me crazy enough to forget all that. Crazy enough to forget the rules."

My breaths were shallow. The air between us heated. And if he lowered his lips to mine, I felt certain that the clash of our skin would cause sparks to ignite. I knew I should deny it. That I should get the hell out of my closet and tell Parker to go home.

Instead, I reached up and grabbed the collar of his shirt, pulling him toward me. "You drive me crazy too."

His lips crashed into mine, and the second we met, it was like pure, raw energy shot straight through me. This was so much more than just sparks. It was a detonation. I didn't know how to think. How to breathe. All the hatred, the lust, the hidden desire flowed through us. And the more I wanted him, the more I hated him for making me feel this way.

But as quickly as it started, the kiss was over. The two of us broke apart and I pushed through the closet door, desperate for air. What had I been thinking, kissing Parker? Had I completely lost my mind? The problem was, as he followed me out, I wanted to do it again.

"That was . . ." I stopped, feeling lost.

"If you can't find the words," he said, "we can always try that again."

"I was going to say, that was a mistake." I shook my head. "A stupid, one-time thing. It won't happen again."

The corner of Parker's mouth lifted like he saw that as a challenge.

"I just needed to get you out of my system," I added. "Like you said."

"And did it work?"

"Definitely."

"Right," he said, with a small nod. "Same. I can't think of anything worse than kissing you again."

But he was looking at me differently. Like that kiss hadn't solved anything. Like it had only made the attraction between us stronger. It didn't help that I was lying through my teeth, too.

"Good," I replied. "You better get out of here before my dad comes back."

"Yeah, I guess." He went to the window, but turned back to

me as he climbed out. "I'll see you tomorrow. School cafeteria. Seven a.m."

And then he was gone.

Had that really just happened?

I turned my attention to the box on my bed. Yet another thing I didn't know how to handle. I wasn't sure I was ready to confront my dad about my mom's past. But I couldn't exactly pack the box away and pretend I'd never seen it, either. My mom was more like me than I'd known, and tonight she'd come to life for me in a way I couldn't ignore.

That was the problem with opening boxes that were meant to remain closed. Once you'd seen their contents, there was no going back.

Chapter 27

PARKER

"Good morning, Devils!" I grinned as I stood in front of my teammates. When they didn't reply I blew out a frustrated breath. "You're supposed to say, *good morning, Parker*."

"Dude, what's going on?" Seth asked through a wide yawn.

He wasn't the only one who looked half asleep. It probably wasn't my best idea to call a meeting first thing on a Monday morning. But this conversation with my team couldn't wait.

"Fine. I'll get straight to the point." I paused and held out both hands for a little dramatic effect. "We suck."

"We got out of bed early for *this*?" Cullen groaned.

"Yep. We've lost our first three games this season, and it's not good enough."

"Not *all* of us suck..." Elliot pushed his way to the front of the group. "I'll be back in the number one jersey soon. That'll make all the difference."

"This isn't about any one player, Ford," I replied.

"Yeah, right," he scoffed before glancing obviously at Mackenzie.

I started to respond, but Mackenzie got there first.

"You're still hobbling around in a boot, Ford. All you've proved this season is that you know how to throw an average party. Besides, this is a team sport. We win and lose as a team."

Elliot sneered, but he didn't try to argue. How could he when it was true? A few mutters of agreement sounded amongst the guys.

My eyes flickered in her direction. I'd been doing my best not to look Mackenzie's way this morning. When I did, I was only reminded about how amazing last night had been and how badly I wanted to kiss her again. I'd never felt like this around any girl before. She made me lose control, and more than that, she made me want to lose control again and again.

She was still scowling at Elliot, but when she caught me looking her expression blanked, and she nodded for me to continue. It was as if our mind-blowing kiss had never even happened. Maybe she really had gotten me out of her system. Meanwhile, mine clearly needed another attempt to fully reboot.

"You were saying?" Seth prompted.

"Right." I cleared my throat as I focused on the rest of the group. "I was saying that we *all* need to improve. Anyone who thinks they don't, please feel free to go back to bed, but don't bother showing up for practice tonight. Like Mackenzie said, this is a team sport. Right now, we're not playing like a team."

"Bit rich coming from you, Parker," Elliot piped up again.

"What?"

"You're like a one-man show out there," he continued. "Maybe try passing instead of shooting all the time."

I nodded. "You're right." A few mumbles rippled around the group and Ford looked surprised. "You're right," I said again. "I need to work on being a better teammate too. I've been trying too hard to do everything on my own. Score goals, help the defense, be an enforcer; I thought that was how I could best help the team. But it's actually hurting us."

I found myself glancing back at Mackenzie. I wasn't sure how I expected her to react, but when I saw her smiling at me, I felt more confident.

"Every one of you has a job to do out on the ice. And the best teams trust each other to do those jobs. But I haven't been doing that. None of us have."

Ford looked like he wanted to object, but my admission seemed to have stunned him into silence. More players were beginning to nod in agreement, although some still seemed unsure.

"We have less than two weeks until the homecoming game," I continued. "I don't want to lose to those Sunshine Hills jerks. Do you?"

The mutters of agreement grew louder.

"We're already training hard," Owen said.

"That's true," I replied. "Everyone is working hard at practice. But I'm talking about things that make us a stronger team *off* the ice. Over the next two weeks, I want us doing everything together. We sit together in the classes we share. We eat lunch together. Play video games together, hit the gym, go for a run, have a skate. I don't care what it is, we all need to spend time with *every* member of the team."

"You want us to hold hands and share feelings?" someone yelled from the back.

"If it helps you learn to communicate better, I don't care if you braid each other's hair and give piggyback rides."

Most of the players chuckled. I was beginning to feel like they were getting the message.

"Look, we have nothing to lose by trying this. I know I'm

asking a lot, but you're all great hockey players, and we're the state champions. If we're not winning games, then something must be missing. Maybe it's this."

The guys were all eyeing each other with some suspicion, as if this must be some kind of trick.

"So, who's with me?"

A few of them shrugged, but then I saw heads nodding. Eventually, Owen started clapping, and soon everyone else joined in. Seth even let out a surprisingly enthusiastic, "Let's do this!"

I blinked back my surprise. Had I actually gotten through to them?

"Okay, okay," I said, quietening them down. "I'm glad you guys are on board, because in honor of our commitment to being a better team, I've set up a little exercise. We need to mark ourselves with a visible reminder of our newfound unity and dedication to the team and each other."

There were even more looks of suspicion now.

"We're getting tattoos?" Owen asked, horror in his eyes.

"Well, that *was* my first idea," I replied with a smirk. "But no . . ." I waved toward the table behind me and everyone looked on in confusion. "We're making friendship bracelets."

The way my teammates stared at me, I thought they would have preferred to get tattoos. Their expressions ranged from shock and uncertainty to amusement and even disgust. But I was completely serious.

"Friendship bracelets?" Seth asked.

"That's right."

"This is stupid." Elliot laughed. "We're not Swifties."

The guys all turned to look at him, and I wondered if each of them was thinking the same thing.

But Seth stepped toward the table. "Speak for yourself, Ford. *Reputation* always gets me pumped before a game."

His words seemed to spark the rest of the team into action, and once he'd pulled out a chair and sat down, the guys all moved to follow him. Elliot stayed rooted to the spot, watching all the other players find a seat and get started on their bracelets.

"Seriously?" he asked, his tone incredulous. "This is ridiculous." When nobody acknowledged him, Elliot turned and marched from the room as quickly as his boot would allow.

"Friendship bracelets?" Mackenzie came to stand beside me, and I was instantly aware of just how much space separated us.

"Hey, it was your idea."

"I was joking," she replied. "Besides, we only talked about this last night. You just happened to have a friendship bracelet kit at home?"

"I have a sister, don't I?"

"She doesn't really seem the type."

"She's not." Cammie would never wear something as bright and colorful as the beads on these bracelets. "It was a Christmas present she never opened."

"I knew it." Mackenzie flashed me a satisfied smile. "So, you going to make me a friendship bracelet then?"

"Nope."

"Why not?"

I leaned in close. "Because I don't want to be your friend, Mackenzie."

Her eyes widened, but I walked away before I could say anything else we might both wish I hadn't. I went to join the rest of the team making bracelets, taking a seat next to Owen. Despite their initial uncertainty, everyone seemed to be embracing the idea now, and were already passing completed bracelets to each other. We had about an hour before we had to get to class, and by the time we were done, I had five bracelets gracing my wrist.

Each of them was different. Seth gave me one that alternated red and white beads to match our team's colors. Jansen included my number and a few devil emojis. Cullen gave me one that was such a random collection of colors I had to assume he'd just picked the beads closest to him on the table. Another bracelet, which had been thrown across the table at me, attempted to spell out my name but could only manage 'Parka.' I hoped its designer had just run out of letters.

Mackenzie's wrists were both covered. I shouldn't have been surprised so many guys wanted to make her one. I watched her laugh as she exchanged bracelets with Seth, and I couldn't stop myself smiling with her. There was no guarantee this whole bonding thing would help our team beat the Sunshine Hills Saints, but if it helped Mackenzie feel like she belonged a little more, then it would be worth it.

When the bell rang and we all got up to leave, the guys were still laughing and chatting together, and it continued as we moved out of the cafeteria. It gave me hope this might actually pay off.

"Don't forget, I want to see you all making an effort to spend time with your teammates, today and all week!" I raised my voice to be heard over their chatter as everyone filed out of the room.

Owen appeared beside me and handed me a bracelet. "Couldn't leave without giving you one too."

I frowned down at the bracelet. "GYB?"

"Got your back," he replied.

"Thanks, Cleaver."

As he walked on ahead, I smiled and slid the bracelet into place on my wrist with the others.

A few of the other guys nodded as they passed or flashed their colorful wrists at me, but not Mackenzie. She left quickly, keeping her head down. And while the air fizzed between us as she moved beyond me and out the door, it wasn't the electric zing I'd gotten used to. It felt like the beat of an icy wind, which quickly seeped into my bones and left me on edge. She'd spoken to me earlier like everything was fine, but now something was clearly wrong. Was this about last night?

I followed after her, pushing through the growing crowd of students making their way through the school corridors. "Hey, Mackenzie!"

Either she couldn't hear me over the throng of the crowd, or she was ignoring me, because she continued forging on.

"Mackenzie, wait up!"

Again, she didn't stop, so I jogged to catch up, and when I fell into step alongside her, she kept her eyes looking straight ahead.

"What's going on?"

Silence.

"I know it may seem like I know everything. But, funnily enough, sometimes I don't. If I do something wrong, you need to tell me."

"It's nothing," she said, still marching down the hallway. "Everything's fine."

"Then why are you ignoring me?"

"I'm not."

"Good, so you *will* talk to me." I gently took her arm to stop her, and she reluctantly turned to face me.

"I have to get to class," she said.

"Just for a minute." I could see the nearest classroom was empty, so I waved toward the door. "In private?"

She gave a small nod and allowed me to guide her into the room. I closed the door behind us, and she went to lean on the teacher's desk. She folded her arms and glared at me. It was far sexier than any girl had a right to look, especially at school.

"So . . ." I said.

"So?" she shot right back.

"Clearly you're annoyed about our kiss . . ."

She scoffed and shook her head. "I'm not annoyed about our kiss. Like I said, it was just a way to get you out of my system. Mission accomplished."

Not for me.

"So, if it's not the kiss then . . ."

Her eyes lowered to the floor. I waited, knowing she'd have to break eventually. I'd happily wait all morning for her to tell me the truth.

Finally she sighed and looked back at me. "Is being my

friend really such a terrible prospect?" she asked. "Do you really despise me so much?"

"No." I took an instinctive step toward her. "I don't despise you at all." The emotion in her words had taken me by surprise, but the truth in my own shocked me even more.

"But you still don't want to be friends with me. Can't even bring yourself to make me a stupid bracelet." She shook her wrist in front of me, the beads our teammates had given her rattling against one another.

I closed the remaining distance between us and reached up to take hold of her wrist. "I can't bring myself to make you a bracelet because I'm selfish. If I made you a bracelet, I'd want mine to be the only one on here."

She stilled.

"That kiss might have gotten me out of your system, but you're still completely consuming mine. So, no, I don't want to be your friend, Mackenzie. I don't want to be your friend. I want *more*—and I hate it."

She stared up at me, but I couldn't tell what she was thinking; whether she was about to run from the room or pull me closer like she did last night. Her face was a battlefield of uncertainty, and her gaze seemed to flicker between defiance and desire.

"Would it really be such a bad idea if we gave in one more time?" I murmured, dropping my hand from her wrist and placing it on the desk beside her.

"Terrible," she whispered back. Her hand was still hovering in the air, but she slowly lowered it until it was lightly resting on my chest. The air between us hummed as her eyes dipped to my lips. We were standing so close, and it took every ounce of resistance in me not to bridge the small gap separating us.

"Tell me what you're thinking," I murmured.

Her breath turned shallow as her gaze lifted once again. "I'm thinking that, maybe, you're not out of my system yet either."

I had no idea who moved first, but her lips were against mine in an instant. I gathered her face in my hands as I deepened the kiss, and she wrapped her arms around me. Still, every part of me wanted her closer. It was just as intense as our kiss last night. Every bit as overwhelming and overpowering. God, how I loved getting burned when it was Mackenzie lighting the match.

Someone cleared their throat behind me. Mackenzie jolted back, but I was far less eager to pull away. With an irritated sigh, I turned to the door.

A terrified-looking freshman was poking his head through the entrance. "Uh, is this English class?" he stammered.

Mackenzie's cheeks were bright red. My lips twitched and I struggled not to laugh.

"No idea," Mackenzie replied. "We were just leaving."

She practically dragged me from the room. I'd never seen her move so fast before. Not even when she was chasing down the school bus.

As soon as we were in the corridor, she whacked me on the arm. "You think that was funny?"

"I mean, it was kind of funny."

"It was not." My smile faded when I realized just how much she was freaking out. "What if it wasn't some kid who walked in on us?" she went on. "What if it were one of our teammates? They're *finally* starting to accept me."

As she continued, the panic in her voice grew. "Or what if it was a teacher? What if my dad heard about this? He wouldn't even give me another game to prove myself. I'd be kicked off the team, for sure."

Her words hit me like a bucket of cold water. My reasons for staying away from Mackenzie had originally been to protect my place on the team. But I had her place to worry about, too. I didn't want the guys to think less of her for being with me. And while I might be happy to risk Coach Foster's wrath myself, I didn't want to be the reason Mackenzie was banned from playing the game she loved. Not again.

We both went quiet, but I could tell from the look in her eyes that she'd come to the same conclusion as me.

"Don't say it," I murmured.

But she didn't hesitate. "That can't happen again."

Maybe I didn't enjoy the pain she brought me after all.

"It's out of our system now," she continued. "It has to be."

I didn't have a choice but to agree. Neither of us did.

I rubbed my face and let out a groan. "Guess I better go make one more friendship bracelet then."

Chapter 28
PARKER

I knew Mackenzie and I had agreed not to kiss again, but it was all I could think about for the next few days. I wondered if Coach Foster could read minds, because he pulled me aside after our practice on Thursday and I prepared for the worst.

"Nice work today, Twelve."

It took a second for his words to register. "What?"

I must not have heard him correctly. I felt like I'd been playing well below my level this week. Maybe because I'd spent too much time focusing on how the rest of the team was doing, and not enough on my own performance.

"You made some nice plays out there," Foster said.

I really couldn't work this guy out. Maybe I was dreaming. Though if I was, I'd rather dream up a world where Mackenzie hadn't skipped training with me for the third time in a row that morning. Things wouldn't be awkward between us. And we certainly wouldn't be trying to just be friends.

She was coming off the ice right then and I couldn't focus on what else Coach Foster was saying. Mackenzie pulled her helmet from her head, sweat making her hair stick to her face. She looked exhausted from a hard practice, and yet my heart only beat harder at the sight of her.

I'd noticed a big improvement in her game this week. In fact, the whole team had impressed me. Our sessions seemed more intense, with players working harder than ever. And Mackenzie was benefiting. Our teammates were putting far more heat on their shots, shouting words of support and encouragement, and listening to her instructions on defense without hesitation. Maybe team bonding was actually working.

She looked over and caught me watching. She didn't smile, but she didn't frown either. When our eyes met, I felt desire burning low in my gut. But there was also another, more powerful sensation. A stupidly warm feeling bubbling up in my chest. One that made me want to do something—*anything*—to make her smile.

"Are you listening, Twelve?"

My eyes shot back to Coach Foster, who was glancing between Mackenzie and me with suspicion.

"You don't need a reminder to stay away from my daughter, do you?"

I most definitely did, but I quickly shook my head. "Don't worry, Coach. She'd rather punch me again than come near me."

"*Again?*"

"Uh . . . it was just a misunderstanding."

"What kind of misunderstanding?" he growled.

Shit. Shit. Shit. He looked like he wanted to kill me. Upside: if I survived, Coach Foster would go to prison, and Mackenzie and I could live happily ever after. Downside: I might end up dead.

"Parker returned my keys to me in the parking lot," Mackenzie said, appearing beside us. "It was dark. I got scared and punched him. No big deal."

That was easy enough for her to say. She wasn't the one on the receiving end. Still, I was relieved she'd explained so

I didn't have to.

Foster rubbed the bridge of his nose like we'd both just aged him ten years. "Why didn't I know about this?"

Mackenzie stiffened. "You don't tell *me* everything, Dad."

She turned and walked away before he could reply. It was obvious Mackenzie was referring to the secret she'd discovered about her mom, but judging by the confused look on her dad's face, he clearly had no idea. I made a quick exit before his confusion turned to frustration and he took it out on me.

I caught up to Mackenzie before she reached the girls' locker room.

"Hey," I said, stopping beside her. "Thanks for getting me out of that."

She turned to look at me. If I was a dog, I was pretty sure my tail would have been wagging simply because she glanced my way.

"It's what friends do, right?"

Friends. I preferred it when she hated my guts. I'd spent years watching Grayson in the friend zone with Paige, and I'd do just about anything to avoid that hellhole. I'd take a warzone with Mackenzie over the friendzone any day.

"Right," I grunted. "How was your run this morning?"

Despite the fact she'd been finding reasons to train without me, she hadn't stopped putting in extra sessions. At first, she'd insisted she could go to the weights room alone. Then she set up a session for herself with Seth and Owen. Today, it had been a run. I knew exactly why she was doing it, but I hated it all the same.

"Uh, yeah, it went well." She glanced away, watching as

some of our teammates passed us. It was for the best if we didn't spend time together. I'd merely looked in her direction tonight and her dad had started freaking out. Even now, I probably shouldn't be talking to her, but I couldn't seem to resist.

"Things don't have to be weird between us," I told her. "You know that, right?"

"Yeah, I know."

"Because I think training together is important. You still want to prove your dad wrong, don't you?"

"Of course I do." Finally, she looked at me again.

Mackenzie really had improved thanks to our work together. I didn't want to let a little awkwardness jeopardize her chances of staying on the team. And while it was a little selfish, I was also looking for any reason I could to spend time with her.

"So, we'll meet at the rink as usual tomorrow morning?"

She hesitated.

"I promise I won't try to kiss you again."

That pulled a gentle smile from her lips. "Okay. Tomorrow morning."

I was distracted as her dad walked into view further down the corridor. He was deep in conversation with his assistant coach, so he didn't see us. He soon disappeared around a corner, but I could feel Mackenzie tense at my side.

"What you said to your dad before," I started cautiously. "Have you talked to him about your mom yet?"

"No," she murmured, looking at the floor. "I'm still trying to wrap my mind around it. I don't even know what I'd say."

"Dumping the box on his desk and asking, 'what the hell is this?' could be a good place to start."

"Yeah, probably." Her shoulders sagged. "It's hard. I'm still on probation. He's barely talking to me."

"I know."

"I'm not sure I even want to hear what he has to say," she continued, more firmly this time. "And I'm a little scared of how I might react." She shook her head, almost as though she was disappointed in herself. "I don't know. I'll talk to him eventually. I just want to focus on getting ready for the next game."

"I get it. But if you need anyone to talk to . . ."

Her mouth started to curve. "You want me to spill all my deep dark feelings to *you*?"

I moved closer, our proximity causing my chest to thump. "That's what friends do, right?"

"Right." She nodded, but I could have sworn her smile faltered slightly.

She started to turn away, but before she could disappear inside the girls' locker room, I said, "I'm organizing a team party on Saturday night. It's at Cullen's family lake house."

"Sounds fun," she replied. "For you guys, at least. There's no way my dad will let me go."

"Then don't tell him."

"You're a bad influence, you know that?"

"Are you only just figuring that out now?" I grinned at her before walking away.

My bravado only lasted until she was out of sight, and then I found myself slumping with a sense of defeat. Why couldn't I just forget we'd kissed and move on like I had every other time I'd kissed a girl? Why was it so hard to stay away from her?

I didn't do girlfriends or dates or commitment; I never had. And yet, it bothered me that those things weren't an option for us. I should probably be grateful. Even if we could be together, Mackenzie and I would likely kill each other. Still, I couldn't ignore the small voice deep inside that thought maybe we'd be perfect together.

*

"I talked to my stepmom." Mackenzie took a seat beside me near the end of our art class on Friday. Her arm brushed against me as she did, and I tried my best to ignore the trail of warmth it left behind.

We'd trained together before school today for the first time that week, but she'd convinced Owen to come along too. I'd been annoyed at first. I didn't like third wheels, especially when I felt like the third. And it wasn't as though Mackenzie and I needed supervising. Then again, I was sure she'd returned a few of my heated looks, so maybe it was a good thing Owen had been there.

"I told her I'm having a sleepover at Jaz's house tomorrow," Mackenzie continued. "And she was only too happy to say yes. So, I'm in for the team party."

"That's great." I struggled to hide the excitement in my voice.

"But just a heads up," she continued. "Jaz fully intends to gatecrash. She claims I need a chaperone with all you boys around."

"Sure, Jaz is more than welcome."

She nodded at my tablet. "How's your project coming along?"

"Good." Although I was happy to change the subject, I pulled my tablet away so she couldn't see the screen. "But it's not finished yet."

"Are you . . ." Mackenzie tilted her head, her eyes dancing with amusement. "Are you, Parker Darling, hockey superstar, too shy to show me your work?"

My attempt to hide it from her hadn't been subtle, and, if anything, it had only made her more intrigued. There was no way I was letting her near it until it was finished though—perhaps not even then.

"Totally shy," I replied. "Then again, I probably should have thought twice before deciding to paint myself naked."

"You're joking?"

"Nope." I jumped from my seat. "But I'm glad you've finally realized you're in the presence of greatness. Hockey superstar; I liked the sound of that."

"Where are you going?" she asked.

"To see what Mr. Green thinks."

"You're happy to show *him* your naked self-portrait?"

"It's art, Mackenzie. He can see beyond my chiseled abs."

Her gaze instinctively dipped to my stomach, but she quicky returned her attention to her desk. I was smiling to myself as I made my way to the back of the room and knocked on the door to Mr. Green's paint-closet office.

I poked my head into the room. "Mr. Green, do you have a sec?"

"Sure." He gestured for me to enter, so I eased myself into the tiny space and sat in the chair across from him. I felt far more nervous than I'd expected.

"What can I help you with, Parker?"

"Uh, I wanted to run my project past you. I've made a few changes since last time."

"Excellent." He held out his hands, and I passed him my tablet.

I wasn't nervous because there was a naked drawn selfie on the page. No, that might have almost been easier. I was nervous because, for the first time, my art actually felt inspired by something—by someone. And I worried I hadn't done them justice. That I was too much of an idiot to ever capture something that mattered and illustrate it in a way that could mean something.

Mr. Green was silent as he looked over my work, and my fingers dug into the edge of my seat as I waited.

"So, what do you think?" I'd never been very patient.

Mr. Green was frowning at my tablet but then he lifted his eyes to mine. "You've chosen a new main character for your comic. No more hockey-playing superhero?"

His brow was creased, and he looked as though he had many more questions to ask. As I suspected, he thought it was stupid. But training with Mackenzie had sparked an idea, and I hadn't been able to let it go.

"Yeah." I swallowed, trying to sound confident. It was probably the dumbest thing he'd ever seen. "I've taken it in a different direction. I've only done the first couple of pages, but I've already mapped out the rest of the story."

Mr. Green shook his head at me but was still smiling. "It's definitely original, and it shows some promise. The panels flow nicely, the line work is clean, and I love how expressive the characters are. I think with a few tweaks it could be really strong. Can you tell me a bit more about your inspiration? What message are you trying to convey?"

For once, I knew exactly what I wanted to say with my art, but explaining my newly discovered deep thoughts to my teacher wasn't so easy. "I guess I just felt like maybe you don't have to be a superhero to inspire and help people. Anyone can do that. And sometimes it's the people who are always underestimated that surprise you the most." I shook my head. "Sorry, I'm not sure if that makes any sense."

"No, it does," Mr. Green nodded, his eyes still drifting over my illustrations. "I like it. You're demonstrating how people can be more than meets the eye."

"Yeah, something like that," I murmured. I was used to receiving a lot of praise when it came to hockey, but somehow getting a compliment from Mr. Green about my art hit differently.

He handed the tablet back to me. "I look forward to seeing more."

"You do?" I did little to hide my surprise and I quickly cleared my throat. "I mean, great, thanks."

"And I'd like you to try and complete it by next Friday. I'd love to include it in the exhibition we're displaying at the Ransom Community Center."

"Really?"

"Yes, I think it would be a great addition."

The bell rang as I left his office, and I was still reeling as I packed up my things.

"So, Mr. Green liked your naked selfie?" Mackenzie asked as we left the room.

"Yeah," I replied. "I think he did."

"Wait, you didn't actually draw yourself naked, did you?"

"I guess you'll find out when it's finished."

I started off down the hallway and was surprised when Mackenzie stayed by my side. She was supposed to be avoiding me.

"You're walking with me," I pointed out.

"We're headed in the same direction."

"You also talked to me in class."

"I figured I should tell you I can come to the party this weekend."

"I thought you were trying to stay away from me."

"It's harder than you think," she murmured.

We reached her locker, and she pulled it open. I leaned against the locker next to hers.

"I like it when you walk with me and talk to me," I said. "I like it when you're kissing me too."

She pushed her locker shut. "You said I was out of your system."

"I said I wouldn't try to kiss you again. I never said I didn't want to."

"You don't know how to give up, do you?"

"No, I don't," I agreed. "I've never walked away from something I want. You can keep pretending there's nothing between us; that we're just friends. But just so you know, I'm not going to act like being near you doesn't drive me crazy; I'm not going to pretend that I can't stop thinking about kissing you. I know we agreed it shouldn't happen again. But that doesn't mean I'm going to ignore what I'm feeling."

"It's easier when you pretend," she said in a quiet voice.

"It's not easier for me."

She swallowed, and her green eyes looked hopelessly up at me. "I miss hating you."

"Yeah, I miss it too."

Chapter 29

MACKENZIE

Why was it when one part of your life started to go well, another lost its way entirely? It felt like my extra hockey practices were beginning to pay off. My fitness and my game were improving quickly, I was growing in confidence, and I was feeling more like a valuable part of the team. It was all thanks to Parker. But he was also part of the problem.

We were still training together, but now we'd agreed to be just friends, I had to constantly convince myself I was okay with that. But the pull toward him was undeniable.

He was the main reason I was questioning my sanity when I arrived at the lake house for the team party on Saturday night. The old wooden house was tucked away in a forest of pine trees outside town. Jaz parked her car with the others on the long driveway, and we followed a gravel path flanked by softly lit torches around to the back of the house. A light dusting of snow crunched underfoot, and there was a welcome glow coming from the bonfire that had been built out back.

We were running a little late and most of the team was already here. My gaze immediately went to Parker, who was standing on the far side of the flames. He glanced up at me as I approached and a smile slowly pulled at his lips, making my traitorous heart flutter.

Yeah, I probably should've stayed home.

"We're completely outnumbered," Jaz said as we slowly

made our way to join everyone. "It's a sausage fest."

"What did you expect?" I laughed. "This is a boys' hockey team party."

"I know, I know. I just figured I wouldn't be the only girl to invite myself."

"I'm glad you did."

"Yeah, me too. I don't know how you've managed to survive on your own this long." She grinned. "How *is* the team bonding going?"

"Good, I think." I was certainly feeling closer to my teammates. Some of them had made an effort to sit with me in classes we shared or invited me to their table in the cafeteria. I'd even been roped into a pickup game of basketball one lunch period. It was nice to finally feel accepted, but it also made the prospect of being kicked off the team harder.

"Foster!" Seth called as we neared the fire. A few of the other guys cheered my arrival too and beckoned us to find a seat.

"Certainly seems like it's working," Jaz said as she watched the guys all laughing and joking around the bonfire.

My eyes were drawn back to Parker, who was watching me. His smile always hinted at trouble, but tonight it seemed to also hold a promise: we weren't done. Not by a long shot.

"And you and Parker . . ."

I turned back to Jaz. "Me and Parker, what?"

She twisted her lips as she looked between the two of us. "What's happening with you guys?"

"Nothing. We're just friends."

"Just friends?"

"Yep."

"I thought you hated him."

"I do. I mean, I did."

"You did?" She was eyeing me closely. "What happened?"

"Nothing," I said as innocently as I could. "He's just a bit like a fungus. Irritating, but when you can't get rid of him, he grows on you."

Jaz burst out laughing. "Yeah, I can see that."

"Punch?" Seth asked, coming over to us with a red cup in each hand.

I happily took one, but Jaz looked skeptical. "Is this team-bonding punch or Seth on summer break punch? Because I'm driving."

"I wish it was Seth on summer break punch, but unfortunately it *is* a team-bonding night."

"Sounds great," she said. "Thanks, Seth."

"You're welcome."

"Have we missed anything?" I asked. "I know we're a little late."

"Well, we already did the hair braiding and piggyback races."

"Bummer." I laughed. "Please tell me I didn't miss out on the trust falls."

"No." Seth looked deadly serious. "I think they're coming later."

I glanced back at Parker and found myself wondering, would he catch me if I fell? But I didn't have to question it. I knew he would. When Jaz asked what had happened to make me stop hating Parker, I'd avoided answering because I didn't know what to say. I couldn't pin it to any one moment.

Maybe it was sometime during our endless hours of training, or when he'd defended me during the game against the Chargers. Maybe when he'd climbed the wall of my house just because I hadn't said goodbye and kissed me in my closet as though he'd been waiting years for that very moment. Maybe it had happened further back than that, without me even realizing it, when he'd shown such blind faith in my ability as a hockey player that he smuggled me into his team's tryouts, knowing full well it might completely ruin his reputation with my dad. Whenever it was, I hadn't just stopped hating him. Somewhere along the line, I'd gone and decided to trust him.

"Parker seems pretty intent on getting you guys back to winning ways," Jaz said.

"Parker doesn't know how to lose," Seth replied. "Winning is in his DNA. Plus, he *really* hates the Saints."

"Well, hopefully all this team bonding works."

"I think it will." Seth started to grin. "And if it doesn't, I can happily walk away from the experience knowing at least I got a friendship bracelet from the great Mackenzie Foster."

I smiled. "So, it wasn't all for nothing, then."

"Definitely not."

The music suddenly stopped, and Parker whistled, drawing everyone's attention as he leaped up onto a log. "Thanks, everyone, for being here tonight. You might be pleased to know, there are no set plans for the evening. I'm really proud of the way you've all stepped up this week and embraced team bonding. And how hard you've worked in practice. I know it's all going to pay off next weekend when we crush the Saints."

The boys around the fire cheered loudly in response.

"So, tonight, I just want everyone to hang out and enjoy yourselves."

More cheers rang through the cool night air.

"What about the feelings circle?" Seth called out once everyone quieted down.

Laughter echoed and Parker grinned. "You can share your feelings if you like, Seth."

"Nah, I'm good," he replied.

"Really? Nothing you want to get off your chest?" Parker teased him. "No deep, dark secrets?"

"Well, actually, there is one thing . . ." The corner of Seth's mouth lifted as mischief danced in his eyes. "There's this girl I've got a crush on, but I haven't told anyone."

Intrigued looks appeared on all the boys' faces and whispers rippled through the group.

"Who's the lucky girl?" someone shouted.

"She's a junior," Seth started. "Dark hair. Blue eyes. Kind of mean." He was grinning at Parker now. "Incredible skater. Looks *great* in spandex. She's got three terrifying older brothers, though . . ."

There were a few nervous laughs, as everyone followed Seth's gaze to Parker, who was glaring at his friend.

"I've got some feelings I'd like to share myself," Parker growled. "I think I need a new best friend."

There was more laughter as Seth turned to me. "If you ever want to piss off one of the Darling boys, just check out their sister. They go feral."

"You've got a crush on Cammie?" I asked, shocked.

"No." Seth laughed. "I wouldn't dare. Didn't you see the look on his face? It's just fun to mess with him."

Parker might want a new best friend, but unfortunately for him, I thought he and Seth were perfect for each other.

"Anyone else got some feelings they want to share?" Parker shouted. His eyes met mine, making my heart flutter. But then he turned to the rest of our team to add, "Before I throw Seth in the lake?"

The guys snickered and looked Seth's way. He held up his hands in surrender but was still grinning broadly.

When no one else spoke up, Parker jumped down from the log, the music kicked in again, and the party started for real.

Jaz nudged me. "What's up with Elliot?"

I looked in the direction she nodded and saw Ford sitting on a log with a bunch of other players. He was on the end, looking down into his red cup as though he was wishing it was a bottle of tequila.

Everyone else was chatting and having fun, but Elliot looked like he wished he were anywhere but here. He certainly didn't look interested in team bonding. When Parker had first pitched the idea, Elliot had walked out in a huff, and I hadn't seen him spending any extra time with his teammates. He'd made absolutely no effort with me. I wasn't sure if it was because I was a girl, or because I was playing his position, but the guy clearly didn't like me.

As if he'd heard my thoughts, Elliot glanced up and saw me watching. His eyes narrowed before he stood from the log and walked off.

Jaz nudged me again, but this time when I turned to see

what she was looking at, I found Parker standing there.

He gave me a soft smile. "Hey."

How could one little word feel so powerful? Why could I feel it resonating in the depths of my soul?

"Hey."

His eyes darted to the ground and then back to me. He almost seemed nervous. "You didn't feel like sharing your deep dark secrets?"

I was staring at my biggest one.

"Nope. I'm an open book." I gave Parker a tight smile and moved past him. "I need to refill my drink."

My cup was still full, but I had to get away. All week I'd been trying to keep my distance from Parker. And all week I'd been failing. But the way he was looking at me tonight, I worried I might do something stupid if given half the chance.

I needed to clear my head. So, I placed my cup down on the drinks table and walked beyond the fire. I started down a path that led through the trees toward the lake, leaving the warmth of the party behind me. It was freezing tonight, but I kept moving.

The trees thinned out as I reached the lake and found an old wooden dock. I buried my hands deeper into the pockets of my coat as I stopped to look out at the view. The water was frozen, and with the moonlight shimmering across its surface and a sky full of stars sparkling above, it was the perfect spot to still my mind. And yet, all my thoughts were back at the fire with Parker.

"You must be freezing." I repressed a shiver as he came up behind me, but it had nothing to do with the cold.

"No, I'm fine."

"Here." He placed his jacket over my shoulders.

I eased out a breath as I glanced up at him. "Now you're the one who's going to freeze."

"Nah, I don't really feel the cold. Dad says us Darling boys are part yeti."

"Ah," I nodded. "That explains the hairy feet."

"I don't have hairy feet."

I laughed and shook my head. "You should see your face. I'm only teasing."

He reached up and lightly ran his fingers down a loose strand of my hair. "I like it when you tease me."

"Parker . . ." I warned. "We can't kiss again."

Disappointment clouded his eyes, and he slowly lowered his hand. "Who says I was trying to kiss you?"

I lifted an eyebrow.

"Okay, maybe I was trying to kiss you." He flashed me that damn cheeky smile of his.

"You know we need to stay away from each other."

"Yeah, I don't think that's going particularly well . . ."

"No," I murmured. I pulled my gaze from his and looked across the frozen lake. "It shouldn't be this hard. We don't even like each other."

"You're lying." He touched a hand to my cheek, and my ability to resist him dissolved. I leaned into his touch. When it came to Parker, I was powerless.

"Okay, maybe I like you just a little bit," I admitted.

"Only a little bit?"

"I'd like you more if you never opened your mouth."

He laughed softly and leaned down so his forehead pressed against mine. I was surrounded by the scent of him. By the feel of him. He was pure heat against the icy cold, and I was one wrong move away from getting burned.

"Why'd you follow me out here, Parker?"

"Because I wish things were different." He drew in a breath. "We're going to win our game next week, and your dad's going to put you on the team permanently."

"Isn't that a good thing?"

"Of course. I want that more than anything. But I also know it will only make it harder for us to be together. And I just..." He paused, and I felt his arm wrap gently around my waist. "I guess I just wanted to keep dreaming that things were different a little longer."

"We're alone out here," I replied softly, sliding my hand up to rest on his chest. "Maybe we can pretend just for a while..."

He lightly brushed his lips against mine. My whole body seemed to sigh in response. This was so different than the heated kisses we'd shared before. It was heartbreakingly beautiful and painful all at once, because we knew we weren't just getting it out of our system. We were saying goodbye. One final kiss and we'd be done.

When we broke apart, my chest ached in response. I wasn't ready to let him go. Not even close.

He wasn't either. Barely a second passed before he pulled me against him again. I came happily, eagerly. His hand was in my hair. The other gripping my waist. All softness and hesitation gone, replaced by pure desire.

His kisses made me feel as if my feet no longer touched the

ground. They had my body vibrating like the stars above were igniting beneath my skin. I never wanted this moment to end.

When it did, I was left breathless. *Wrecked*. That kiss had carved a trail of destruction through me, fracturing my resistance into the smallest of pieces.

I took a step away from him. I had to.

"We should head back to the party."

Parker nodded, his gaze still raw. I quickly pulled his jacket from my shoulders and passed it to him before turning from the lake. I hurried up the track toward the bonfire, even more desperate to escape than when I'd first taken the path down to the dock.

Chapter 30

PARKER

I returned to the bonfire, watching as Mackenzie walked ahead. Even now, I couldn't seem to take my eyes off her as she sat on a log with Cullen and Jaz. I wished more than anything I could be next to her. Hell, I'd happily lie on the ground as the log if it meant I could be close by.

Our kiss before had felt final. It had felt like saying farewell to all the things we couldn't be. I knew that my feelings for Mackenzie went far beyond just desire. Staring at her now, I didn't just want to kiss her. No, I wanted to know her thoughts. I wanted all her scowls and smiles. I'd even take her punches, if it meant she could be mine.

I cared about Mackenzie. More than I could have ever thought possible a few weeks ago. And that was why I had to let her go.

"Where did you disappear to?" Owen asked, coming over to me.

"Uh, we needed more firewood."

Owen laughed as he glanced at the roaring bonfire. "I think we probably have enough."

"Yeah, probably," I agreed.

I hated lying, especially about Mackenzie. I didn't want to hide the way I felt. I wanted to shout it from a top floor window of the school. But I couldn't. And the fact Owen had noticed I was missing only confirmed that kissing Mackenzie down by the lake was a mistake. Not because it hurt. But because we could have been caught. It wasn't worth the risk of the rest of the team finding out or word getting back to her dad.

Owen was still smiling as he looked around the party. "Tonight is really great."

"You think?"

"Yeah." He nodded and scratched the back of his neck. "You know, I've spent a lot of time worrying about my place on the team this season," he continued. "Last year, I was always just Matt's younger brother, and I barely got off the bench. I felt like I only made the team because of him. Even without him here, I still felt like I didn't deserve my spot. But spending extra time with everyone outside of practice, getting to know the team, well . . . I guess I just feel a little more part of things, you know?"

My heart warmed, but his words saddened me too. "You deserve your spot on the team just as much as anyone here tonight. You know you've always been a big part of things for me, right?"

"Yeah, I know."

"Also, I always thought of Matt as just *your* older brother. Not the other way around."

"I'm sure that's not true," he said, though he gave a shy smile. "Anyway, I just thought you should know that even if we don't win next week, what you've done for the team, it's made a difference to me. Even if Coach Foster can't see it, you're the one who's leading the team. You're *our* captain."

I cleared my throat, which for some reason felt like it was closing up. "Thanks, man. I think we just aced team bonding. Do we hug now?"

Owen laughed and batted my outstretched arms away. "No, I think I'm good."

"Thank God."

A few of the guys called him over, but Owen hesitated.

"Go," I encouraged. "If you compliment me again, I might just cry."

"Darling Devils don't cry," he said with a laugh, before heading to join our teammates.

It was a little bittersweet hearing the name. I wasn't sure I was a big bad Darling Devil anymore. With my brothers gone, I was just Parker. And I was beginning to feel okay with that.

Instead of rejoining the group I went over to where Seth was leaning on a tree watching the roaring fire.

"I'm still looking for a new best friend," I told him. "But lucky for you, the lake's frozen solid, so I can't throw you in."

He didn't look at all concerned. "You couldn't possibly replace me."

"I feel like Owen would do a pretty good job. Bonus, he's terrified of most girls and wouldn't dare hit on my sister."

"I didn't hit on your sister. I just said she's hot."

"You really don't like living, do you?"

Seth laughed. "Owen's too nice. He couldn't survive being your best friend."

"Yeah, you're probably right. I guess I'm stuck with you."

"I guess so."

We both stared at the crackling flames. Standing with my friend, the sounds of the team's laughter filling the air, was almost peaceful. At least, as peaceful as I could feel with Mackenzie sat only a short distance away.

"So, Elliot's been causing trouble again," Seth eventually said.

"What now?"

"He tried to stage a walkout a little while ago. Said the party sucked. I'm surprised he even showed up, to be honest. He hasn't exactly been acting like part of the team."

"Huh. Did anyone go with him?"

"Nope, he left on his own." Seth paused and turned to look at me. "Wait, did you miss all this? I didn't realize you were gone that long. Where have you been?"

"Uh, firewood," I muttered. Was it just Seth and Owen who had noticed I'd disappeared or was everyone else onto us too?

"Yeah, your hair's giving real I've-been-collecting-firewood vibes."

I could still feel the way Mackenzie had gripped the ends of my hair as we kissed. Damn, that was hot. My hands itched to run through my hair and tame it. But I resisted. "Don't lie, my hair's fine."

"Was Mackenzie 'collecting firewood' too?"

"Uh..."

Seth lowered his voice. "You know you're not supposed to be making out with her in the woods, right?"

"Since when are you the voice of reason?"

"Since you went and lost all of yours."

"It's fine. It was the last time."

"Yeah, sure."

"It was." I tried to sound convincing.

"I don't want to tell you what to do," Seth continued. "But you should probably stop before it gets out of hand."

I had a bad feeling that it already had.

"There are other girls," he added with a shrug.

I didn't want other girls. I wanted the girl that pissed me off. The girl who called me on my shit. The girl who laughed or threw a middle finger up when I called her on hers. I wanted the girl who was fiery and determined. The girl who took up so much space in my head, even when she wasn't around, it was a miracle I could think of anything else.

So, no, there weren't other girls. There was only her.

"Whatever, man," I said. "I'm not focused on girls right now, anyway."

Seth snorted.

"What?"

"Dude, you're always focused on girls."

"That was before Mackenzie."

He shook his head, his eyes filled with concern. "Shit, you really like her."

I paused as I looked at him. "Have you ever hated a song the first time you heard it?" I said. "And the more it comes on the radio, the more it drives you insane? But then, after a while, you start humming it everywhere you go. You know all the words. It's on all your playlists. And somehow, despite everything you thought before, it becomes your favorite song?"

"Uh . . ."

"Mackenzie's my song. And I have no idea what I'm going to do."

Seth didn't have a witty retort this time, just a look of sympathy. "You do what's best for her," he said. "You walk away."

I didn't answer. Instead, I stole Seth's cup of punch and

downed it, wishing for a moment that it was spiked. I could still feel the heat from my last kiss with Mackenzie coursing through me, and I hoped the drink might wash the sensation away. I knew I needed to let her go. But hearing it from Seth made it all too real.

I spent the rest of the party hanging out with my other teammates, making sure to talk to every player. I knew I'd started this whole bonding thing to give us a shot at turning this season around. But I also really liked the guys I played with, and the more I got to know them, the more I wanted to spend time with them outside of practice. Friendship had never really entered the equation for me when it came to hockey, but I had to admit, it wasn't the worst thing.

When the party started to die down, and people began to go their separate ways, I walked to my truck with Seth. Mackenzie, Jaz, and Owen were just behind us. It was the closest I'd been to Mackenzie since we kissed. I'd been avoiding her. And she'd done the same to me. But a quiet ache settled in my chest at the thought of letting her leave without saying goodbye.

Before we reached my truck, I handed Seth my keys. "I'll be right back."

Seth glanced over his shoulder at Mackenzie. "Be good," he warned.

I turned and jogged back toward her before I could think better of it. "Hey, Mackenzie, got a sec?"

She hesitated a moment before sharing a look with Jaz.

"I'll meet you at the car," Jaz said, as if she knew exactly what Mackenzie was thinking. Owen gave me an encouraging smile before he followed his sister further up the path.

"Can I give you a ride home?" I asked, when Mackenzie turned to face me. Maybe I wasn't going to behave after all.

But she shook her head. "Thanks, but I'm staying at Jaz's house tonight."

"Ah, of course." It was probably for the best. I really wanted to do the right thing by her—no matter how hard it might be.

"Was that what you wanted to talk about, or..." Mackenzie's voice drifted off.

Before I could reconsider, I reached into my pocket and pulled out the friendship bracelet I'd made. I weighed it in my hand a moment, desperately not wanting to give it to her but knowing that I should.

With a sigh I held it out to her. "I made this for you."

She frowned. "Is that a friendship bracelet?"

"Yeah. I said I was going to make you one."

She hesitated. She knew exactly what this meant. It was my acceptance of the fact we could only be friends. "You've had this with you all night?"

"I've had it with me for days."

Sadness flickered across her face. But then she reached out to take the bracelet, and my heart cracked at the edges.

"Thank you," she murmured, turning it over in her hands. She gave me a sad smile as she peered up at me. "Why'd you go with the green beads?"

"It's my favorite color." Never more so than right now, as I stared into her eyes.

"And the letters? What does RWYA stand for?"

"They were out of P's, 4's, and M's."

"Seriously, Parker."

"It means ready when you are."

"Ready when I am?" Her voice was barely louder than a whisper.

"I know being with me could mess with our places on the hockey team. But I also know that a few obstacles have never scared me before."

I drew in a deep breath before I continued, "I would sneak around with you, if you wanted. I would shout about us from the rooftops, if you asked. But you deserve to be with someone who isn't some secret. And you shouldn't have to worry about your place on the team. Our timing is terrible. But I refuse to discount tomorrow, or the next day, or the day after that. Even if it's months from now, or years, I'm ready when you are. Just give me that bracelet back, and I'm happy to say to hell with everything else."

Her eyes glistened and she stared down at the bracelet. But then she ever so slowly slid it onto her wrist. It was the right decision, but it felt like a punch to the gut.

"See you for training Monday morning?" she said.

"Yeah, I'll see you then."

I'd really thought it wouldn't be too hard to give her the bracelet. That once she had it, I could simply move on. But there was a hollowness inside me that hadn't been there earlier tonight.

As I watched her walk away with the bracelet, I felt something else leaving me. A sense of hope. Of excitement for what might be possible. Everything about this was tough, but I thought that might be the hardest part.

Chapter 31

MACKENZIE

I wasn't sure if it was the bonfire, the bracelets or all the extra time we'd spent together, but I felt a tangible shift in our team practices the next week. We were playing better and enjoying it more. Even my dad threatened to break into a smile.

"Nice work tonight, everyone," he said, clapping his hands as he called us together at the end of our Thursday night session. "You're starting to look like a real team. Keep this up and we'll start winning again."

I glanced in Parker's direction. And I wasn't the only one. We all knew the improvements were thanks to him. He was smiling as he listened to my dad, but didn't seem to notice the recognition from his teammates, as though all that mattered to him was ensuring the team became the best it could be.

"Rest up tonight, you know how important the big homecoming game is tomorrow," Dad added, with a confident smile.

As the team started to disperse, he pulled Owen aside, and I overheard their conversation as I passed. "Why have you all been wearing those bracelets the past two weeks?"

Owen grinned and nodded in Parker's direction. "Maybe you should ask him."

Dad only frowned before grunting and walking off the ice. He didn't ask Parker anything. Not that I was surprised.

When I got home that evening, I went straight up to my

room as usual. My dad might have made it clear that he was pleased with the team's efforts at practice, but he hadn't said anything to me about my performance, or my chances of surviving probation. We still weren't talking, even though I had plenty of questions for him.

I sat on my bed and pulled the picture of my mom and her hockey team out from under my pillow. As much as I needed answers, I wasn't sure I wanted to hear them yet. It didn't stop me from wondering why Dad had kept this from me all these years, though.

There was a knock at the door, and I stuffed the picture back under the pillow as Tessa poked her head into my room.

"When we first moved into this house, I didn't realize it came with its very own ghost," she said. "I've always wanted to live in a place that's haunted."

I laughed softly. "Sorry, Tessa. I realize I haven't been around much."

She walked across the room and sat on the bed beside me. "I know you're having a hard time with your dad," she said. "He won't talk about it with me, either. I get that hockey is important to you both, but this has got to stop."

Tessa couldn't have known the issue was about more than just hockey now. It felt like there was a gaping chasm between me and my dad. One I didn't even know how to begin to cross.

"I don't know what to say to him," I admitted.

"Will you try?" she asked. "I know he's stubborn, but this is never going to get better if you two don't talk." She took in a breath to compose herself. "Just think about it," she added.

I nodded.

Her expression was thoughtful when she looked back at me. "Do you know how proud I am of you, Kenzie? It's hard enough to go after the things we want in life. But it feels impossible when we don't have support from the people we love most. Keep going, honey. I know your dad will come around eventually. And in the meantime, know that I'm cheering for you."

I smiled up at her. "Thanks, Tessa."

As she left my room, I pulled out the picture of my mom again. Maybe Tessa was right. This was something I couldn't hide from. Something he couldn't hide from either. It was time to talk.

I headed down to my dad's office, clutching the picture, nerves running up and down my skin and making my hands shake. Hovering outside his slightly open door, I wondered for a moment if I was brave enough. I didn't usually back down from anything, but seeing my mom in hockey gear just like me simply meant too much. I didn't want anything my dad might say to ruin it for me.

"Mackenzie?" Dad called out. "That you out there?"

I stepped into the doorway. "Yeah, it's me."

He hesitated when he saw me, like he was uncertain how to start. When his eyes caught on the bracelets on my wrist, he nodded at them. "Can you explain why you're all wearing those?"

I instinctively reached out to touch them. It almost felt like the one Parker had given me was burning against my skin. It didn't belong there. But I couldn't take it off.

"Parker had us make them."

"He did?" Dad sounded confused. He was probably worried

they were a sign of Parker leading a team rebellion against him.

"Yeah, he called the team together last week and told us our communication on the ice needed to improve. So, we've been working on team bonding outside of practice."

Dad's eyes widened. "Why didn't I know about this?"

"Maybe because you make it hard for the team to trust you," I said. "You have me on probation. Parker's convinced that if he looks at me wrong, you'll bench him, and yet he's been helping me train anyway."

"What are you talking about?" Dad growled.

"Well, I wasn't getting any support from my coaches, was I?" I snapped. "And Parker will do anything to help the team win. He's a clear leader, but you still haven't named him captain. Why? Because I kissed him a few years ago?"

"This isn't about that. Parker Darling only cares about his own game. He's not captain material."

"He cares about the team more than anyone!" I threw my hands in the air. "And if you just opened your eyes for one moment, you'd see it."

"You're not a coach, Mackenzie. You don't see the same things we do. You're looking at that boy through tainted lenses."

"I thought you said this wasn't about the fact we kissed." I shook my head. "Why are you still so hung up on that?"

This time, my dad didn't have a response. Instead, he glanced away.

I shook my head. "I came in here hoping we could have an open conversation, but yet again, you're closing up on me. Just like always." I marched up to his desk and put the picture of my mom down in front of him. "What lie are you going to tell me about this? Or will you just not say anything, yet again?"

He stilled as he stared down at the picture. Ever so slowly, as though his body was resisting, he reached out and gently gathered the frame in his hands. "Where did you get this?"

There was no longer anger or argument in his voice. Instead, it was replaced by a tone I'd rarely heard from my dad before—pain.

"The wrong moving box was in my room. It was filled with Mom's things."

He nodded, his eyes still unable to pull away from the picture.

"Why didn't you tell me she played hockey?" I did my best to stop my voice from breaking as I spoke.

Finally, my dad managed to lift his gaze, and I was surprised to find grief pooling quietly in his eyes. "She wouldn't have wanted you to know."

My heart ached at his words. "Why?"

He didn't answer.

"Please, Dad. You can't shut me out of this."

"I know." He closed his eyes, as if he was taking a second to gather himself. When he opened them again, I could have sworn they were glistening slightly. "I just wasn't sure when we'd have this conversation, if ever. But, it's probably long overdue." He walked around from behind his desk and leaned against the front of it. "Have I ever told you how your mom and I met?"

"Uh, yeah, I guess. At college, right?"

"That's right," he said, with a rare warm smile. "I was walking through campus one day and saw she had climbed a tree to rescue a cat. The cat was okay, but your mom was stuck. I went to help her get down and she fell right on top of me. She was so beautiful, I pretty much fell in love at first sight."

I listened carefully. He'd never told the full story before, and I longed to hear more.

"I soon learned Abby was also bold and smart and kind and so incredibly strong. I often felt like it was a miracle she even noticed me. But it wasn't all smooth sailing in those early days."

"Why not?"

"Because your mom hated hockey more than anything," he said. "And there I was, hockey-obsessed, about to enter the draft. The game was my entire life, and I wanted her to be a part of it. Luckily, she liked me a little more than she hated it."

I shook my head; it didn't make sense. "But if she hated hockey, why did she play?"

"She didn't always hate it," he explained. "In fact, I think once upon a time she loved it as much as me. But her high school didn't have a girls' team. She played with the boys, and that came with many challenges."

He ran a hand through his hair, his forehead creasing as he continued. "She never felt accepted by the boys, and she was bullied by the girls. She had to prove herself every single time she stepped out on the ice and, although she didn't like to talk about it, I know it eventually became too much for her. Before the end of high school, she'd quit hockey for good."

"She gave up?"

"Yes, and I don't blame her. I know I've always said I wanted to protect you, Mackenzie, but the blows we take mentally can sometimes take longer to heal than the physical ones. Hockey put your mom in a dark place, and she locked those memories away for years for the sake of my career. When you were born, she made me promise to do everything I could to prevent you from experiencing what she went through."

I swallowed, my throat closing up. "*She's* the one who didn't want me to play?"

He nodded. "We both thought it was for the best."

"But I was a baby when she said that, Dad. I understand you wanting to respect her wishes and look out for me, but I'm not a kid anymore. You don't know how she'd feel about it now."

"I thought you loved your art. Isn't that enough?"

"I do love art," I replied. "But there's nothing wrong with wanting more than that. What happened to Mom was a long time ago. Things have changed. Have you seen the attention the PWHL is getting? There are women becoming coaches and refs. They're in management and executive roles for NHL teams. Hockey is changing."

"Maybe it is . . ." Then he shook his head. "But it hasn't come far enough. As much as I love this sport, it's mostly still an old boys' club. And it's my job to protect you from being subjected to the same heartache your mom went through."

"I'm old enough to make that decision for myself," I insisted. "And if you're right, if the sport hasn't moved forward enough, then maybe I can be part of the push to make it better."

My dad didn't respond. Instead, he was looking at me intently, as if he were seeing me clearly for the first time.

"I know you and Mom had good intentions," I added, "but I've told you before, and I still feel the same way, I don't need your protection. I need your support."

Dad swallowed and he took a moment before he replied, "When did you go and grow up on me?"

"I didn't go and grow up on you, Dad. I'm still the same me. I'm just not afraid to stand up for myself anymore. And I'm strong enough to deal with whatever hockey throws at me."

I was getting too emotional to keep arguing, so I turned and left, sadness and anger propelling my legs up the stairs to my room. I hated that my dad had kept all that from me. And it hurt to know that the sport I was so desperate to play had caused my mom such pain.

I'd been stupidly staring at her picture every night since I found it, wondering if she'd be proud of me for following in her footsteps. Now I knew she'd be anything but. I just wished I could talk to her. Show her that hockey would be different for me. Explain how much I needed it.

I lay on my bed and stared at the ceiling. I could finally understand Dad's apprehension about me playing, but nothing else had changed. I still wanted to play.

There was a soft knock at my door before I heard the sound of footsteps retreating down the hallway. When I went to open the door there was no one there, but I found a tray of dinner on the floor. Tears gathered in my eyes again. I may not have my dad's support or my mom's, but I wasn't totally alone. Tessa wanted me to succeed. And so did my brother. Parker and the rest of the Devils had my back, too.

I might not be able to change my mom's mind, but I could prove to my dad he was wrong about me. And I still had one last chance to do it.

Chapter 32

MACKENZIE

Our art class spent the morning at the Ransom Community Center, setting up an exhibit to display everyone's most recent works. I didn't have anything new to show. Instead, I hung one of the pieces I'd finished before my move to Ransom. It felt a little like cheating, but Mr. Green didn't seem to mind. I think he was just happy to have another piece to brighten the walls.

"I thought you were doing something with mixed media," Parker said, coming to stand beside me. It hurt to have him so close, knowing I couldn't reach out to him. But it hurt even more when he stayed away.

He took his time as he looked over my artwork. The painting was of my brother in action on the ice. I'd spent countless hours perfecting it, and, although I was proud of the final product, I was a little sad I hadn't been able to finish the new project I'd been working on.

"I like this one, though." He finally turned to me. "Makes me feel like I'm on the ice right beside him, ready to pass the puck. It's Max, right?"

"Right," I said with a smile. "And I *am* working on a mixed-media piece, but I didn't get it finished in time. I've kind of been rethinking it anyway."

"Yeah?"

"Yeah, I—"

We were interrupted as the door to the dance studio down

the hall opened and a gaggle of lively old ladies spilled out. They were chatting loudly and animatedly as they walked toward us, and I started to smirk when I recognized Dominic the hoop dancing instructor bringing up the rear. He was helping two of his elderly students from the room, though I wasn't sure they'd given him much choice. They looked like they were gripping him so tight they might leave a mark. I didn't dare to look down at what was happening in his pants today. Jaz would be so disappointed in me.

"I guess hoop dance is for all ages."

"Hoop dance?" Parker frowned as he glanced at the crowd of women slowly moving this way. Apparently, the class was just as popular with the seniors of Ransom as the moms.

I smiled and shook my head. "Jaz took me to a class a couple weeks ago. It's like extreme hula hooping."

"Why would anyone want to do that?"

"Someone has probably asked the same thing about people who put on skates, push a puck around with sticks, and get into fights on a big piece of ice."

"Yeah, probably," he said with a laugh.

"Aw, look at that cute couple," said one of the old ladies walking past, not-so-subtly pointing us out to her friend.

"They'd make very pretty babies."

"Oh, no, they're too young for that. I hope they're using protection."

Parker spluttered out a laugh, but my cheeks flushed with embarrassment. Why did some old people feel like they could say whatever came to mind? And they weren't finished.

"I wish Earl still looked at me like that boy's looking at her," the first one said. "Like she's the only one in the room. These days, he only looks at his dinner that way."

"Well, you are a very good cook."

As the group moved out of earshot, I turned to Parker, and my heart swelled when I found his eyes already on me.

I glanced back at my painting. Parker cleared his throat. "Uh, you were telling me about your mixed-media piece," he prompted. "You're rethinking it?"

"I am. I just . . ." My voice drifted as I tried to search for the right words. "My idea was to display the changing face of hockey over the years. The base layer was a collage of old hockey team photos, but whenever I looked at it, it just made me mad."

"Why?"

"Because it was covered in boys' faces."

He nodded with understanding. "So, what are you thinking?"

"I'm thinking, screw the boys. I should be creating something that champions the girls who play hockey. The ones who paved the way over the years for people like me."

The feeling had been cemented last night after talking to my dad. Now that I knew what my mom had gone through, I didn't want it to be hidden or forgotten. I wanted to tell her story, and honor other women and girls who played this sport.

"So do it." Parker slowly started to grin. "Throw the old piece out and start again."

I laughed softly. "That easy, huh?"

"Why not? That's what I did with my project. My initial concept wasn't working, but then something else inspired me."

"You changed your mind about the naked selfie?" I pretended to look disappointed.

He shook his head, still smiling. "I went with something I think you'll like a lot better." But a moment later his eyes dropped to the floor, as though he was suddenly less confident that was true. "Do you want to see the final piece?"

For some reason, I felt nervous. Perhaps it was because he seemed a little unsure too. Parker didn't often show vulnerability, but right now he wouldn't meet my eyes.

"Do you *want* me to see it?" I asked.

He hesitated. "Yes, of course, I do . . ."

"And you're sure it's not a naked selfie . . ."

"What's the problem? It's not like you haven't seen me naked before."

"I'll have you know I've scrubbed that encounter firmly from my mind."

His head tipped forward as he chuckled. I loved it when he laughed that way; unguarded and unfiltered. It was like catching a glimpse of the real Parker. The one who hid beneath layers of flirty lines, smirks, and mischief. The one I was falling for.

"Well, if you ever need reminding, there's plenty of photographic evidence."

"Are you showing me your artwork or not?" I said.

"Yeah, it's this way." I swore Parker blushed as I followed him across the room. He'd been awfully secretive recently about whatever he was working on and, despite a few attempts in class, I hadn't managed to catch a glimpse of it yet.

When he finally stopped by a piece on the wall, Parker said,

"It's not very good."

I frowned at him, still wondering why he was acting so nervous. But as I looked up at the wall, my breath caught. I was immediately struck by Parker's talent. He'd created a comic strip that was so good it looked professional. I stepped forward to get a closer look, and stilled when I saw the first frames.

There, drawn with beautifully vivid colors and painstaking detail, was a cheeky-looking raccoon. In the first frame it was waking up and climbing out of its dumpster, and in the second frame it was stealing someone's clothes. I glared at him.

"Just keep reading it." He smiled back.

The next frames were just as bright and fun, and the details were so intricate. It had so much life, and I could see the care he'd drawn it with. His raccoon easily brought a smile to my face as it trailed dumpster food around the streets, got into scraps with other animals and, in one frame, splashed in a puddle.

But then, the story became even more familiar. The raccoon showed up at an ice rink for hockey practice. Its teammates, who were all monkeys, looked shocked as it took to the ice and they grew more and more frustrated as it littered the rink with trash, chewed on other players' sticks, and struggled to find its rhythm in the first game. There was even one frame which included the team's coach, a huge silverback gorilla, yelling at the raccoon from the bench. I couldn't stop the smile on my face from spreading even further.

It was the final panels that truly resonated with me, though. The raccoon stepped up to score the winning goal of the game, succeeding despite everyone's doubts.

"It's . . ." I didn't have words.

"Sometimes, people surprise you," Parker said softly. "Sometimes, they may not seem like they belong, but they're exactly where they're supposed to be."

I blinked up at him.

"And sometimes," he continued, "the most chaotic, stubborn girl you've ever met skates into your life and proves you wrong about *everything*."

"I'm not stubborn."

"Don't say that. It's one of my favorite things about you."

I swallowed the lump in my throat. More than ever, I was desperate to tear the stupid friendship bracelet from my wrist. And staring at Parker's illustrations only made me wish I could be worthy of the story they told. That I was the kind of player who could flip the narrative and shatter everyone's expectations. Who belonged despite their differences. Tonight, I'd get my last chance to do just that.

I blew out a weary breath as I stared at the pictures. Even if I could score the winning goal tonight, it may not make a difference.

"What's wrong?" Parker asked softly.

"Unfortunately, I think I inherited my stubbornness from my dad," I admitted. "We had a big fight last night."

"I'm sorry to hear that."

"I finally showed him the photo I found of my mom."

"And . . ."

"And, he gave me an explanation, but a part of me wishes I didn't know the truth."

"What did he say?"

My throat tightened as I recalled our conversation. I was usually pretty good at clamping down any emotions when it came to talking about my mom. But right now, it all felt a little too raw.

"It's okay, you don't have to tell me," he murmured.

"No, I want to." I looked into his eyes. "My mom was the one who didn't want me to play hockey."

His lips parted in surprise as I explained how she'd been bullied for playing on the boys' team—how she'd asked my dad to protect me from suffering the same way. My voice broke as I spoke. "I feel like I'm going against her wishes. And how can my dad ignore what he promised her? Even if we win tonight, it feels like there's no way he'll let me stay."

I felt like an idiot for even thinking I could get through to my dad. And worse, it felt like I was about to break down in front of our entire art class. And Dominic's hoop dance groupies.

"Hey, it's going to be okay." Parker swept me up in a hug before I could object. He was so warm, his smell so inviting. Everything felt a little easier as he held me.

"We'll make him realize you deserve to play. That things change and sometimes it's okay to let past promises go," Parker said. "Even if I have to show your dad my terrible art to convince him."

"It's not terrible." I laughed. "I love it."

"Parker, Mackenzie." Mr. Green came up beside us. "Is everything okay?"

"Yes," we both quickly responded, pulling back from one another.

"Then you should probably get back to work. We need to finish up soon, and you're causing a bit of a scene..."

I glanced over my shoulder and saw one of the old ladies from the hoop dance class. She was looking at us and fanning her face. Another was pulling out her rosary beads. They could handle Dominic, but two teens *hugging* sent them into meltdown?

There was a wicked grin on Parker's lips. "Sorry, Mr. Green. I couldn't help it. My art just really moves people."

I smothered a laugh as our teacher shook his head. "Yes, well, perhaps you can use your skill for *moving* things to help us pack up. We're almost done setting up here."

"Sure, can do."

Mr. Green set off, but Parker lingered. "You know, I can think of a few ways we could really cause a scene."

"Have I told you how impossible you are?" I asked him.

"Not today," he said. "But then again, it's early."

He walked away, amusement pulling at the corners of his mouth. I returned my attention to his comic, trying to stifle my own smile. Parker *was* impossible. Impossible to ignore. Impossible to despise—no matter how hard I tried. But, more than anything, he made it impossible to be just his friend. Bracelet or not, every time I was with him, I was only reminded how much more I wanted us to be.

Suddenly someone was beside me. "Moving, huh?"

I frowned up at Elliot. He hulked over me, peering at Parker's work. "I don't see it."

He was standing too close, making the hairs on the back of my neck stand to attention. I fought the urge to walk away, and instead stood my ground.

"My ankle's feeling better, you know," he continued. "Doctor thinks I should be able to return to hockey soon. Great timing, since it's your last game tonight."

"You don't know that." I faced him. "I have every intention of staying on the team."

"Sure, you might make the team," he agreed. "But once I'm back, will you even get to play?" Elliot gave me a smug smile. "I think we both know that everyone will feel much better when I'm guarding the net again."

"You're not back yet," I replied with much more confidence than I felt.

His eyes narrowed and he stalked away. As much as I wanted to ignore what he'd said, Elliot's words continued to swirl in my mind. Between my mom's wishes, my dad's probation and the harsh reality of what would likely happen once Ford was back playing again, it felt like the odds were stacked against me.

But as I glanced up at the comic Parker had drawn, inspired by me, I felt a flicker of hope. All was not lost just yet.

Chapter 33

PARKER

"It's game day and *that's* what you're eating for dinner?"

I happened to think it was perfectly acceptable to eat Cheerios at any time of day, so I stayed firmly focused on my cereal. "Go away, Reed."

"You'd think he'd be a little more excited to see us," Grayson said. "We came all this way to watch the homecoming game."

"It's like he doesn't even care," Paige chimed in cheerfully.

"Maybe the sugar's gotten to him." Even Violet was here, flown all the way from California just to give me shit along with everyone else.

I looked up from my bowl to see they were all smirking happily at me from the other side of the kitchen bench. Reed had an arm slung over Violet's shoulders, while Grayson had his wrapped tightly around Paige's waist. If I were to draw them right now, I'd call the piece, "Whipped."

"The options were cereal or Mom's leftover meatloaf. Clearly, I had no choice."

"Clearly," Reed said, coming over to swipe the cereal box and take a handful of Cheerios for himself. "You ready for tonight?"

"Yep."

"Because, no pressure, but the losing streak ends here. You need to destroy the Saints."

"Yeah, we hate those guys," Gray added. "No offense, Violet . . ."

"None taken. Just be glad you never dated any of them." Violet pretended to shudder but then laughed as Reed's eyes narrowed.

"Don't remind me," he grumbled.

"But you have such a cute scowl," she replied.

"Well, as fun as this is," I interrupted, "I *do* have a game to go win."

I placed my bowl in the sink, grabbed my hockey bag, and headed for the door. Reed patted my shoulder as I went past. "You've got this, bro."

Grayson nodded. "Do us proud."

"Good luck," Violet added.

"We'll all be cheering you on," Paige said. "And we're going for pizza after if you want to celebrate your win with some real food."

"Thanks, guys." I replied. "If we win, I'll be there."

"*When* you win," Reed called after me.

How come every time someone said 'no pressure' you instantly felt like you were drowning in it? Still, after a good week of practice, I was feeling more confident. Today was the day we turned things around. It had to be. Not just for Mackenzie and not just for me, but for everyone on the team.

I'd started the season thinking that becoming captain and winning the state championship was all that mattered. But those things didn't seem quite so important anymore. I was so used to being the hero, it often felt like I'd failed if I wasn't the star of every game I played. But, through training Mackenzie and working to improve our team, I'd realized this game wasn't only about standing out. There was something special about helping other people shine brighter than they thought possible.

It was raining when I left the house and downright torrential by the time I arrived at the arena. Hopefully it wasn't a bad omen. Even though I raced across the parking lot, I was still soaked when I entered the rink.

Mackenzie better not have been lying when she'd insisted she could drive herself here every day this week. She'd told me she would borrow her stepmom's car for our morning trainings and get a ride with Jaz for team practices. I figured it was because she wanted to keep as much distance between us as possible, so I didn't question it. Still, I wouldn't forgive her or myself if she'd walked here in the pouring rain.

I was making good time, so I made my way to the girls' locker room. I respected the fact Mackenzie wanted space, but there was something she needed.

When I reached the locker room, I knocked on the door. There was no immediate answer, so I cracked the door slightly. "Hello?"

Still no response. Feeling a little braver, I opened the door wider. "Mackenzie, you in here?"

"Parker?" She stuck her head around the corner, and I was instantly glad to see that her hair wasn't wet. "What are you doing?"

"Well, I thought it was about time I got my revenge. Give me your towel and your clothes..."

She grabbed hold of my sweatshirt and yanked me into the room. Thankfully, we were alone in here, but Mackenzie glanced out the door to check we hadn't been seen before she closed it firmly behind her.

"Seriously, do you *want* to get in trouble?"

"Always." I grinned. "And I wanted to see you."

"If you're worried about me getting nervous, don't. I'm planning to win today, no matter what." Her words were determined, yet I caught a flicker of uncertainty in her tone.

"We will." Nerves didn't usually get to me before a game, but I could understand why she might be feeling that way. There was a lot riding on tonight. "I always heard comeback stories were exciting and romantic, but I'm a little tired of playing the underdog now."

"Same," she said. "So, why did you want to see me? Is something up?"

"I realized you've been missing something the last few games..."

Her brow creased just a fraction. "Something else I need to work on?"

"More like something you need to wear." I placed my gear bag on the ground and pulled out a brand-new Devils jersey. "Here."

Her expression softened as she took it from me.

"You're an important member of this team, Mackenzie, and, whatever happens today, as far as I'm concerned, you always will be. It's only fair you have your own official Ransom Devils jersey."

She stared silently at the jersey for what seemed like minutes. When she finally glanced up at me, her eyes were filled with emotion.

She cleared her throat. "You got me my own jersey?"

"Look at the back."

When she turned it over and saw her name printed across the top and the number below, she went still.

"Thirty-three," she whispered. "My mom's number."

"I hope that's okay."

"Of course it is." Tears were starting to gather in her eyes, and I stepped forward. I longed to reach out and comfort her, but I knew I shouldn't.

"We can't change what happened in the past. But you belong out there on the ice, and it sounds like she did, too. Maybe we can give this number a new chapter? Write the kind of story your mom deserved."

"I like the sound of that." Mackenzie was still staring at the jersey, and as she looked up a tear escaped and fell down her cheek. I gave into my urges and reached across the gap between us to wipe it away with my thumb. She tensed for a split second but then closed her eyes and sighed.

"Thank you, Parker," she whispered. "For everything."

The tremor in her voice struck me deep inside.

"I should leave you to get ready," I said, dropping my hand.

She nodded. "I'll see you out there."

As I made for the door, I glanced back at Mackenzie one last time. Her eyes were still wet with tears, but joy sparkled through them as she lifted her jersey to admire it. The sight only intensified the warmth in my chest. Just a few weeks ago I craved her scowls and her anger, but now I knew there would never be anything more addictive than watching her smile because of me. It felt like I could spend a lifetime doing small things to make her happy and never grow tired of it.

Once I'd finally dragged myself out the door, I hurried to the boys' locker room to get ready. I greeted my teammates before sitting next to Seth. He was eating a very suspect-looking burrito.

"Where the hell did you get that?" I asked as I unzipped my bag.

"Gas station on the way here. You want some?"

"I think I'm okay." And Reed had thought my pregame meal was bad. I was usually down to eat just about anything, but even I knew there were limits.

"You sure? I already had two."

"Nope. All yours." It wasn't often that I felt smart, but sometimes Seth made me feel like a genius.

"Suit yourself." He shrugged. "Your brothers back for the game?"

"Yep. They've been making sure I remember just how important it is to win tonight—like I could forget."

"Pfft. We don't need reminding. We'll get this done."

"Yeah, we will."

I heard the door swing open and frowned when Elliot entered the room. "Ford, what are you doing back here?"

"I've got good news." He held his arms wide and raised his voice so everyone could hear. "Doc says I'm cleared to play. Isn't that great?"

The room went quiet. No one seemed relieved or excited; instead, they all looked confused. Elliot hadn't practiced with us for a month, and I knew everyone had noticed how he'd mostly avoided our team bonding efforts.

"You're really back?" Owen asked.

"Yep."

"I thought you were out for a couple more weeks at least," I said.

"I'm obviously a medical marvel," Elliot said with a smirk.

"Maybe so, but you don't just front up to a game after weeks without practice and expect time on the ice."

"Why not?" he scoffed. "It's not like you want the *girl* out there. I'd be a better bet even if I was still injured. Right, guys?" Elliot looked around the room for support, but it was severely lacking.

The team had finally started to accept Mackenzie as one of us. We knew how hard she'd been working to level up, and in the last few practices it was plain to see how much her skills had improved. I'd always thought she was better than Ford, and it seemed the other players on the team were beginning to realize that too.

When Elliot didn't get the response he was looking for, he simply shrugged and a smug smile returned to his lips. "Guess we'll just see what Coach Foster has to say."

He had me there. Coach Foster had never wanted Mackenzie to play, and with Ford back, I knew he'd be more than happy to swap her out.

There was a knock on the door before Mackenzie entered the room, shielding her eyes with her arm. "You guys better all be dressed. I do *not* want to see your ass again, Seth."

No one responded and Mackenzie lowered her arm to reveal a concerned look on her face.

"What's going on?" She glanced around, her eyes finally

landing on the smirking Elliot.

Mackenzie stepped close enough to mutter to me, "Parker, what's going on?"

I didn't get a chance to give her an explanation, though, because Coach Foster walked in. "Evening, everyone," he said, barely looking up from his clipboard. "We've got a big game ahead of—" He stopped short as Elliot practically danced up to his side.

"My ankle's all better, Coach. I'm back and ready to play." Elliot handed him a piece of paper that I assumed was a note from the doctor, but Foster didn't so much as glance at it.

"I'm glad to hear you're on the mend, Ford," he replied. "But I'm afraid you'll have to sit today out. You haven't practiced in weeks."

I felt my lips twitch into a smile, and when Elliot saw it, he glared at me. But he powered on. "I'm ready to go, Coach. I can play."

"We can talk about this later, Ford." Coach Foster's voice was firm. "Right now, we have a game to prepare for."

"But you'll lose without me." Elliot's voice rose, and a few of our teammates recoiled in shock. Did he have a death wish? "Especially with *her* in goal. I know she's your daughter, but come on."

Yep, definite death wish. There were a few grumbles of dissent amongst the guys, but I was only interested in hearing Coach Foster's response.

"Like I said," Coach replied, somehow remaining calm. "We can discuss your place on the team another time."

Elliot's hands bunched at his sides as Coach Foster moved

past him. He only got half a step before Elliot thrust his phone into Foster's hand. "She's not even here to play hockey! Look!"

My heart sank as Elliot shot me a knowing look. I had a bad feeling Mackenzie and I wouldn't like what was on that screen.

Foster clenched the phone tightly. When his eyes flashed in Mackenzie's direction it looked like a storm was building inside them, ready to unleash. But then his expression softened, and I realized he'd noticed the number displayed proudly on the shoulder of his daughter's jersey.

There was a pained look on his face, but I got the feeling he couldn't bring himself to look away. Seconds of silence that felt like an eternity passed before his face became unreadable once more. He handed the phone back to Elliot.

"So you can see she doesn't belong here, right?" Ford demanded.

Even though she was still standing a few feet away, I felt Mackenzie stiffen. I wanted to reassure her but feared it would only make things worse.

"Ford . . ." Coach's tone was full of warning, but Elliot continued.

"She's only playing because she figures it's a way into our star player's pants. And this is proof." He held his phone for everyone else to see. There was a hazy picture of Mackenzie and me down by the lake at the team party. Despite the low light, it was clear we were kissing. I was surprised Coach Foster hadn't already killed me.

"Not my best angle," I said, earning a few sniggers from the guys. Mackenzie shot me a glare. It wasn't as piercing as the one from her dad, though. I did my best to ignore it and stood up.

"Yes, that is Mackenzie and me kissing. But it's got nothing to do with hockey. I hate to break it to you, Ford, but hockey is probably the only reason she *hasn't* been in my pants."

"Not helping, Parker," Mackenzie muttered.

"What? It's true. Mackenzie and I kissed that night, but we haven't since. Because she cares more about this team, and wants to make sure that everyone here respects her for the incredible player and person she is."

"Cares about the team?" Ford scoffed. "We've been losing because of her! This is a boys' team, and she's a distraction."

"I play just fine with her here, and I'm the one who's in love with her."

That really shut everyone up. Mackenzie's eyes widened. I never knew when to stop talking, did I?

"*Love*?" she mouthed, when I risked a glance her way.

I shrugged. What else could this impossibly warm and all-consuming feeling in my chest be?

I turned back to our coach. "If you're going to kick her off the team, you'll have to kick me off, too."

"Yeah," Owen added. "Mackenzie is one of us."

The other guys were nodding.

"She's better than Ford anyway," Cullen added, before the other players all joined in.

"*Way* better."

"And she's improving every game."

"She's brave too."

"She might be a girl, but she's *our* girl!"

Seeing the guys stand up for Mackenzie meant more than anything.

"Coach, we don't care if her and Parker like to swap spit," Seth said. "That doesn't make her any less of a player or any less of a teammate."

"Enough!" Coach Foster barked. The room seemed to tremble as everyone fell silent. "This isn't the kind of behavior I expect on my team."

I knew I was totally screwed. I couldn't bring myself to regret speaking up though. Or regret kissing Mackenzie. I'd dealt with the consequences of kissing her once before, and I was willing to do it again. I just wished I hadn't gotten her in trouble.

Coach Foster went to speak, and I braced myself for him to confirm that Mackenzie was out, and Ford was in.

"I expect everyone to support their teammates," he began. "To have their backs at all times." But then he turned to Elliot. "I don't expect them to use blackmail to get their way. If you think any player in this room will trust you on the ice after this, Ford, you're mistaken. I want to see you in my office first thing Monday morning. We can discuss your reintegration with the team on a... probationary basis."

Elliot was still panting from the exhilaration of his dramatic reveal, but Coach Foster's words slowly began to sink in. "*What?*"

"You heard me, Ford. *Leave*. We have a game to win, and right now you're the one distracting the team."

Everyone was staring at Elliot, mouths open in shock. He was just as stunned into silence as everyone else. He stood for a moment, as though he was trying to think of one final argument to fight back with. Then he dropped his head and slowly turned for the exit. The team watched him walk out, but my eyes were only on Mackenzie. She stood strong and purposeful, her eyes glistening with emotion. There was a time when I would have loved nothing more than to see her struggling. But now, her unshed tears felt like they were gutting me.

Coach Foster slowly turned to Mackenzie, and I could see why he had been so hard on her all this time: because he cared about her deeply.

He stepped toward his daughter. "Mackenzie, I'm sorry I stopped you playing hockey. I wasn't protecting you; I was protecting myself. But I'm not going to hold onto the past anymore. I know your mom didn't want you to go through what she did, but if she could see you right now, she would be so proud."

Coach Foster took in a slow breath before continuing. "You have already proven to me that you deserve your place on this team, and it looks like you've proven it to everyone else here as well."

"But my probation doesn't end until after today," she said softly.

"I never should have put you on probation in the first place," her dad replied. "It's clear that you are exactly where you belong—you're a permanent member of this team."

The room erupted in cheers, and a few of the guys close to Mackenzie patted her on the back.

Her forehead creased, and she opened her mouth as though her instinct was to argue back, but then her shoulders relaxed and she started to smile, her eyes lighting with pride. She'd done it. She'd actually done it. My own smile was so big it felt as though I'd just won the state championship game.

"And that's not all," Coach Foster shouted over the sound of our celebrating teammates. "I have another announcement to make."

Shouts and cheers turned to low whispering as Foster faced me. "Despite the information recently brought to my attention, I want to acknowledge the efforts over the last few weeks of one individual who helped bring this team together. It has made us stronger during a challenging time, and I'm confident we will only get better if he continues to show such selfless leadership this season. I'm pleased to introduce your new captain, Parker Darling."

The room exploded once again as my teammates mobbed me. Still, it took a moment for Foster's words to land. Captain? He'd really made me captain of the team? After what he'd just learned about Mackenzie and me? Was he nuts?

Not that I objected. This was everything I'd ever wanted. Then I thought—glancing at Mackenzie and seeing the smile brightening her face—perhaps it wasn't *everything*.

When the guys finally released me, I stepped toward Coach Foster and shook his outstretched hand. He gripped it firmly and leaned forward, his low voice still as deep and menacing as ever, despite the subtle smile on his face.

"Congratulations, Parker," he said. "I know how much you've done to help this team. And my daughter. Keep it up."

I was afraid to ruin the moment by opening my mouth, so I just nodded.

"Now, enough theatrics," Foster said, turning back to the group. "We've got a game to win!"

"Coach is right," I said, moving to stand at his side. I'd never been someone who liked to hesitate, and I'd already missed weeks of captaining this team; I wasn't missing another second. "The Saints are our biggest rivals. We showed them who was boss at the tournament last year, and we'll do it again tonight because we're the better team both on and off the ice. So, let's show those snooty, elitist, private school jer—"

Coach cleared his throat.

"Uh, private school *guys* how to play." I glanced at Foster to check whether he approved of my adjustment, but he was glowering same as always, so I pressed on. "We are the Ransom Devils, so we're going to go out there and do what we do best—win!"

The guys cheered as we all charged out the door. I was the last one into the hallway, just behind Coach Foster, when Mackenzie grabbed me and pulled me aside.

"You love me?" She was still gripping my jersey, like she was worried I might escape to avoid the question.

"Oh, that." I'd kind of been hoping she might have forgotten, given everything else that had just happened. It wasn't exactly the smoothest way for me to declare my feelings for her. Who wanted to tell a girl they loved them for the first time in front of her angry, terrifying father?

"Yes, that."

"I mean, are you really surprised? The first time we met, I told you I'd fallen in love at first sight."

"I'm pretty sure you were joking."

"Yeah, well, now I'm not. I love you, Mackenzie Foster."

She slowly started to smile. The way it lit up her face and

made her green eyes sparkle was so ridiculously beautiful, if I wasn't already in love with her, I would be now. "Then I guess you'll be needing this." She opened her hand to show me the friendship bracelet I'd made her. "I don't want to be your friend. Because I love you too, Parker Darling."

I started to lower my lips toward hers.

"Parker! Mackenzie!" Coach shouted down the corridor at us. "It's bad enough I had to see that shit once today! Get yourselves on the ice, now!"

Mackenzie laughed as her dad stormed off. "Guess that's as close as we're going to get to having my dad's approval."

"Actually, I think he's starting to like me," I said, with a grin. I leaned in again, but she placed a hand against my lips.

"Maybe don't push your luck just yet," she replied. "Come on, captain. We have a game to win."

Chapter 34

MACKENZIE

There wasn't a spare seat in the building as we hit the ice for our game against the Sunshine Hills Saints. The stands were packed with students and fans from Ransom, but there were just as many people in the crowd wearing the bright white and gold of our opposition. The energy in the arena was at fever pitch as the crowd cheered and heckled in equal measure.

I spotted Parker's family quickly. His parents were here, along with his siblings. I recognized Paige next to Grayson, and Reed's arm was draped over a pretty redhead's shoulders. My brother sat right behind them with my stepmom and little sisters. As Max caught my eye, he leaned down to whisper something to Daisy and Skye. They both gave him a serious nod before turning and lifting the posters they'd made with my name high above their heads.

I stood a little taller as I lifted my glove and waved back at them. It was hard not to get emotional seeing my family all here supporting me. Especially now that I finally had my dad in my corner too.

There was still a lot riding on this game though, if we wanted to turn the Devils' season around. But the pressure on my shoulders felt different now. I wasn't on probation anymore. I was a real member of this team, and, thanks to Parker, I had my own jersey and number to prove it. My mom's number. I desperately wanted to win and to do her proud. For the first time, I felt like both were truly possible.

Warm-ups went by quickly. And, before I knew it, I was skating to the net for the faceoff. I took slow, steady breaths. This game wouldn't be like the others. I was going to make sure of that.

As everyone took their positions, Parker slid alongside me. "Time to win?"

"Time to win," I repeated.

"Just try not to outshine me," he added with a smirk. "Despite everything I've said and done these last couple of weeks, I still want to be the star of the team."

"That sounds like a challenge."

"Looking forward to it." He gave me another wicked smile before he skated to center ice.

The game started, and I quickly realized it would probably be impossible to outshine Parker tonight. From the moment the puck dropped, he was everywhere. Chasing down loose pucks, slamming Saints players into the boards, firing off shots and setting up opportunities for his teammates. It was no surprise when he opened the scoring with a brilliant goal.

Sunshine Hills were no pushovers, though. I could see why they'd played in the championship game last year. And I could also see why there was so much animosity between the two teams. The Saints were tough, aggressive, and skillful. But so were my teammates—and so was I.

I wasn't the same goaltender I'd been just a few weeks ago. I was stronger and faster. All the extra training I'd done with Parker was finally clicking into place. Every early morning, every sore muscle, every mistake; they had all led to this moment. And I felt unbeatable. I saved every shot that came my way in the first period, and it filled me with satisfaction to see the frustrated looks on the Saints players' faces when we reached the first intermission.

The rest of the team were playing well too, clearly benefiting from our recent team-bonding sessions. They were working harder for each other, making fewer mistakes. It seemed like every single pass was finding a teammate. There was no confusion, more confidence, and, even if the scoreboard didn't reflect it at the end of the game, I think I still would have felt like we'd won something today.

The second period was just as intense, and I continued to make save after save, but the Saints finally broke through my defenses. While Cullen scored another goal for us, Sunshine Hills got two. The scores were tied.

The locker room was tense during the second intermission. Every player catching their breath, checking their gear, and visualizing how they could help to bring home the win. My dad said a few words, and so did Parker. But we didn't need encouragement. We all knew exactly what was on the line.

I glanced up at the stands as I headed across the ice to take up my position for the start of the third period. My pulse fluttered with adrenaline at the cheering crowd. They seemed even louder now, more anxious, as everyone prepared for the decisive final period.

"I've been thinking..." Parker said, skating up to me before play restarted.

"About the game, I hope."

"Well, sort of." He grinned. "I think we should make a bet."

"You want to bet *now*?" The scoreboard was counting down to the end of the intermission; we had less than a minute left.

He shrugged. "This game isn't tense enough; we should up the stakes."

"Isn't tense enough? We're tied two goals each in the final period against our biggest rivals. How high do you want the stakes to be?" But then my eyes narrowed and I started to smile. "Actually, don't answer that," I said. "I know guys like you. You're probably going to say something like, 'loser has to take off a piece of clothing' or 'if you score, I have to kiss you.'"

Parker laughed, and his eyes glowed with mischief. "Well, we've already kissed, and I seem to remember losing a lot more than one piece of clothing because of you. No, I have a much better idea."

"And that is?"

"A date," he replied. "If I score another goal, you go on a date with me."

"Go on..."

"And if you keep the Saints from scoring any more, you go on a date with me."

"It sounds like you just really want us to go on a date."

"Pretty much."

All the other players were in position, and I nodded to center ice. "Parker, the game's about to start."

"They can wait."

"Parker..."

One of the refs was waving frantically at him. Only ten seconds left on the clock, but he didn't look like he was planning on moving anytime soon. He seemed happy to wait me out.

"Okay, fine! You're on. Just get to the faceoff."

"So, it's a bet?"

"Yes, it's a bet!"

When the game restarted, I felt renewed energy flowing through me. Nothing quite motivated me like beating Parker Darling. But the Saints were motivated too. The third period was too close to call, like a tug of war between two evenly matched opponents; neither willing to budge an inch. As the minutes ticked by, I was on track to win my bet, but Parker needed to step up if he wanted to win his. He needed to find a way past the Saints' goalie, who had saved even more shots than me.

The anticipation in the stands and on the ice only grew.

Suddenly there were just two minutes left.

Then there was one.

With the clock now racing toward zero, a Saints winger stole the puck, and before anyone could stop him, he was on a breakaway. He streaked over the blue line toward me. Our defense couldn't keep up. And while Parker was probably the fastest player on the ice, there was no way he could make up the ground in time. It was all on me.

The arena fell silent. My heart pounded in my ears and my eyes lasered in on the puck. The Saints forward flicked his wrist and shot. I could practically feel the puck vibrating through the air as it left his blade and flew toward me. I reacted instinctively, dropping to the ground like lightning and blocking it with my leg.

The puck spun on the ice in front of me, perfectly placed for a Saints player to pounce on the rebound. I could have smothered it with my glove and stopped the game, but from the corner of my eye I saw Parker skidding to a halt by the boards. Like we'd practiced countless times together during these last weeks, I flicked my stick against the puck, shoving it away from the net and right to him.

He gathered it up and took off like a rocket before the Saints players knew what was happening. There were only seconds left. If he was going to score, he'd have to do it fast. He closed in on the net at the far end of the ice and went to take a shot. But then, he slid the puck across to where Owen was just arriving. The perfect pass. Owen snapped a wrist shot. The Saints goalie was stranded. The puck hit the net, and the final siren blared.

The arena erupted. We had won. Owen stared at the net in shock as Devils players descended on him to celebrate. Seconds later, he was being carried across the ice as we chanted his name. Parker was celebrating harder than anyone. He could have taken the final shot himself; he could have been the hero, but, instead, he'd done what was best for the team.

I was glad to still be wearing my helmet so no one could see the tears at the corners of my eyes. Winning the game meant more than anything. I'd finally proven to everyone that I was worthy of my place on this team. But more than anything, I'd confirmed to myself I deserved to play the game I loved so much.

Even when Owen was finally lowered back to the ground and the celebrations subsided, there was still an excited buzz in the air. The guys congratulated me on the win and praised my crucial save. I pulled my helmet from my head and ran a hand through my hair as I watched them all make their way to the bench. But one player remained at my side.

"I told you not to go and outshine me," Parker said, smiling as he pulled his helmet off too. "That was some save at the end. And the way you cleared the rebound to set up our winning play. Now who taught you that?"

"Uh, I think it was Owen. Or maybe Seth..."

He growled under his breath, making me laugh.

"You know, now that I think about it, there's also this hockey captain whose been helping me train..."

"Wow, he sounds like a great guy. Probably good-looking too, right?"

"Well, I thought he was a bit of a jerk at first, but I'm starting to wonder if maybe he's not so bad."

"Oh, really?"

"Except, unfortunately, I don't think he wants to go on a date with me."

"Why do you say that?"

"He didn't score. He lost the bet."

Parker dropped his stick and gloves as he skated in close. He reached out to gently take my face in his hands. I could feel myself melting into him, despite the fact that we were standing in the center of the ice with a packed arena surrounding us.

"What are you doing?" I asked.

"Showing you how much I want to date you."

"You know we're not alone here."

"I've always liked an audience watching me win," he replied.

"My dad's out there."

"Yeah, but I think we're besties now."

I released a breathy laugh as he dipped his head close.

"I'm not hiding my feelings for you anymore, Mackenzie. Not from anyone." He pressed a kiss against my lips. The crowd around us burst into cheers once more, and there were also a few whistles from our teammates on the bench.

My cheeks flushed as our lips parted. But Parker was smiling brightly. Could anything embarrass this boy?

"Come on," he said. "Let's go check if your dad still likes me."

We skated off the ice together to meet our teammates, friends, and family. No longer a secret. No longer enemies. Definitely not friends, but something teetering on the precipice of so much more. We'd either end in disaster or we'd be epic. And I knew I wouldn't have it any other way.

ACKNOWLEDGMENTS

I've never written a romance quite like Parker and Mackenzie's. They constantly had me grinning at my laptop like an idiot, and I had the best time writing their story. I always knew Parker was going to be fun to write about, but Kenzie now has a special place in my heart too. I'm going to miss them!

This book wouldn't be what it is without the help of so many people, and I'd like to extend my gratitude to everyone who played a part in bringing *Wild Darling* to life.

A huge thank you to my agent, Lauren Spieller, and the rest of the team at Folio, for all your support, advice and expertise. I am so lucky to have you in my corner!

To the team at HarperCollins, you have been amazing to work with once again. Thank you to everyone at Electric Monkey and Avon A for your enthusiasm for this series and your tireless work behind the scenes. Special thanks to my editors, Liz Sellen-Bankes and Amanda Maciel, your keen eye for detail and thoughtful edits made *Wild Darling* shine!

Thank you also to the HarperCollins team in Australia. It's been a joy to work with you on this series, and I loved meeting you all in Sydney last year. Special thanks to Maraya Bell, who spent countless hours driving me to bookstores for signings and guiding me through my first big speaking events!

Thank you, Andra Murarasu, who illustrated the beautiful cover of this book. You are incredibly talented, and I'm still in awe of how perfectly you captured Parker and Mackenzie.

I really wanted to make sure the hockey elements in this book and Mackenzie's experience playing for the Devils felt authentic, so I owe a huge thank you to Debrah Jaggard whose fascinating insights and deep knowledge of coaching and playing hockey were invaluable. Your tips on coaching girls were especially helpful, and I hope you enjoyed Parker's training sessions!

To my friends, who hype me up, keep me sane, and constantly inspire me. Love you, girls! One of my besties has been asking me to name a character after her for as long as I can remember. Nessie, you finally made it! And yes, I might have cackled just a little as I wrote Vanessa in.

To my family, thank you for always believing in me. Your endless encouragement is why I never give up. You are the reason I dream big, and why I always work so hard to achieve my goals. When you are juggling small children and work, you need a village. And I'm so lucky mine shows up for me when I need it!

To my three beautiful children. Ava and Harry, you turned two while I was writing this book. Archie, you turned four. You are all still so young, yet each day I am made so proud by how kind and thoughtful you are (if sometimes a little cheeky). You are the light of my life and I'm so lucky to be your mum.

To my husband, Pete. If the world was filled with guys like you, we'd have no need for book boyfriends. You are the ultimate support of both our family and the worlds I dream up. None of this would be possible without you.

Finally, to my incredible readers, I am eternally grateful to you for giving my books a chance. Each time I see your posts, comments and messages, it makes my day. I hope you love Parker and Mackenzie as much as I do! And I'm so excited for you to see what comes next…

ALEXANDRA MOODY

is an Australian author who writes romance novels for young adults. She lives in Adelaide with her husband, their three kids and naughty dog. When she's not busy writing, you'll find her reading or spending time with her family. She loves to travel, is addicted to caffeine and has a love/hate relationship with the gym.

Instagram or TikTok: @amoodyauthor
www.alexandramoody.com